MIND GAMES

ESTHER K. BOWEN

Esther K. Bowen

ISBN:152331446x
ISBN-13:9781523314461

Soli Deo Gloria

ACKNOWLEDGMENTS

A special thanks to my family for their patience, encouragement, ideas, and their willingness to listen. Also, thank you to my editor, Danielle Seybold, and my cover artist, Kelli Neier, for answering my questions and emails, and for their hard work making this book better.

Loyalty to family is Betrayal of the State. Those who devote themselves to their biological relatives inevitably neglect the Family of the World.

— Fact 97, Citizen's Handbook

Chapter 1
Daughter of the State

The State will be divided into five branches: Security, Development, Government, Natural Resources, and Human Resources. Under these will be the Ministries. It is the duty of all citizens to attain the highest level possible in their assigned ministry.
— Charter of the International Administrative State

"The Ministry of Information is the heart of the State," the Director began. She spoke slowly and with reverence. "It is artistry. It is beauty. Fluid and adaptable, yet in some ways never changing. It is like water."

The twenty students in the classroom sat at quiet attention. Meagan, uncomfortable in her plastic chair, nervously twirled her short red-brown hair, and tried to ignore the clenched feeling in her stomach.

"There are five ministries under Security," the Director continued. "Defense, Public Security, State Security, Justice, and then us, Information. We are not like the others."

Meagan noticed that Frankie, the small blond girl sitting beside her, had tears running down her cheeks. Normally, Meagan would have rolled her eyes, but today the girl's discomfort just increased her own. Meagan wasn't used to feeling nervous. She never received high enough grades to care about exam results. She knew she would never get anything higher than a C. It was a reminder.

But today was different. Under the governance of the IAS, everyone was placed in a level that determined their station in life, and the privileges that went with that station. Students entered their level at age four, and some would stay in that level for the rest of their lives. Meagan was lucky. She'd been considered smart enough to be placed in the tenth level of the Information Ministry. Any level below that and she wouldn't have been taught to read. The Information Ministry required enough skill that it did not even make use of some of the lower levels. Its students started out at a higher station than many people would ever attain.

That was not enough for Meagan, however. Through the course of her schooling, she had risen two more levels. All the students in this room were Level Eight, which, out of twenty levels, was a decent position. But this was their biggest test. Level Seven was a mobile position in the Information Ministry. Not many students attained that level, but if Meagan did, if Level Seven or higher was given to her on graduation, then she could continue to advance. Maybe she could even buy her way into Level Three, which was a privileged position, attained more often by birth than by skill.

"We do not patrol the streets or sentence criminals from high benches." The Director leaned forward over the weathered desk. Her crisp blue suit seemed out of place in the drab room. "We do not do these things. It is not our function. The other ministries, their work is hard, solid as stone. They crush and tear and leave no threat to the safety of the State. Here our work is soft. Our work is beautiful; it is water. It flows. It bends around time and events, smoothing them, shaping them, slowly and with grace."

Meagan shifted slightly in her seat. Why did the Director have to make them wait through a speech? Did she enjoy making them all suffer while she droned on and on? Out of the twenty students in this classroom, only three would advance. For the rest, this would be their station in life. This was the final chance to rise in the ranks of the Ministry of Information.

"Our ministry is unlike any other. Public and State Security, Justice, Defense, these are all responsible for the bodies of the people they so carefully watch and protect. They have the liability for the physical actions of the populace."

Would the Director never be finished? Meagan glanced around the small room. She was in the back row. Luckily, she was tall enough to see over most of the others' heads. The two Instructors, the ones responsible for the day-to-day teaching of the students, were standing behind the Director. Instructor Seldeen, the short, trim woman who aside from teaching was responsible for the ten girl students, smiled happily as she listened to the Director's words. Meagan resisted the urge to gag. Seldeen was a vicious, petty woman, who probably believed every word the Director said. Instructor Dolman, the boys' supervisor, looked bored. Meagan didn't blame him. She'd be bored too, if she didn't feel like she was going to throw up. She had to advance. She could not spend the rest of her life with these people.

"We, as the Ministry of Information, have a different calling, a higher calling." The Director smiled deliciously as she said this. "We are responsible for the hearts of the people. We hold the task of giving them their loves, their hates, of teaching them what is good and what is evil."

Meagan clenched her hands in her lap and reminded herself that she was the best. No one in this room was a better propagandist than she was.

"As you students train, as you learn, you are not simply completing projects so you can write glittering prose; you are the future of this sacred obligation, this grave duty."

Meagan stifled a nervous laugh. If the talent in this classroom was really the best of the best in the propaganda industry, then the future of the International Administrative State was doomed. Some of these people couldn't write an interesting piece to save their lives. So why was she so nervous?

"Think of that, dear students," the Director concluded, "as we all learn the results of your sixteenth year exam."

That, of course, was the heart of the matter. This was her chance. Everyone was soon going to see that she was the best. The students' works had been sent to the government seat of the city. The city's Head of Information himself read and scored these writings. He had not known her past. He would not keep her grade low so that other lesser skilled, but more socially correct, people would stay ahead of her. Meagan resumed twisting her hair. Now was her chance to leave all this behind.

The Director hit a button on her hand-held computer and all eyes focused on the wall behind her where the images were projected large enough for the whole room to see. The Director scrolled down the page.

"The highest scoring student," the Director said, "is Student Meagan."

Two students gasped. Meagan felt a slow smile of triumph curl across her face. She could have laughed out loud. She was leaving. She had made it. She was above all these students. They could mock her, but in the real battle, she had come out on top.

"The second highest is Student Alice."

Meagan's smile was replaced with a sinking feeling in her stomach. She had hoped that Alice would be out of the picture altogether after this. Now she would have to put up with at least two more years of competition with that girl.

Several students clapped, but behind the applause was terror. It charged the room like the air before a storm. Only one place remained.

"The third-highest score belongs to Student Tyde."

Meagan was not surprised that the small, wiry boy had been chosen. He was a quiet boy who kept to himself, but he was wicked with words, and possessed a vicious streak that rivaled her own.

"We are grateful to the Head of Information for this assessment," the Director said. Was she talking to the students, or to the security camera at the back of the room?

"Sometime this week, all of you will receive your new living assignments. For three of you, it will be the next step in your education. For all of you, remember this: society is like a great machine and we are its pieces. Some of you have found where you fit in. Everyone must work at what they do best to make this world a better place tomorrow. For now, here at the school, everything will continue as it always has. Until you move out, nothing changes."

The Director finished, and left the room. Instructor Seldeen stepped up behind the desk.

"You have your assignments already. Turn them in first thing tomorrow morning. You have this hour before lunch to work on them. You're all dismissed."

The students rose and the front row filed out. The best students were at the front of the class, in the best seats. Since Meagan was considered one of the worst students she was in the back, in the corner, and had to wait until everyone else had gone. While she waited, she picked up her notebooks and papers and ignored the muffled sobs coming from some of the girls. They would probably have a huge pity party tonight, crying all over each other. Meagan did not even try to conceal the smirk on her face. She had proven that she was the best, no matter what the Instructors said.

"Meagan," Instructor Seldeen called. Meagan glanced up. There was an intensity to the Instructor's voice that put Meagan on guard. She pushed her way into the aisle and strode up to the Instructor's desk.

"Meagan, I was told that you cheated to accomplish this paper. You copied someone's old paper."

"It's a lie," Meagan answered. She knew that she was not supposed to speak unless the Instructor gave her permission, but if the Instructor had her way, Meagan would not even have a chance to defend herself.

"Lie is a strong word, Meagan," Instructor Seldeen said softly. The unspoken warning and unspoken threat were clear. "You are not the best student in this class, so for you to score the highest, well, don't you think it's rather strange?"

Meagan's temper flared. "Yes, it is strange. I actually got an honest grade for once. You can't stand that. How in the world would I be able to copy an old paper? Did you actually consider the facts, or did you just take Alice's word for it?"

"That's enough, Meagan," Instructor Seldeen said.

A small part of Meagan screamed at her mouth to shut up, but she ignored it.

"You can't stand to see me be better than Alice, your favorite, because of my parents." Meagan leaned forward, planting her hands firmly on the desk. "Well, I'm not my parents, and I am a better propagandist than all of you, even you Instructors. One day, I'll prove it, and you'll all be sorry."

Instructor Seldeen jumped to her feet and slammed her fist down on the desk. It gave a creak, and Meagan was surprised that it did not fall.

"You will never speak like that again! You are an insult to the State. Think about that while I decide your punishment."

Meagan straightened. Her heart was racing and she felt blood rush into her cheeks. She clenched her hands at her sides. She knew she should be afraid, Meagan only felt burning anger, and strangely enough, a fierce triumph.

"You may leave," the Instructor said in a controlled voice. Meagan stormed out of the room. Instructor Seldeen would enjoy making her wait to hear her punishment. Meagan gritted her teeth. She didn't care. It didn't matter anymore anyway. She had succeeded on the exams. She would be leaving. The Instructors could fume all they wanted, but there was nothing they could do about it. They could try to make her life miserable until she left, but she could take it. Soon she would be gone and that was what mattered.

The School of Information had been an old house before the city converted it into an educational facility, and Meagan hated every inch of it. The house's three stories, including the attic where the girls slept, were connected by a narrow staircase lit by a single florescent bulb. The old stairs groaned and squeaked like a family of mice. It was Meagan's firm belief that they were kept that way to hide the rustlings of the real mice that made their home in the walls. The cramped kitchen and eating areas were on the ground floor, as was the sleeping room used by the boys. The two classrooms, along with the rooms for the two Instructors and the Director were on the second floor. Meagan supposed she should be grateful the girls slept in the attic because it was larger than the room the boys shared, but it was colder in the winter, and sweltering in the summer. Just like everything else, the Director had to prove that the boys and girls were treated equally.

Meagan climbed the narrow stairs to the attic, heading for the study room. She pushed the door open and strode into the sleeping quarters, which occupied half of the attic.

Ten metal beds lined the walls, five on each side. One student was taking a notebook out from under her bed; two others were curled on their beds crying.

Meagan hurried past. She was in no mood for people. However, she hesitated when she noticed a group of girls talking in a tight knot. They looked up at her with flushed faces.

A tingle of warning ran up Meagan's spine, and her muscles tensed. Nevertheless, she strode forward, head held proudly. She was halfway across the room when Alice stepped out of the group and came toward Meagan, followed by the other girls. Meagan's fists clenched.

"Congratulations, Meagan," Alice said.

"Stick your face in a blender," Meagan retorted.

Alice crossed her arms. "So much for being a good sportsperson. But I guess you wouldn't know much about that anyway."

"Shouldn't you all be working?" Meagan asked the assembled

girls. "You shouldn't start the first day of the rest of your lives by slacking."

There was a sharp intake of breath, and several of the girls stepped closer.

"Watch yourself, Meagan," one said.

"You have a big mouth," said another.

"Do you feel bad about cheating on the exams?" Alice asked softly.

"That's a loaded question," Meagan shot back. She would not give Alice the satisfaction of seeing her defend herself.

"I don't think you realize what you've done," Alice continued. "When you cheated, you stole the future of these girls. One of these girls could have moved on, but you robbed her of that."

The girls around her muttered their agreement. Meagan counted six, plus the three on the beds. Two continued crying, and the third girl, Lucie, was watching with wide eyes.

"I don't think you realize just how many people you've hurt with your uncooperative actions." Alice's voice was rising now. Meagan glanced behind her. Yes, there were six girls. But she could forget about Alice. Alice didn't like to get her hands dirty.

"Are you even going to answer?" Alice demanded. She looked to the girls around her. "You know, I think Meagan knows perfectly well what she did. I think she planned to cheat us all along." Alice stepped closer to Meagan. "You're just like your criminal parents." Her voice hardened. "Too bad you weren't killed with them."

Meagan's backhand sent Alice sprawling.

"I am nothing like my parents," Meagan said, her voice low and dangerous. That should have been enough to give the others pause, but they were looking for a fight. That was okay. Now Meagan was too.

"You'll pay for this, Meagan," a girl named Susan snarled. The other girls started yelling and closing in. One of them shoved her from behind, and another tried to slap her face. Meagan caught her wrist, and laughed tauntingly as she ducked another blow. Most of the girls' attacks were open-palmed slaps. She could block or dodge most of them. She jabbed her elbow into the stomach of one of the girls then brought her fist up into the jaw of another. She was bigger than all of them, and she suspected she was older too.

She didn't know her age, not even the Director knew. But Meagan thought she was at least a little older than these sixteen-year-olds. The girl she'd hit fell to the floor. Meagan's lips twisted into a smile.

Suddenly, one of the girls kicked her legs out from under her and another shoved her forward, making her land hard on the rough floorboards. She threw her hands over her head, shielding herself from the blows. She could do nothing about the kicks aimed at her side and legs and back.

Meagan gasped in pain as one of the girls' kicks connected with her shoulder blade. She clamped her mouth tightly shut and twisted away, trying to push herself to her feet. One of the girls stomped on her hand. Another kicked her in the side of the head. Meagan's vision blurred, and she tasted blood in her mouth.

"We have rules about violence here!" The shriek came from across the room.

Immediately, the blows stopped, and Meagan's vision cleared. Everyone turned to see Instructor Seldeen standing in the doorway. Meagan shoved herself to her feet. Alice stood behind the Instructor, blood trickling from her nose. Instructor Seldeen strode over and stopped in front of Meagan.

"Did you hit Alice?" she demanded.

"Alice was hit?" Meagan let her eyes widen in surprise. "I think she was that ugly to begin with."

"Shut up, Meagan," Seldeen said softly, her voice low and cold. Meagan knew that voice. She was really in trouble now. Seldeen drew herself up to her full height, her eyes about even with Meagan's nose.

"Student Meagan, for your many acts today against this class, the selection process, and the State, you will be Shamed."

Chapter 2
The Fate of Criminals

There can be no half-measures. Anything less than full allegiance to the State is sedition, radicalism, and shows a hatred for the people of the State and our glorious institutions. Anyone who does not follow the State is a criminal.
— Fact 625, Citizen's Handbook

Meagan's face went hot. Alice just smirked at her, but several of the other girls gasped. Everyone was afraid to be Shamed. They were gullible little mice. All of them. So afraid of punishment that they obey without question. Meagan had been Shamed before. In her twelve years of education, she had been Shamed twenty-eight times. She had just stopped caring. She would never be able to please the Instructors, so there was no reason to try.

Instructor Seldeen stabbed a button on her personal, a hand-held computer and communication device, then raised it to her mouth.

"Dolman, get your students up here now," she snapped. She grabbed Meagan's arm and shoved her toward the center of the room.

"Get ready," she commanded.

Meagan removed her gray jumpsuit and shivered in only her thin white tee shirt and black shorts.

Instructor Dolman led his students into the room. The Director followed, a switch in her hand. Meagan's jaw clenched. They would all pay for this. Someday, she would make them sorry they had underestimated her.

"Step forward, Meagan," Seldeen said. Meagan did so, hands clenched at her sides, head up, her eyes snapping defiantly. That was what the Instructors couldn't stand. Defiance.

"Form a line," the Director commanded. The students lined up, one behind the other, facing Meagan.

The Instructor handed the first student the switch.

"What were your crimes, Meagan?" Seldeen asked.

"I was accused—" Meagan began, even though she knew it wasn't the correct response.

"Stop," Seldeen demanded. "There are no accusations. There is only justice, swift and perfect."

Meagan said nothing.

"Repeat it, Meagan."

"There are no accusations, only justice, swift and perfect. Fact 709, Citizen's Handbook," Meagan quoted in proper fashion.

Seldeen smiled. "Better, Meagan."

She nodded to the first student in line, a girl named Helen. Helen brought the switch down across Meagan's left shoulder. It stung, but Meagan did not flinch. Helen handed the switch to the next girl in line.

"What is your role in life?" Seldeen snapped.

"I serve the State. Fact 13," Meagan shot back just as quickly. The switch slapped across Meagan's arm. Still, she refused to flinch.

"What happens when people fail to follow the rules?"

"People destroy their bodies with unhealthy practices. They destroy each other. They destroy government with their demand to do things their own way. They destroy the earth by constantly taking and never giving. Fact 84."

The switch struck her shoulder, already sore from where she had been kicked. Meagan bit her lip.

"Who is a criminal?" Seldeen demanded.

"Anyone who does not follow the State. Fact 625." The switch struck her again. Meagan watched the girl pass it to the next in line. It was Alice. She took the switch and smirked up at Meagan.

"What is the fate of a criminal?" Seldeen asked.

"A criminal's fate is punishment. Fact 743," Meagan answered. Alice raised the switch and slapped it across Meagan's face, hard. Meagan couldn't stop her reflex. Her head turned away and she gasped in surprise and pain. She recovered quickly, jerking herself erect, chin up and nose in the air. She could feel blood on her face, tickling her cheek as it ran down to her chin. Alice looked at her and shrugged, passing the switch to the next student.

"What were your parents, Meagan?" Seldeen asked smoothly.

"I have no parents. Fact 96." Meagan hardly felt the next blow. Seldeen smiled at her, a patronizing smile.

"Correct answer, Meagan," she whispered silkily. "But we all know that you did have parents, and they were criminals."

And that was it. Every C she'd received on every paper, glaring up at her, reminding her that she was to be punished every day of her life for her unknown parents' crime.

Meagan clenched her jaw and snapped back every answer as quickly as Seldeen asked the question. When all nineteen students had taken a turn, Meagan felt sick. Her arms, shoulders, and face ached. The Director stood in front of her. Meagan knew what question she would ask. It was the same question every time, the same question the students answered every night before going to bed. Her Shaming was almost over.

"Meagan," the Director asked, "to whom do you belong?"

"The State is my father," Meagan answered flatly, "and the Earth is my mother. I belong to them. Fact 1."

"Very good, Meagan. Your Shaming is over. You will accept whatever punishment Instructor Seldeen prescribes for cheating on the exam. That is all."

The Director turned on her heels and left the room, followed by Instructor Dolman and his students.

"Back to work, girls," Seldeen said cheerfully. The girls dispersed. Meagan grabbed her jumpsuit and began to pull it back on.

"Meagan," Seldeen said. "The downstairs rooms are looking a bit untidy. We wouldn't want a surprise inspection seeing our school untidy, would we?"

"No, Instructor," Meagan mumbled.

"Make sure it is clean before tomorrow," Seldeen said, then turned and left the room.

Meagan finished zipping her jumpsuit. She glanced around the room, but Alice was nowhere in sight. That was just as well. Meagan didn't know what she would do if she saw the little creep, but it wouldn't be pretty. Whatever she did, Meagan would take her time conjuring up some way to get back at Alice. She would make her terrified to ever cross Meagan again.

Meagan drew her hand across her face, trying to wipe off the blood. She would make Alice suffer. The thought comforted her as she stomped downstairs.

Meagan grabbed a bucket and mop from the closet. She would start by cleaning the boys' room while it was empty. Everyone was either in the classroom or the study room working on assignments.

Meagan allowed herself a wry smile. The irony of the situation was that it didn't matter how well those students did on their assignments, or that, after all the cleaning she herself would only have minutes tomorrow morning to finish hers. She would move up and they would not.

Meagan ducked out the back door with the bucket and crossed the school's small yard to the back of the next house. The school's water was carefully rationed by the Ministry of Water Resources. For cleaning, Meagan filled the bucket from a spigot that came from the neighboring house. The green and silver tape wrapped around it marked the spigot as a communal water source shared by several houses. It was not rationed, but it was carefully monitored. The water would not be shut off, but anyone who used more than necessary would be in big trouble.

"Y'know what your problem is?"

Meagan turned at the voice. Tyde leaned against the wall of the school, arms folded across his chest.

"As if I cared about your opinion on anything," Meagan answered. She lifted the bucket and started back toward the door.

"You're relying on talent to get you through."

"Oh and you're not?"

The dark-skinned boy smiled.

"Did you know I could have come in ahead of Alice if I wanted to?"

Meagan rolled her eyes. "I doubt it. While Alice is a hideous stain on the face of humanity, and an awful writer, she's still better than you."

Tyde's smile widened. "Yeah, but what you don't know is that the Information Head is particularly fond of good wine."

Meagan stopped dead in her tracks. "You bribed the city's Information Head?"

"It wasn't easy."

Meagan set the bucket down. "How?"

"Like I would tell you that." He lowered his voice. "You know what else I wouldn't do?"

When Meagan didn't answer, he said, "I wouldn't have come in first."

Meagan felt a sinking feeling in the pit of her stomach.

"Why is that?" she asked softly.

"Everyone watches out for the person who scores highest," Tyde said. "Now, I'm guessing you were your usual self, and got insanely high scores." He nodded at her like she had just signed her own death warrant. "Guess who everyone will be watching? Guess who everyone will try to take out?"

"But—"

"It won't be hard either," he said. "Alice will have you out of the running in no time. I'm not the only one who knows how to bribe people. And the Director already doesn't like you. She thinks you're a troublemaker, and you do nothing to help your case."

Tyde laughed. "How do you think your new Director will respond when she reads your file? How you weren't properly raised. How you got dumped off in this ministry after going through—well, you know. How you might not even be the right age."

Meagan's cheeks grew hot. Her hands clenched at her sides. The worst part was that Tyde was right.

He continued, "She'll read all this, then Alice will come in and talk to her. Maybe give her a piece of chocolate. Tell her how much of a troublemaker you really are. And you, idiot that you are, will play along." Tyde sighed. "You really have no people skills, Meagan."

Meagan finally snapped. "How'm I supposed to get any when no one will even talk to me?"

Tyde shrugged. "Not my problem. I'm not your psychiatrist."

"Then why are you telling me this? Are you just gloating?"

Tyde shook his head. "You and Alice are big players. Neither of you are subtle, and both of you will likely not go any further, even if you manage not to kill each other first. Still, I wouldn't mind you sticking around for a bit, Meagan. I could use someone drawing attention, while I quietly move up levels. Of course, you're not going anywhere unless you learn to cheat a little."

"I'll keep that in mind." Meagan picked up the bucket and yanked the door open. "I'll also know to watch out for you. Things may not be so easy for you next time."

Tyde rolled his eyes. "Please. For someone so good, Meagan, you really are an amateur in the ministry."

By the time she'd finished scrubbing the kitchen, Meagan was exhausted. Her shoulders were burning, and her entire body ached. She was feeling faint, having missed both lunch and dinner. But even worse was her realization that Tyde was right. She was in serious trouble. She did not doubt her skill, but how could she compete against a class full of cheaters? Level Eight had been hard enough; how would she survive the next? She had been so focused on winning that she had neglected to plan for the even more difficult battle to come. Well, she was the best at propaganda. Now she would learn to be the best at cheating.

"Fifteen minutes to curfew," the Director called. Meagan felt a small surge of triumph. She had finished everything. She was sure Seldeen hadn't expected her to finish nearly as quickly as she had. Meagan's smile vanished. Seldeen had probably hoped that Meagan would be caught outside after curfew. If Meagan had an arrest on her record she would be disqualified from advancement.

Meagan glanced out the kitchen window at the darkening sky. She still had time before the Director walked through the house, making sure everyone was in bed. Meagan slipped outside to empty the bucket for the last time, hurrying across the yard in her soft gray shoes. A streetlight across the road lit the yard, making the dirt and clumps of grass appear strange and discolored. She hurried to the spigot, dumped out the bucket, and rinsed. The cold water raced over her hands, and she allowed herself to close her eyes for a moment.

Clang.

Meagan spun to her left. It sounded like something had knocked over a trash can. She turned off the water and peered down the narrow space between two houses, but it was too dark to see. From the shadows came an uneven shuffling, like feet dragged along the ground, and she thought she heard a gasp. Everything grew quiet.

Meagan straightened and turned slowly back toward the school. Then she froze. A dark figure reeled out of the alley and collapsed.

Chapter 3
The Code

We must never regress to the dark times of the War of Sedition. We must move forward into a bright new era. To this end, the State will take whatever actions are necessary to ensure an everlasting peace.
— IAS Charter for the North American Continent Regions

For a moment, Meagan didn't move. She stood frozen, eyes wide, heart hammering in her chest. Then she crept to the side of the unmoving figure.

It was a man. He lay on the ground gasping for air, his chest rising and falling sporadically. She didn't have time for this. Meagan glanced back at the door standing ajar, waiting for her. She knelt down beside the man.

"Are you okay?" As soon as she said it, Meagan knew it was a stupid question. The man did not answer. Meagan leaned forward for a closer look. His hair was gray. He looked about fifty. That in itself was a little unusual. Around here, middle-aged men were not common.

The man's green eyes darted back and forth, and he seemed confused.

Meagan glanced over the rest of his body. From the green trim on his orange jumpsuit, Meagan knew he was from the Science and Technology Ministry. What was he doing in this section of the city?

Thinking she could listen for a heartbeat, Meagan leaned over and opened the brown jacket he wore over his jumpsuit. She recoiled in surprise. Blood leaked out of two holes in his chest and continued to soak his already sodden jumpsuit. Meagan took two deep breaths to calm herself. The man must have been shot. There may have been more damage, but Meagan couldn't tell in the dark.

Meagan glanced cautiously around, muscles tensing. Who was this man, and why had he been shot? Were the people who shot him still near? She listened, but did not hear anything out of the ordinary. The man took a deep, shuddering breath. He blinked several times.

"Water." His voice and eyes pleaded with her. She gave him a small smile.

"I'll be right back."

Meagan raced to the kitchen. No one was in the small room. Everyone must be getting ready for bed. Meagan hesitated. She should just close the door and leave the man to his fate. She had no obligation to him. Still, something inside her rebelled at the thought. Meagan sighed and grabbed a glass from the cupboard. Racing back out, she filled it from the spigot and knelt back down beside the man. Meagan slipped her arm under his head and raised it enough to pour a little of the water into his mouth. As he tried to swallow, his body was racked by a fit of coughing. Meagan gasped when the sleeve of her jumpsuit was spattered with red. He was coughing blood. She lowered his head to the ground and stood hastily. She had to get help.

"Wait. In my shoe," the man gasped. "Wild Card, you have to … It's in …" He coughed again. Meagan glanced back toward the school. She wanted to run for help, but she couldn't leave this man alone. The man whispered something that she could not hear. She dropped back to her knees.

"It's all right," she said gently. Through her fear and confusion, she felt a strange compassion for this man. The minute she felt it, she hated herself for it. Those kinds of feelings only got her into trouble. She really needed to get back. She was about to stand up and march right back into the house and let someone else handle the situation, when the man grabbed her arm.

"For you," he whispered. "Won't find you. I lost them for …" His eyes became unfocused. "I'm sorry," he whispered, almost to himself. "Tell the Defiance …" His face twisted and he stopped breathing.

Meagan reeled back, gasping. Her mind spun, and she grew cold all over. The nameless man's body lay in front of her, his eyes staring vacantly at the starless sky. Already he didn't look human, but like some life-size wax mannequin. Meagan bit her lip. She had never seen anyone die before. Or had she? Images leaped into her mind. They were hazy, only a blur of colors. Dark blues and black under harsh, white light. Shouting. A shot.

Meagan gulped huge lungsful of air. She stared at the drab side of the house in front of her waiting until the feelings—the memories—of panic and screaming subsided. She shoved the images down deep inside, into a part of her that she tried to forget existed. Hadn't she stopped having these feelings years ago?

A cold fear rose in her chest. The man had mentioned the Defiance, an insurgency group committed to the overthrow of the IAS. The public was told that the movement had been completely wiped out a few years after the War, but the government had to take strict measures to ensure they never came back. Well, apparently they were back, or, Meagan thought wryly, they had never been completely destroyed.

The full meaning of the situation began to dawn on her. She was sitting beside the body of a criminal, and not just any criminal, but a Defiance member and a dissident against the International Administrative State. Now she wasn't only on the verge of breaking curfew, she was also in danger of being connected with the Defiance.

Meagan leaped to her feet. The last thing she needed was to be caught outside after curfew with a criminal. She had enough trouble as it was. It was bad enough that her parents were criminals, now this one had to come and die right in front of her.

Meagan heard the growl of an engine. It was coming her way. She heard shouts farther down the street. She needed to get back inside, and fast. But then the thought hit her. What had the man said about something in his shoe? Half of her brain screamed not to think about it, that she needed to leave now. But the other half, the one that got her into trouble, demanded she know the answer. Hardly believing what she was doing, Meagan crouched back down and removed the man's shoes, sliding her hand into first one, then the other. She heard the sound of pounding feet coming toward her. Her fingers felt something hard. She grasped the object and pulled it out. Without looking at it, she thrust it into the pocket of her jumpsuit. Sure that this man's pursuers were going to burst into the alley at any minute, Meagan shoved the shoes back onto the man's feet, snatched up the bucket and cup, and ran into the house.

Meagan had just closed the door behind her when she heard a shout from outside. Light suddenly flooded in through the kitchen window, as a spotlight shone on the yard. Meagan looked cautiously over the windowsill.

Men wearing the white uniforms of Public Security ran into the yard between the houses. Meagan watched as two approached the motionless form lying on the dirt. One of them knelt and appeared to be checking him for signs of life. The kneeling man spoke to the other man, who said something into a radio.

A third man, dressed in a black suit, approached the body. From the way the other men treated him, Meagan knew he was in command. He knelt beside the body, and, opening the jacket with disdain, glanced briefly at the wounds. Then he gave a command, and the two in white began searching the body.

The commander glanced up briefly, and looked directly at Meagan. She dropped down below the window. He couldn't have seen her. It was dark in the kitchen. He wouldn't have been able to see in the window.

Still, she couldn't shake the fear that gripped her chest. She stepped away from the window. Grabbing a dish towel, she scrubbed the cup clean of any evidence.

"What are you doing?"

Meagan almost dropped the glass. She turned to face the Director.

"Just finishing some clean up."

The Director looked at her suspiciously. Meagan hastily put the glass away and shoved the bucket into the closet. She smiled at the Director.

"Wouldn't want to be late for curfew."

Meagan slipped into the darkened sleeping room. A sliver of soft streetlight shone through the tiny window high on the wall and silhouetted the dark forms curled in the beds. The sound of gentle breathing filled the room. The only hint of the unusual events unfolding below was the tardy presence of Meagan herself, but no one was awake to notice. At least, as far as Meagan could tell, no one else was awake. Even though she was burning with curiosity about the device in her pocket, she slipped into her bed without even so much as a glance at it.

She did not sleep. Her mind would not stop buzzing. That man had stared into her eyes. His cold fingers had wrapped around her arm. Meagan shivered and forced herself to think of something else. Tyde was right. She would have to learn some tricks if she was ever going to advance. Alice would have her kicked out of her new school before two weeks were up. And she still had that man's blood on her sleeve. What had he been trying to say? Who or what was Wild Card? What had she taken from him?

Under her thin covers, Meagan ran her fingers over the plastic object. It was circular, about twice the width of her thumb and about as thick. On one side, it felt as if there was rubber in the middle. A small, flat lump had been taped on the other side. Meagan slid it back into her pocket.

Ten minutes crawled by. Meagan counted them out. Everyone in the room was breathing easily and deeply. She waited, making sure she didn't hear any noise that might indicate the Instructors were still awake. When she was satisfied that she was the only person not asleep in the school, Meagan quietly climbed out of bed and crept down the hall into the bathroom. She shut the door and felt in the darkness for the worn mat that lay on the tile floor. Her fingers closed on the grimy material and she pulled it against the bottom of the door to block any light. Meagan flipped on the switch. The cold, florescent bulb barely lit the small room. Meagan sat cross-legged on the floor and pulled the mysterious disk out of her pocket.

It was a black, circular, plastic object, smooth, with a button on one side. A folded piece of paper had been taped to the other side. Meagan peeled off the tape and unfolded the thin strip of paper. She frowned at the writing, which appeared to be a string of letters and numbers in no particular order.

TD28wDaRIas105wW5cTA2

What did it mean? Since it belonged to the man, could it be something from the Defiance? A code of some kind? Meagan thought back. The man had said it was for her, but she was sure she didn't know him. What had he called her? Wild Card? Meagan shook her head. He must have been delusional.

She refolded the paper and put it back in her pocket. Next, she tried pushing the button in the middle of the plastic device. A small light flashed green. Meagan waited, but nothing happened. She pushed it again. The light flashed red. She pushed it one more time, this time holding the button down while she counted to five. She wasn't really surprised when the green light flashed again and nothing more.

Meagan breathed a sigh of frustration. She had no idea what these things were. Too bad they hadn't turned out to be something useful, like extra ration cards or a train pass. Now she was stuck holding onto strange objects she did not understand. For a moment, she thought about going to the Public Security station and turning the items over to them, but she quickly discarded that idea. She would have to explain where she found the things, and why she had not given them to the authorities sooner. She would also have to explain why she had been out near curfew with a man who was a member of the supposedly destroyed resistance to the world government. No, she would keep these things with her. It wasn't like anyone would know the difference.

Chapter 4
A Thief and a Wild Card

Food is a basic right. As such, its distribution and consumption is too important to be left to the judgment of the masses. It is evil for some to feast while others starve. Food equality must be attained if we are ever to achieve the highest goal: True Equality.
— Fact 125, Citizen's Handbook

Commander Val Ultan was not in his office when his personal signaled an incoming call. He also was not at home, in bed, which is where most citizens would be at this hour. He was jogging along the canal that ran through the Development sector of the city. The sun had not yet risen, though the sky grew steadily lighter. Ultan stopped on a bridge that spanned the gray water and took his personal out of the pocket of his exercise slacks.

His lieutenant spoke. "Sir, you were correct. Our fugitive, Henry Lark, did have a location device."

"On his body?"

"No, sir. But Tech confirmed a traceable locator signal. They just broke the encryption, so we don't know how long it's been on. However, we can act on it until it is turned off or the encryption changes."

Ultan nodded to himself. His hunch had been right. "Are you at the office?" he asked.

"On my way now, sir."

"Very good. I'll meet you there."

Meagan woke the next morning feeling ill and unrested. She couldn't get the events of the night before out of her head. In her mind, she could still see the eyes of the dying man staring into hers, pleading with her, calling her "Wild Card," whatever that meant. She needed some time alone, time to think.

A smile creased her face when she checked the weekly chore roster hanging in the kitchen. Supplies Day was in two days. The school's weekly ration of school supplies, toiletries, cleaning supplies, and other miscellaneous necessities except for food and water, would arrive, and the school would be restocked.

Meagan was responsible for going and signing for those supplies, which meant that she had a long two days ahead of her, but it also meant that she would have some glorious hours of relative freedom.

First she would have to pick up the ration cards. The city contained three main areas and two trains. One of the trains circled the administrative center of the city. The second train ran in a larger loop around the production area. Outside of that was housing. The circles were divided roughly like a pie, with each of the five main branches of the State occupying a wedge-shaped sector that radiated out from the center.

The office that issued the ration cards was in the administrative center of the city, in a Government sector. Government actually had two smaller sectors opposite each other, instead of a single large one like the others. The office that issued ration cards was in its southern sector. Meagan would catch the production train and ride it around its circle until she came to one of the stations by a highway, on which she could take a bus. The city had three highways. Two crisscrossed it like a giant X, and the third shot north from the intersection of the other two. From the bus station, Meagan would have to walk to the rations office.

Meagan had heard that the most important people of the city were allowed to have cars, and that they could take their cars on the highways. But of course, they would have to, since there was really no other easy way to leave the city. Even though the Information Ministry was under Security, Meagan lived in the Human Resources sector of the city, because she was a student. Meagan had never been outside the loop formed by the production train. Nevertheless, she was determined to someday leave the city. She would be so powerful that she would have her own car, and then she would be able to go wherever she wanted. She would go to other cities, or maybe a beach somewhere.

But if she was ever going to get away, she needed to do what Tyde advised. She needed to cheat, and that called for resources and allies.

Meagan pondered this as the Director scanned all the proper authorization codes into Meagan's personal. Everyone had a personal. It was identity papers, phone, rations, and computer all rolled into one. Being caught without one was a very serious crime. The Director handed the personal back to her and Meagan headed out the door.

It was a beautiful, crisp fall day. Good walking weather, even though she would mostly be spending it inside. Once she reached the rations office, she would have to stand in line with all the other people waiting for rations. By the time she finally got through the line, and the ration cards had been downloaded to her personal, she would have about fifteen minutes before curfew. Meagan was not allowed a nighttime pass, so she would have to spend the night in a nearby hotel. For people stuck out at curfew, there were hotels scattered throughout the city with free rooms available for those with a pass, which the Director had secured for Meagan and loaded onto her personal. The next day, Meagan would have to redeem her ration cards at an office in the northern Government sector, where the Transportation Ministry had their distribution office. Again, she would have to wait in line most of the day, before making her way back to the school, which was within walking distance. The rations would be delivered later.

Most people at the school thought it was one of the worst jobs ever, but Meagan relished the hours of escape. Not that she didn't find it boring, tiring work, but she would have done almost anything to be away from school and the people in it. Besides, if she was not sent on this errand, the Director or one of the Instructors would just have found other boring, unpleasant work for her to do.

The wind had a chill to it, but the sun was warm. At least for now. It was practically impossible to predict what the weather would be. The climate was as wild and capricious as the bureaucrats who ran the city.

Meagan was one of the few people out on the street. All of the houses here were one kind of school or another, and most of the students would be at their lessons. Several other kids were going, as she was, for supplies. Meagan maintained her distance.

Finally, she reached the train station. Meagan stepped up to the counter behind which sat a lady dressed in the pink colors of the Transportation Ministry. Meagan waved her personal over the sensor in the lady's computer, transmitting the pass. The lady nodded and hit the button that allowed Meagan access to the station.

Meagan joined the line of people waiting to file through the metal detector. Suddenly, she felt an uneasy pang in her stomach. Was she being watched? Don't be ridiculous, she told herself. Of course she was being watched. With just a casual glance around, Meagan spotted three security cameras. There had been cameras on the way here, too. There were even cameras in the school. So why did she just now feel like someone was spying on her?

Meagan turned ever so slightly to peek over her shoulder at the people in line behind her. A woman, dressed in a blue suit that marked her as an Instructor, stood behind Meagan, and behind the woman waited a man wearing the purple of Supervision. Nothing unusual there. Still, Meagan couldn't shake the feeling.

After she'd passed through the metal detector, she stepped onto the platform. Soon a white train approached and hissed to a stop. The line shuffled forward. Someone bumped into Meagan. Normally, she would hardly notice, but she was already on edge, alert to even the slightest threat. Meagan's hand shot out just in time to catch the arm of a man reaching for her pocket.

It was the man in the purple suit. His eyes widened. Meagan knew he was surprised that she had caught him, but he shouldn't have been. Meagan was not a bad pickpocket herself, and she'd sensed something funny about the way he bumped her.

"Thief!" Meagan screamed. She saw men in the white uniforms of Public Security hurrying toward her.

"That man," she added, pointing to the man who was raising his hands in surrender. "He tried to steal my personal."

The white uniforms shoved their way through the gathering crowd. Meagan didn't wait. If they stopped to question her, she would miss her train. She ducked between two bystanders and hopped onto the train. It wasn't until she was on board that she realized her personal was in her other pocket. The man would have taken the strange device given to her by the Defiance man. Meagan checked her pockets once more to make sure she had everything, before moving back through the car, looking for a seat.

Ultan's personal beeped.

"Yes, Lieutenant?" he said.

"Sir, the girl is on the train and she still has the locator. She caught our agent and avoided Public Security."

Ultan leaned back in his office chair. The girl was smooth.

"Do you want our agent on the train to approach her? Get it back?"

"No, but keep her under surveillance," Ultan said. "Inform me if there is a change in the situation."

Ultan scratched an eyebrow thoughtfully and glanced down at the information he had pulled up on the screen of his personal:

Meagan Brent
Female
White
Age 16 or 17*
Ht. 5.6, Wt. 110
Hair: brown, Eyes: green
Ministry: Information
Student
Level 7
*see acquirer's report

He scrolled down, continuing to read. Her record didn't seem to indicate that she was involved in any sort of rebellion, but confirming that would obviously require a more thorough investigation. This was an interesting development.

The train car was almost full. In the blend of colors, Meagan saw four other passengers wearing the gray jumpsuits of the Information Ministry sitting near the back. Meagan shuffled toward them. The seats held two people each. Meagan would have preferred to sit next to someone else in the Information Ministry, but there wasn't room. She slid into the empty seat behind them. There was no law that said she had to sit by people from her own ministry. The IAS even suggested that people mingle with other ministries. But they also didn't do anything to discourage the rumors that circulated about the oddities of ministries outside one's own. Meagan was also aware of the fierce rivalry that existed between some of the ministries, and even within different divisions of the same ministry. Information had a longstanding contempt for the Culture Ministry, which oversaw things like theaters and parks.

The Information Ministry was responsible for providing the written material for the movies, plays, monuments, and more or less everything else that Culture had to implement. The need to work closely together fomented a great deal of hatred. Meagan felt more comfortable with others from her own ministry. Looking around, she knew that nearly everyone else did too.

She felt a strange tingling down her spine, and once again surveyed the people around her. No one appeared to be watching her. Still the feeling persisted. The last few passengers boarded the train and the doors slid shut. Meagan looked out the window at the bright colors of the station. This was certainly turning out to be a strange day. First, some guy tried to rob her, unusual because of the harsh punishments for crimes, and now she couldn't shake the feeling of unease that had settled in her stomach.

"May I sit here?"

Meagan jumped as someone stopped beside her seat.

With some distaste, she let her eyes travel up the brown jumpsuit that marked this person as a member of the Construction Ministry. He was a laborer, an unskilled worker of the lowest level. Then her eyes met his face.

He was surprisingly young for his station; he appeared to be about her age, maybe a little older. His dark brown hair actually looked clean, and although his boots and jumpsuit were spattered with mud, there was no evidence of the unwashed smell that tended to accompany people of his level. Furthermore, there was not a shred of deference or humility in his stance, nor in his brown eyes that seemed to appraise her just as she analyzed him.

With a start, Meagan realized that he was still waiting for her to answer his question. She slid over a seat.

"It's against regulations to deny anyone a seat," she murmured, still watching him. She was above him and was allowed to watch him if she wanted. Normally, she would not have given him a second thought, but it annoyed her that the more she stared, the more he stared back, eyebrows raised, a questioning smile on his face. He should have the decency to look away from his betters.

"Stop staring at me," Meagan said.

He winked at her. "I'm just following your lead."

Meagan opened her mouth and raised her eyebrows. Then she

turned away and faced the window.

"Don't be rude," she said with a smirk.

The doors closed, and the train pulled away from the station. At the front of the car, a large, flat-screen television began broadcasting. Meagan recognized the movie. It was a documentary of how the train had improved their city. Lucie, a fellow student at her school and the only one Meagan even remotely liked, had written the script for this movie. It was common for the students' work to be used in this way. The city had to do something with the students' work and, instead of just throwing it away, this provided an inexpensive way for the government to plaster the messages of the IAS all over the city. This documentary wasn't bad. She preferred a good story herself, but many students found that to be too challenging. They favored the straightforward statement of their message, as opposed to the careful weaving of the message into a story. To Meagan, a story, in some strange way, felt more genuine, more powerful than reality.

Out of the corner of her eye, she again glanced at the stranger sitting next to her. Why was he here, beside her, instead of with the others like him? She didn't really mind him sitting here. He was actually somewhat handsome. Not that she cared. She was simply observing a fact; it wasn't like she actually had any feelings for him. Meagan sighed. It was going to be a long trip.

"Do you have it?"

Although it was spoken so softly that she barely heard the words, she almost jumped out of her seat with surprise. Meagan looked at the young man next to her, but he was looking straight ahead, watching the movie.

"What?" Meagan asked.

Now he did look at her, but he kept his voice low. "It's all right. I'm Wild Card."

Meagan felt her jaw drop. Did he just say he was Wild Card? Did that mean…

The young man continued, "I'm your contact. You have some information for me."

All at once, understanding hit her, and her heart started racing. She had made a terrible mistake, taking items from a dying insurgent and thinking no one would notice. The young man sitting beside her was the dead man's associate, part of the notorious

Defiance. By taking those small items she had identified herself as another member. Meagan realized, as a story she had read years ago came back to her, what the small object she had hidden in her pocket was. It was a locator. If she turned it on, a person with the right codes in his personal could find out where she was and track her. She must have turned hers on.

Meagan swallowed hard, hoping to hide the fear that suddenly twisted her stomach. Her first thought was to jump up and put as much distance between herself and this dangerous man as possible, but she was on a train. Where could she go? She had no idea what this man would do. Indeed, she had no idea what he was capable of doing. Her second thought was to dash away and call for Public Security. There should be at least two on the train. But this too she rejected. She would have to explain why she had the locator in the first place. She was a whole lot more afraid of Public Security than she was of some crazy dissident. Meagan took a small breath. She needed to take control of the situation.

"What is it you want?" she asked, keeping her voice calm.

He looked at her sharply. "The password," he answered. "You weren't supposed to activate your locator until you had it."

His answer confirmed her suspicions. That old story she had read about spies and counterspies was set during the time of the War. More details came back to her now.

"What about the payment?" she demanded.

"Not until I see what you have," he shot back. He looked away and resumed watching the movie. Meagan turned to look out the window, keeping a smirk off her face. She could not believe he was actually buying this. She was feeling very much less afraid now. This Defiance member was just a boy; he wouldn't dare try anything. Everyone knew that there were Public Security officers on every train. He couldn't do anything to arouse their suspicion.

Meagan dug in her pocket and pulled out the small slip of paper that had been taped to the back of the locator. Keeping her hand down, out of sight of anyone watching, she slid the paper across to the boy. She wondered if this paper really contained the password he wanted so badly or if it was something else. If it wasn't what he wanted, would he fall for it? The boy reached over and took it. Keeping his hands low, he unfolded the paper and glanced at it. Meagan was sure that she was going to be caught.

But he slipped the paper into his pocket and acted as if nothing at all had happened. Meagan breathed an internal sigh of relief. She was not going to get killed by some crazy member of a group that had supposedly been stamped out years ago. Now he would leave and not bother her.

The young man took out his personal and began to work on it, ignoring Meagan. Suddenly, Meagan's personal vibrated in her right-hand pocket. She pulled it out, and when she looked at the screen, she barely kept her jaw from dropping. A plane ticket to Chicago was the first thing she saw. Those weren't easy to obtain. When the IAS had come to power twenty-eight years before, they declared the old national boundaries obsolete which resulted in a ten-year war. The world had been redivided into regions and each region had a capital city overseeing it. So while Chicago wasn't the world capital—that was New York—it was the capital of this region, and therefore, harder to obtain permission to travel to.

But that wasn't what interested Meagan. What caught her eye was the two weeks' worth of rations that had just been transferred to her name. The rations were not for the crummy, cheap food the school rations provided, either. Some of the food Meagan had never heard of before, like peaches and cider. Some of the food Meagan recognized, but had never eaten. The students were banned from eating food like cake because it was unhealthy.

Meagan felt a slow smile slide across her face. Tyde and Alice and the other cheaters had just met their match. How often was it that someone just gave her rations? She wasn't about to waste an opportunity as good as this. Meagan leaned back in her seat. She still had two days away from the school.

"Have another job for me?" she asked. The boy looked at her, startled. His eyebrows drew together. Meagan's heart beat a little faster. Had she said something wrong?

The boy said, "I could use a partner tonight."

"Just tonight, right? I have to be somewhere tomorrow."

"Yeah."

Meagan's eyes narrowed. After tonight, when she had finished with this naive boy, she would turn him over to Public Security. She might even get a reward.

Meagan smiled. "It looks like you've got yourself a partner."

Chapter 5
The Invitation

To those who still assert that we are the enemy of freedom, we say:
Is this freedom? All the killing, all the economic and environmental disaster? This war that you brought down upon yourselves?
What good is freedom to the dead?
— IAS wartime propaganda

"Sir, the girl has been approached by a boy," the agent on the train reported to Commander Ultan.

"Is this the 'Wild Card' we've been looking for?" Ultan asked.

"I believe so, sir," his agent said. "Hold on," she added. After a minute, she said, "I believe the girl gave Wild Card the code."

"Continue to follow her," Ultan replied. "I'll put a tail on this Wild Card."

"Yes, sir. I ran his face, and I'm sending you the information we have on him."

"Very good."

Name Unknown
Male
White
Age Unknown, looks about 18
Ht. 5.9, Wt. about 130
Hair: brown, Eyes: brown
Ministry: Unknown
Occupation: Unknown
Level: Unknown
An operative against the IAS, not connected to the Defiance or known criminal element. He has worked with the Defiance before.
It is assumed he is an operative for someone higher up.
Organization: Unknown
Background: Unknown

There was more, Ultan noted, scanning the information. Places the boy had been seen, people he may have worked with. For a world where travel was restricted, this Wild Card seemed to get around. Most reports said his last known location was Chicago, based on information over four years old. But here was something original. This report, only six months old, had Wild Card in Rio de Janeiro. Ultan shook his head. How could the boy move around so much, and the State still know so little about him?

The train slowed as it reached Meagan's stop. As the music swelled in the final scene of the movie, the boy leaned over to Meagan.

"I need your height, weight, and preferably, a photo," he said.

"What?" Meagan turned to look at him.

"You're going to need something other than that." He waved his hand at her jumpsuit. "I have a contact who can get me some things for you, but she'll want your height, and weight, and a picture at least."

Meagan shrugged. "Why not?"

"Oh, and I need your address."

Meagan hesitated, but this was really going much better than expected. She gave him the address of the hotel. She would have sent it to his personal, but everyone knew that those messages were intercepted and read by security forces. She wondered briefly if the boy's transfers to her had been noted. They better not have been. This boy had better be smarter than that.

People began to file off the train. Both Meagan and the boy stood, and he surreptitiously snapped a picture of her with his personal. They exited the train.

"I will contact you," the boy said. He didn't wait for a reply. Before she knew it, he was hidden in the crowd. Meagan looked around her one more time. She had not been able to shake the feeling that was hanging over her like a wet blanket, the feeling that someone was watching her. But, just like every other time, she saw nothing out of the ordinary.

It scared Meagan a little how easy it was for her to slip into the role of Defiance member. She wondered briefly if she should feel guilty for her actions. She realized that she did not care. Making connections was the only way she would be able to get where she wanted in life. Hard work was for people trapped at the bottom, and not even talent would see her through. No, she needed resources and friends.

Of course, the wrong friends could ruin everything. She must not be caught with this boy before she turned him over to Security. It was a risk, but there was no reward without a little risk. Meagan smiled grimly. This would be fun.

The setting sun worked its way through the spaces between the buildings of the city, its rays turning the drab white concrete walls of the hotel golden. Meagan blew a strand of hair out of her face and pushed open one of the two glass doors that led inside. The clerk behind the counter glanced up as Meagan entered.

"I have a room for the night, number 14C," Meagan said. She held up her personal and transmitted the relevant information to the clerk. The middle-aged woman, who, in Meagan's opinion, had to weigh more than was allowed by IAS health standards, hit several buttons and then held a key out to Meagan.

"Enjoy your stay." She sounded like she meant the opposite.

Meagan took the key and started up the stairs to her room, twirling the key ring on a finger as she went. It was an old-fashioned key that would actually go into a keyhole instead of a card to swipe, but this did not surprise Meagan. Cards were more expensive, and the State was still struggling with the effect of the War on the economy. They tried to keep it hidden from the public, but Meagan was not an idiot, and, as someone higher than Level Eleven, she was allowed to read. She was not allowed to read a lot, but she had access to more books and articles than the average person. The students were supposed to examine the papers only for style, but Meagan read for content. She had not gotten this far by believing everything she was told.

Meagan entered her assigned room. She flipped the switch and a dismal white light reflected off the white walls and white ceiling. A small bed took up almost the entire room, leaving just enough space for a nightstand and a wooden chair to be crammed in. The door to her right led to the bathroom.

She scanned the room carefully. In her last hotel room, a security camera had been mounted in one corner. To her relief, there was none in this room. This must be one of the older complexes, built shortly after the War, when resources were scarcer. It wouldn't do for her to be caught on camera with the boy she knew only as Wild Card. She had no idea how he would contact her, but she was sure she didn't want witnesses. Meagan plopped down on the thin mattress to remove her shoes and noticed something poking out from under the bed. She lifted up a somewhat flat, medium-sized package wrapped in brown paper. It was not solid, and it felt like there were several things inside. Meagan tore it open.

When she laid the contents of the package on her bed, her mouth dropped open in surprise. What was she supposed to make of this? She held up the first item, a dazzling blue dress, short and off the shoulder. Meagan's eyes widened. This was no everyday outfit, even for the privileged. The drab hotel room seemed to brighten up a little just having something so beautiful in it. The second item was a pair of blue high-heeled shoes to match the dress. Finally, there was a small matching handbag. Meagan held it up, and her wonder grew as she realized it wasn't empty.

Unbuttoning the sequin that held it closed, Meagan discovered the purse was full of makeup. She poked through it, finding eyeliner, mascara, blush, lipstick, a comb, and deodorant. Meagan also discovered earrings, ones that clipped on, since her ears were not pierced. The purse also contained a glossy silver personal and a piece of paper. Meagan lifted out the paper. A message had been written in black ink.

Meet me outside the First Official Hotel at 9:00 tonight. Come dressed for a party.

Wild Card

Meagan's heart started pounding. This was really happening. She ran her hand through her hair. What was she doing? There were so many risks, so many laws she was breaking right now. The best thing she could do would be to forget the whole thing and pretend like it never happened. For a moment Meagan was tempted, but then her lips curled up in a smile and her eyes narrowed. There was no going back. She had made her gamble, and she would see it through. It was only one night after all. The risk of being trapped at her level, of serving cruel and exacting superiors, always feeling the fear, the hatred, the despair, that was the real risk. No. She would rise above it all, no matter the cost.

Meagan looked at her personal. It was seven thirty. She would have to hurry. The bathroom had no shower, only a toilet and sink. Meagan scrubbed her face clean and dried it on the provided towel. Then she checked the gauge that showed how much water she had left. She shrugged, deciding it was enough. She put her head under the faucet, letting the cold water run through her hair. It didn't take long for her to finish, which was one of the reasons all the students were required to keep their hair short. Meagan shook the water out of her hair. She was feeling better already. Then she took the comb to her thick auburn tresses.

Meagan frowned in the mirror. Her hair wouldn't behave. Some locks curled around her face while others flew out at odd angles and wisps. She pursed her lips and tried to force her hair into something presentable. She had never been to a party before, but she still remembered eight years ago when the Director had let the students watch news coverage of a party that was thrown by the Minister of Interregional Relations. It was a celebration of the tenth anniversary of the end of the War, and all the really important people had attended. Watching it, Meagan told herself that one day she would attend fancy parties like that. This was her chance, and she wasn't going to blow it.

Meagan began daubing on the eyeliner. At school, they were not allowed to use makeup, so most of the girls probably would not even know how to apply it. Meagan smiled. She had always planned on wearing makeup someday, so a few years ago, she had secretly watched the Director putting her makeup on. Meagan observed this for a week. Then, when the Director was away, Meagan took her makeup and put it on. It had looked pretty good, too. She had been so pleased with herself. Until the Director found out.

Meagan shuddered when she remembered the Director's rage. For a week, her punishment had been to recite the section from the Citizen's Handbook on personal vanity working against the good of the community. She had to recite for half an hour each day in front of the students and teachers during lunchtime. This, of course, meant that she missed the meal. She had been too careless. One of the first rules Meagan ever learned was don't get caught.

When she had finished putting on her makeup, Meagan

slipped into the midnight-blue dress. The silky material swished as she pulled it on and fit close around her body. Even in the washed-out florescent light, the dress shimmered when she moved. Meagan loved it at once. She twirled in front of the small mirror admiring herself. Yes, she looked hot. Her gray-green eyes and short hair went well with the dress. Had that Defiance boy bought it for her? Meagan raised her eyebrows. He and his cohorts had probably stolen it. Still, whoever picked it out had good taste.

Meagan glanced at her personal. Already eight ten. Her smile vanished. She didn't want to be late. Meagan slid the shoes on, but these were a problem. She had never worn high heels before and she had some trouble balancing. Meagan considered leaving them off until she actually left, but she figured that she needed the practice. She wobbled around in a small circle. By her third lap, she'd gotten the hang of it.

Meagan sat back down on the bed. She turned on the personal that she had been given. Her eyebrows rose in surprise. Here was her picture along with a completely false set of records, papers, and identity. Meagan continued looking through the personal. It was full of everything that she would have if she were really, Meagan squinted at the name, Esma Droncht. She opened a file titled "journal" and found all the information she needed about Esma. She was the daughter of a man named Jeffrey Droncht, a respected member of the IAS, and an advocate of space exploration. He lived in New York but had been invited here to a gala at the New Worlds Space Center.

Meagan's excitement grew. The New Worlds Space Center was a museum and research center where scientists worked on the future of space exploration. Even with all the innovations of the last twenty years, humans had not yet seriously explored other planets. The Space Center would change all that. Apparently, Jeffrey Droncht would not be attending, so his daughter Esma was going instead. Meagan expected there to be a high level of security at the party, held in the museum section of the Space Center. She must be very careful not to be caught with Wild Card. Meagan again checked the time, and gathered her things together to leave. Suddenly, she realized that she could not walk out of the building dressed like this. People like Esma Droncht were not seen near these kinds of places. She took a deep breath; she knew what she would do.

First she took the note that Wild Card had written her and tore the paper into tiny pieces. These she flushed down the toilet. Next she pulled her gray jumpsuit on over her dress and zipped it closed. She shoved the makeup and her fake personal into the purse, and pulled off her earrings, dropping those in as well. The purse, along with her fancy shoes and her real personal, she rolled up in her tee shirt and shorts. These she would just have to carry and hope no one became suspicious. She put her gray shoes back on and glanced around to make sure that she had not forgotten anything. She had not. Meagan left the room, closing the door softly behind her.

Anyone exiting the hotel was required to check out before leaving, but the receptionist was on the phone with her back turned. Meagan knew that the doors were locked from the inside unless the receptionist unlocked them, so she simply waited a few minutes until a young man came into the hotel. Meagan acted like she had just come from the receptionist's desk, and, keeping her head down so no one would see that she was wearing makeup, slipped out the door the second before the receptionist turned to greet the newcomer.

Outside, Meagan strode as quickly as she dared, trying to reach their meeting place in time. The sky was already dark, and the few streetlights barely lit the road, which was just as well. It was past curfew. Meagan's eyes darted from side to side, and her ears strained for the sound of feet on the pavement. She stayed near the buildings, ready to duck into a doorway or alley at the first sign of Road Patrol, or worse, a Protector gang. Meagan shivered as a gust of wind raced down the street. Clouds were forming in the night sky, and she wondered if it was going to rain.

As she neared the First Official Hotel, Meagan ducked into an alley and converted back to her dazzling attire. She was unsure what to do about her other clothes, but she certainly wasn't going to just leave them. She kept them with her as she slipped out of the alley.

It was three minutes before nine when Meagan stopped outside the First Official Hotel. She craned her neck to look up at its magnificence. Her hotel was nothing like this. Smooth music drifted out into the street. Even though it was past curfew, the hotel was brightly lit, the warm light spilling out from the windows and the two huge glass doors that sat atop three wide stone steps. Meagan sighed. There were definite advantages to being in the favor of the IAS. She would live like this someday; that Meagan promised.

Meagan looked up and down the street, then back at the hotel. That boy had better get here quick. She checked the time. 8:58. She looked again at the hotel. Was he staying in there, or was this just the spot he chose to meet? Meagan crossed her arms. He could have chosen someplace less well lit.

Meagan's head shot up when she heard one of the doors open. For a moment the street was filled with music, laughing voices, and the delicious scent of food. Then a silhouetted figure left the hotel and hurried down the steps.

Chapter 6
Important People

For a law to be a true law, it must apply to everyone equally. There is no justice in exceptions.
— Fact 704, Citizen's Handbook

Meagan's eyes widened. It was the same boy from the train, but he was no longer dressed in the drab browns of laborers. He wore a sharp black suit with a red tie. His dark hair was neatly combed. Meagan noticed that he no longer moved with the wide, easy mannerisms that he used as a laborer. His movements were more clipped, more precise. His face was determined, his stride purposeful. He would have given the impression of a confident member of the upper class if it hadn't been for the brown backpack slung over his shoulder.

Did she look okay? Her hands rose instinctively to straighten her hair, but she restrained herself and instead smiled alluringly. The boy stopped in front of her. She noticed that his eyes did widen a bit at her appearance. He glanced over her costume.

"You look great," he said.

Meagan couldn't tell whether he thought she looked beautiful or if he thought the disguise was a good one. She held up the gray jumpsuit she was carrying.

"What should I do with this?"

The boy nodded at the backpack he wore. "You can put that in here."

"What will you want me to do?" Meagan asked as she shoved her clothes in the pack.

The boy took her arm and began to lead her down the street.

"I assume that you have read your cover story," he said. "There is a party tonight at the New Worlds Space Center. Officially, I am Ian Windcoff, the son of—" His face blanked and he blew out an exasperated breath. "—of some Finance bureaucrat. Of course the one whose name I can never remember."

He checked his personal. "Linda. Linda Windcoff. Unofficially, that doesn't matter. I just need to get in. You will be my backup. I'm going to attempt to download some information. If

I get into trouble, I might need you to take the information out. Other than that, all you have to do is enjoy yourself."

Meagan smiled. "That sounds good." But her heart raced. What if she was caught?

The boy stopped for a few seconds to hide his backpack in a dumpster set far back in a dark alley. Meagan observed that he checked the street number. She did too. It was Street 84 North. Maybe she could steal the pack later.

The rebel turned to her. "I'm glad you were my contact."

Meagan looked up at him in surprise. "Why is that?"

"Well, if you were some old guy, it wouldn't make much sense for us to stick together at the party, but as it is, we can just tell people that you're my date."

Genuinely confused, Meagan asked, "You want me to be your what?"

The boy looked startled. "Oh. My date. You know, like we like each other and I'm taking you out."

"Isn't that prohibited except under the direction of the IAS?"

Wild Card smiled. "Technically, yes. Dating is prohibited. But a lot of the people at the top, the ones who have the power, ignore their own rules. To them, dating is a quaint old custom that has become fashionable for the upper class. Don't worry, I know what I'm doing."

Meagan looked at him slyly. "Obviously, you do. You seem to be better educated than your average laborer."

"Yes, I am," he answered.

"I don't really know anything at all about you," Meagan prompted. "Not even your name."

"And that's the way it should be."

Her first attempt foiled. Still, she had all night.

"Why are we pretending to be the children of important people?" Meagan asked. "I thought people didn't know who their children were?"

"Like I said before, important people can ignore their own rules."

Another voice rang out. "Stop where you are!"

Meagan and her partner stopped. A member of Road Patrol stepped up to them. He wore the white uniform of Public Security. Meagan caught her breath. The Road Patrol was tasked with keeping the streets safe. Including enforcing curfew.

"It's all right," the boy said. "We have our passes." He took out his personal and brought up his pass. The patrolperson scanned it into his own personal. Meagan grabbed her personal, or rather Esma Droncht's personal, and hastily copied the boy's actions. She'd had no idea having a curfew pass could be so fun. It was like breaking the rules without the fear of being caught. Meagan mentally added that to her list of things she would have when she was Head of Information. Which, she reminded herself, as the patrolperson let them by, was not going to happen on its own. When they were far enough away from the patrolperson that they would not be heard, Meagan again turned to her companion.

"Look," she said, allowing the very real nervousness she felt to creep into her voice, "I know I really shouldn't tell you this, but … well, if anything happens to me I want you to know that I was glad to be able to help you."

Wild Card took her hand and smiled reassuringly. "Everything will be fine. We haven't had any problems so far."

"I don't even know you."

Wild Card didn't answer.

Meagan wrapped her arms around herself. "There … there is no one I can really trust." She brushed a strand of hair out of her face. "I'm Meagan, and I'm glad I could help you."

The boy remained silent for a moment. Then he smiled at her.

"I shouldn't tell you my name, you know."

Meagan tilted her head to one side and returned the smile. "Why not?"

"There are plenty of valid reasons." Wild Card stopped walking and turned to face her. "But, you know what? I don't really care."

Meagan could have cheered; she had finally gotten through his defenses.

"I'm Jacob," he said.

Because the New Worlds Space Center was both a museum and a research facility, it was the perfect place for a gala celebrating the accomplishments of the space program. Guests could wander among the museum displays on the first three floors and marvel at the program's advancement. They would not, however, be shown the actual labs where the technology was being developed.

Meagan and Jacob stopped on the sidewalk outside the cream colored walls that encircled the building and grounds. Meagan knew from a previous visit with her class that there were gates on the north and south walls, each gate with its own guardhouse.

As they continued following the sidewalk around the building, Meagan craned her neck to look up the side of the structure. Spotlights on the ground illuminated its eight stories. She noticed that there were no windows on the face of the building after the third story. Her eyes continued traveling upward. Above everything else, visible even in the dark because of direct spotlights, flew the flag of the International Administrative State. Its green folds snapped in the chill fall breeze. Meagan could just make out the white circle in the middle. Even though she couldn't see them, her mind turned to the stylized images inside that white circle.

She shuddered as she thought of the black fist, clenched to show the might of the State. Two red splashes symbolizing the citizens' hearts and three blue lines for their minds were clutched in the unbreakable fist of the IAS. Meagan's fingers automatically moved to rub the cuff of her jumpsuit where the same image was sewn, but she felt only skin. She wasn't wearing her jumpsuit. Meagan rubbed her arms instead, sure it was going to rain tonight, but the cold seeping into her wasn't just from the night air.

"Almost there," Jacob whispered as they came to the end of the sidewalk. In front of them, a limousine pulled up to the iron gates. A guard came out of the guardhouse, checked the invitations and identities of the people inside, and opened the gates, waving the car through. Then the guard came over to Jacob and Meagan. Meagan's heart started pounding, but she and Jacob showed him their passes and were let through without incident. After they passed the guard, Meagan muttered, "I'm glad that's over with."

"That wasn't the hard part."

Meagan bit her lip. Of course it wasn't. How could she have forgotten? The last time she had been here, she'd hardly taken notice of the security measures. The security hadn't seemed extensive, just routine. Now that she was entering under a false identity, it felt endless.

Meagan took a deep breath. She would take this one step at a time. They were inside the wall now. The manicured lawn was brightly lit and the stone path leading to the front doors appeared to have been polished for the occasion. The limousine ahead of them pulled onto the grass, parking among several other cars. Meagan watched as the driver came around and opened the door for the well-dressed man who stepped onto the grass. A tall blond followed, and the couple started toward the door. Meagan turned and saw that Jacob was several paces ahead of her. She jogged a few steps to catch up, and looped her arm through his. She swung her hips and kept a pout on her face as the other woman had done. Jacob glanced at her and started to laugh.

"You'd fit right in among these important types."

"That's the idea," Meagan replied, and she meant it in more ways than one. Someday, a driver would be opening the door for her.

A young man and woman dressed in the yellow uniforms of the Culture Ministry opened the doors for them. Jacob and Meagan stepped into a room colored with decorative tiles. The room was wide, but not very deep, and a soft music filled it. Several guests approached a window on the right, where they could check their coats. Ahead was the remainder of the security.

A thin brunette woman stood behind a podium directing guests forward. Jacob didn't hesitate, but strode directly to her.

The woman smiled. "Please put anything you are carrying here." She gestured to the conveyor belt behind her. Meagan already had her personal in her hand, so she set her purse down, frantically trying to remember if it contained anything incriminating. She did not put down her personal, and neither did Jacob. The woman didn't expect them to. A personal was more important than anything else. It was their identity. As far as the State was concerned, without their personals, they didn't exist and hence, were criminals.

Another security member came over to them, this time a man, and the first staff person Meagan had seen who appeared to be at least thirty. Meagan's heart skipped a beat. There were two men behind him.

"If you will give your personals to these men, you can step into the scanner," the lead man said.

Meagan hesitated, trying to remember if giving up their

personals was just a normal security precaution, or if the men had become suspicious of the two intruders. Jacob, unfazed, handed over his personal and stepped into one of the two large metal cylinders that would provide the body scan. Meagan breathed a sigh of relief when she saw another one of the guests stepping out of the other cylinder, and a man handing him back a personal. This was normal procedure. She and Jacob were not suspect.

Meagan stepped into the vacated cylinder, spreading her arms as it scanned her, searching for hidden weapons. On the other side, she retrieved her personal from the men who had apparently been checking her identity, and rejoined Jacob. Finally, security let them out of the first room and into the museum.

Now they were done with the hard part.

Chapter 7
The Man Who Spilled the Wine

What good is living to the slave?
— Midwestern Free Press, wartime news

When they stepped into the main room, Meagan could only gasp in amazement. Warm yellow light filled the circular room. In the center, a huge model of the rocket ship that the program was building stretched up four stories. Meagan saw guests on the second floor leaning over the railings to look up at the ship's nose. Running along the wall, peeking out from behind the pillars that surrounded the room, a brightly colored mural depicted the exploration of space that would follow the completion of the program.

The roar of conversation from hundreds of guests overwhelmed Meagan. These guests were themselves a blaze of color. They were not, Meagan noted, wearing their uniforms, but were dressed as she and Jacob were, in gowns and suits of every color. She caught a glimpse of a white uniform and her stomach twisted into a knot. Security wore white. Meagan turned and saw the security overseer talking to one of his men. She turned away and took a deep breath. She was Esma Droncht; she had every right to be here.

Meagan again breathed in deeply. Even better than the smell of perfume and good clothes was the delicious scent of food. Tables set around the room had been loaded with delicate sandwiches and strong cheeses. There were cakes and chocolates and fruits. Meagan looked closer. Some of the fruits she had never seen before, like the bright yellow rings sitting on a plate on the edge of the table nearest her. A bar had been set up and several Culture Ministry hosts were serving drinks. Meagan's stomach growled. She had not eaten since lunch that afternoon. She turned to Jacob.

"Let's get something to eat."

Jacob did not answer. His eyes were darting back and forth, scanning the room. She felt his fingers firmly take her elbow and direct her forward. They mingled with the crowd.

"Impressive display, isn't it?" A large man with a sharp face and gray ponytail materialized out of the crowd. "I saw you arrive," he said, extending his hand, which Jacob and Meagan shook in turn. "I'm Wilson Bet, head of the Commerce Ministry for the city."

"Ian Windcoff," Jacob answered. "My mother is Linda Windcoff, from Finance. And this," he gestured to Meagan, "is Esma Droncht, from SciTech."

Wilson Bet nodded. "SciTech, eh? You're probably more familiar with the good work the IAS is doing here than the rest of us."

Meagan smiled mysteriously at him, hoping he wouldn't ask further.

"Any idea of when the next phase of the program will be finished?"

Meagan's mind raced, trying to remember her previous trip. Had she read anything about a completion date? Her instinct was to glance about the room, looking for a date, but she held eye contact with Wilson Bet.

"We are all aware of the official date the program has released," she answered smugly.

Wilson Bet opened his mouth, but Jacob beat him to it.

"I keep hearing about the food distribution problem that Commerce is having."

Wilson's face twitched. "The problem, young sir, is not with Commerce. We are demanding more gasoline from Resources, but everyone knows they haven't met their quota in years."

Jacob laughed. "You can't seriously blame all your problems on Resources. Not when your divisions are using outdated maps to plan routes and deliveries."

Wilson's face flushed red. "You are just showing your ignorance," he puffed. "Oil production hasn't been able to reach anywhere near prewar levels. That is the fault of Resources."

"Excuses," Jacob said in a singsong voice, shaking his head.

"You want to talk about excuses," Wilson said. "How about the debacle created when your ministry attempted to seize regional assets. Look at all the lame excuses Finance is throwing out for blatant incompetence."

"If you have a problem with that, you should take it up with

Alvo Irmin," Jacob snapped back.

By this point, Meagan was completely lost, but she had to give Jacob credit. Wilson Bet had forgotten his original line of questioning, and she wouldn't get tripped up under his interrogation.

Their argument seemed to resolve when they both blamed the Ministry of Agriculture. Jacob steered them away from Wilson Bet. Meagan frowned thoughtfully. Jacob spoke like he knew what he was talking about. Could Finance be the ministry he really worked in? Not that it mattered. Once she got him arrested, he wouldn't be part of any ministry.

Meagan let her gaze wander over the room. She located several security officers by their white uniforms, but they didn't seem to have noticed the two intruders. Still, what about security cameras? She took a small step back, leaning to try to see past the clusters of guests.

"It's time."

Meagan whirled, her hands already balling into fists.

"Relax," Jacob said, taking her hand and giving it a reassuring squeeze. "I'm going. If I'm not back by the end of the party, leave without me."

He strode quickly through the crowd. Meagan watched him stop beside a satin cord strung across a door hidden in the painted wall. He glanced left and right to make sure no one was watching, ducked under the cord, and waved a card in front of the door. It unlocked, and he disappeared inside.

Meagan rocked back and forth on her feet. If Jacob wasn't back by the end of the party, she was out her payment and a good night's sleep. Well, she couldn't stand here worrying. The smell of food had made her ravenously hungry. She had never been offered food that had not been carefully portioned. Meagan sidled up to the nearest table and began to pile her plate with tiny chicken salad sandwiches.

At the end of the table, three men stood talking and sipping wine. They glanced over at her as she passed, and Meagan smiled at them. Suddenly, glass shattered on the floor. The man standing across from Meagan had dropped his wine. Broken glass lay around his feet and red liquid splattered his shoes. The man didn't seem to notice. He stared at Meagan, his face pale. The two other men turned and looked at him.

He recovered quickly and let out a laugh. "I never was good at handling these tiny glasses. I've always said they should just give us tankards."

The other two men laughed politely, and a young lady who had been serving drinks arrived with a towel to clean up the mess. As they all moved out of the server's way, Meagan looked over the strange man. He was about six feet tall, and although his brown hair was turning gray, he appeared surprisingly fit under his blue suit. His green eyes never left her face, like he needed reassurance that she was really there. Meagan shifted uncomfortably. She was sure she had never seen this man before. The other two men excused themselves and the third extended his hand.

"I guess this is an awkward way to meet," he said, his face still pale.

Meagan shook his hand. She could feel it trembling. "Do I know you?" she asked.

"I don't think so." He swallowed. "I would have remembered you."

That might have sounded nice coming from someone else, but this man looked like he was going to be sick. Meagan shifted nervously. Had she done something wrong? Did he know she was an impostor? She smiled at him, hoping it hid the flash of terror that gripped her stomach.

"My name is Esma Droncht."

Disappointment clouded the man's face, but only for a second. He buried whatever emotions he felt under a carefully constructed social mask.

"I'm Arthur Rand." His eyes stayed on her face.

"You, uh, got some wine on your pants," Meagan said, pointing down, hoping to break his relentless, and somewhat creepy, stare.

Arthur gave a short laugh. "It wouldn't be the first time."

Meagan felt a tug on her arm.

"Ma'am, can I speak to you?"

She turned to find a young man in a server's uniform.

"What is it?" Meagan did not bother to hide her annoyance.

"Um." The server glanced at Arthur. "Um, privately."

"I'm in the middle of a conversation."

"It's important."

Meagan turned back to Arthur, who was watching them both intently.

"Excuse me," she said.

"Of course." Arthur left them, rejoining the crowd.

Meagan set her plate down on the table. "What's so important?" she demanded.

"There is someone who would like to speak with you." The boy's face was pale.

"Who?" Meagan asked.

The boy swallowed hard. "He said to tell you that you can either go up to the fourth floor and talk with him, or he will have you shot as a traitor."

Chapter 8
Black Fists

The Black Fists are the extension of the Will of the State. They must not be feared by the good-doing citizen. But for the criminal, the rebellious, or the fanatic, they are terror realized.
They neither falter nor sleep. They see all.
Through them we will have peace.
— Fact 654, Citizen's Handbook

Meagan's refusal caught in her throat. She looked up, but the off-limits fourth floor was shrouded in darkness.

"He said to take the stairs."

Moving toward the doorway that led to the staircase, she shot a quick glance at the security overseer, but he seemed oblivious to her. Who had summoned her, then? Her heart raced. How had she been caught so easily?

Meagan took the stairs two at a time. Whoever he was, he wanted to talk. He had to give her a chance to explain.

The doors leading to the fourth floor were closed. Meagan pushed the door on the right and it swung open. She stepped forward. The door swung shut behind her.

On Meagan's right the yellow light of the party shone up from below, partially blocked by the low wall enclosing an overlook. On her left, a harsh blue glow from three computer screens did little more than highlight the darkness and cast into eerie shadow the people seated around the table, each watching a monitor. The people at the table wore black, as did the two men standing, watching Meagan. They wore black uniforms and large pistols on their hips. Meagan's blood turned to ice.

The sixth man was different. He stood at the edge of the overlook, his hands planted firmly on the low wall. His black suit did not reflect the light, but made him appear as a shadow that had taken form. He watched guests moving below with a steady gaze.

As Meagan stepped forward, he turned. Beneath his dark hair, his eyes were a hard blue. On the front of his suit was a small, white, circular patch with a black, clenched fist in the middle. Meagan swallowed hard.

The men were Black Fists, feared by every citizen of the IAS. Part of the State Security Ministry, the Black Fists were the government's own secret police. Public Security might make sure that people behaved, but the Black Fists were the ones who did the real dirty work, the work no one ever heard about. Few people had actually seen the Black Fists in action, but everyone knew their reputation. They were the true executors of the government's will, its eyes and hands, and terror of their ruthlessness kept many people, who otherwise might have attempted it, from breaking the rules.

The man walked toward Meagan, his movements methodical. Meagan's eyes widened. She had seen him before. He had been there with Public Security, the night the man died. He was the commander who had knelt to examine the body, and then scared her half to death by looking up as if he sensed someone watching.

Meagan felt herself shaking, but her feet had become a part of the floor. She couldn't move them if she tried. She was an idiot. She had always been an idiot. Had she really believed the IAS would let her get away with playing rebel? Meagan tried to force herself to think, to construct some lie that would save her.

"What are you doing here?" The man's voice was low, but hard. His tone suggested he already knew the answer.

"There is a person from the Defiance here," Meagan said in a small voice.

"I am aware of that. What are *you* doing here?"

Meagan took a deep breath. Laughter drifted up from the party below.

"I discovered that he was from the Defiance," Meagan said. "He thought I was his contact. I was going to play along until I could turn him over to be arrested."

"And profit along the way, of course."

The man returned to the wall and looked down at the activity on the lower floors. Meagan followed. Despite herself, the moving blend of colors caught her eye. Had he stood up here and watched her and Jacob enter? Had his eyes followed them through the crowd?

"We will not discuss how this boy came to believe that you were his associate," the Black Fist commander said. "What matters is that he believes you are. I let him into this building. I do not care that he is here. That is not important. Do you understand?"

Meagan nodded. She didn't understand, but she certainly wasn't going to tell him that.

"What I really want to know is who this boy is," the commander continued, turning to face her.

"You don't know?" Meagan asked.

His blue eyes stared into hers. "You said he was a Defiance member. I know for a fact that he is not. At least, not the Defiance in this city." His finger tapped the ledge; the sound seemed to slice through the clamor of the party. "So, who is he working for? Why is he here? What does he want?" The commander abruptly spun around to face his team, illuminated by the eerie blue glow. "Do you know how I'd planned to find out?" he asked.

Meagan shook her head.

"I was going to have one of my agents act as his contact. That person would have stayed close to this boy and learned everything important about him. I cannot do that now, can I?"

Again, Meagan shook her head. She wondered if he was going to kill her. That was probably one of her better options.

"However, I have a solution to this problem," the commander continued in a slightly less ominous tone. He looked at her. The hint of a smile on his face was disconcerting.

"What is the solution?" Meagan whispered.

"You will find out this information for me."

"Please—" The words caught in Meagan's throat. "Please, I'm a student in Information. I don't know the first thing about this kind of work."

"You've been doing fine so far."

"But I have to get back. My school—"

He held up his hand and her protest died.

"I have seen your record."

Meagan's throat clenched. She thought of all the Cs she had ever gotten.

"I'm aware of your real record. I know how good you are."

Meagan's eyes widened. Who were these people, to know something like that?

"However, because of your past, I can promise you that you will not advance any further in Information."

Meagan clenched her fists. The happy buzz from below

mocked her, an unattainable dream slipping away like smoke and leaving her in the cold. All because of her parents.

"How badly do you want to be a propagandist?" The man shot the question out at Meagan like a jab from a fencing sword.

A saucy comment sprang into her mind, but Meagan bit it back. She sensed that her future depended on how she answered.

"It is everything to me," Meagan began slowly. "If you've seen my record and you know about my past, then you know why my grades don't match my evaluation. I would do anything to put my past behind me and become an exceptional propagandist for the IAS."

She didn't mention that once she obtained power she had a few choice punishments in mind for certain people.

The Black Fist commander hesitated. His eyes darted to his men and back to Meagan.

"What do you know of your parents?" he asked.

"I never knew them," Meagan answered. "I don't know what they did." Her gaze traveled over the scene below. "Whatever it was, I certainly don't approve."

She looked up in time to see the Black Fist commander raise his eyebrows. She leaned forward and locked eyes with the man.

"I am not my parents," she said. "I want nothing more than to forget about them and live my own life."

The commander appeared to think for a moment. One corner of his mouth twitched up in a smile, and Meagan sensed she had answered well.

"Stay with the boy," the commander ordered. "Find out anything you can about him—who he is, who he is working for. If you complete this job *to my satisfaction*, I will have you appointed to a high position in Information."

"And that position would be …?"

"You would be an aide to Nigel Weldon, the Head of Information in Region Seven, based in Chicago. That is a Level Five position, Meagan. A person in that position, who had brains and cunning, who wasn't held back by the details of her past, would be poised to eventually become the Head of Information herself."

A Level Five position! A Level Four was the highest anyone could attain by skill alone. This was her opportunity, her chance to beat the system. Meagan held out her hand. "I'll do what you ask and more. You won't be disappointed."

The commander took her hand, but instead of shaking it, he gripped it tightly and stared hard into her eyes.

"Make sure of it. Remember, I want to know who the boy is working for." Almost as an afterthought he added, "And don't try to contact me. I will get in touch with you when necessary."

Meagan opened her mouth, but before she could speak, one of the men watching a computer screen spoke. "Sir?"

"Yes?"

"Wild Card isn't going for the deposits."

"What about the chemicals?" the commander asked.

"No, sir. He isn't going for anything we predicted."

"Well, what *is* he doing?"

The underling started typing rapidly. "He is hacking into the database—"

"We know that!" the commander interrupted. "He could want information on any number of things. Just make sure he gets the wrong information. I want to know what he's looking for. Right now, for all I know, he could just want information on the space program."

"Yes, sir, he does."

The commander paused. "He wants information on the space program?"

"Yes, sir."

"Interesting. We will have to see what he tries to do with the information we give him."

"Sir," another man said. This one sounded worried. "He bypassed the false information. He's in the real database. He must have had a code."

"Lock him out!" The commander turned to another of his men. "Track him. And you," he addressed one of the standing men. "Get security on the radio. Have you locked him out?" he asked the first man.

"I'm trying, sir."

"Security's on the radio, sir."

The commander nodded and took the radio. "Overseer, this is Commander Ultan." he said. A voice began speaking on the other end, but Commander Ultan interrupted. "I don't care. I want your men on the sixth floor immediately. Get the boy out of there, but under no circumstances is he to be killed. Is that understood?"

After listening to a reply, Ultan handed the radio back to one of his men.

"Sir! The cameras just went out. Something disrupted their signal."

"You." Ultan turned to Meagan. "Get back to the party."

"But—"

"Go."

Meagan ducked out the doors, hurried down the stairs, and was once more surrounded by light and color. She ignored the guests chatting around her. What was she supposed to do now? She turned, looking around the room to see if Jacob was anywhere in sight. He wasn't.

Meagan walked farther into the room. She really wasn't cut out for this kind of work. She had no training and was unsure of her next move. Still, that didn't matter. She would find a way to accomplish the task Commander Ultan had given her. She had to advance. She couldn't spend the rest of her life suffering for her criminal parents.

A hand clamped around her arm. One of the servers yanked her into a sheltered space between a pillar and the wall. Meagan opened her mouth to give the boy a piece of her mind, but he let go of her arm and closed his hand over her lips. Meagan's eyes widened as she recognized Jacob.

"Leave as soon as you can," he whispered. He was breathing hard, and his face was flushed. He pressed his personal into her hand. "Meet me in the alley on 84 North."

With that, he was gone. Meagan smiled grimly. She could call out, right now, and have Jacob arrested. She could stop him. But she didn't. Not yet. She would not let anyone capture Jacob until she had her information. Then she would turn him over to Ultan herself.

Meagan wrapped her fingers tighter around Jacob's personal and strode toward an exit. She frowned. The personal felt odd, sticky. She looked down to see red on her hand, on the personal. Was it blood? Meagan's heart fluttered. What was she getting herself into?

Chapter 9
Just a Graze

For the safety of the world, only highly trained government personnel will have access to dangerous weapons.
— Fact 612, Citizen's Handbook

As Meagan exited the building, a lieutenant showed Commander Ultan the screen of his computer. "This is the information Wild Card stole."

Ultan took a moment to look over the data.

"He stole the real stuff," the man continued. "Should I have my men arrest him?"

"No," Ultan replied. "Let Public Security chase them. We'll keep a close eye on them and grab them when we want them."

"But Wild Card has real information. I thought you didn't want anyone with real information going free."

"He doesn't have enough," Ultan reassured the man.

Yes, everything should be fine. Wild Card would have to be familiar with space exploration research to notice any discrepancies. And even on the off chance that he did, he still had nowhere near enough data to learn about the Project. He radioed the Project's supervisor, Jorn Belwir, and let him know that the situation was under control.

Ultan frowned. The girl, Meagan, was being held back in her ministry, a situation she refused to accept. She was desperate to advance past her circumstances. Resting his elbows on the wall behind him, he leaned back and considered the events he had set in motion. He would give her the power she craved, at the same time binding her to him. She would become his own personal asset in the Information Ministry, a secret weapon to use against threats that might arise—threats that his superiors would not let him counter until he had furnished "proof." Her power would corrupt her, and he could use her for as long as she would serve him.

However, Ultan's main goal was to discover the identity, mission, and employers of Wild Card. But now instead of simply capturing and interrogating him, he would let Wild Card and Meagan escape and use the opportunity, both to learn more about the boy and to transform Meagan into his personal agent.

Ultan raised his personal and contacted Security Overseer Greene.

"Have you captured the boy yet?" Ultan asked.

"No, sir," the man answered.

"Why not?" Ultan demanded even though he wasn't surprised.

"I have my men combing the building, but we think he got out. I'll send most of my force out to search for him."

"I want him found," Ultan said.

One of his men pointed to a screen. Ultan allowed himself a tight smile. Wild Card was working in the kitchen along with the servers. He would probably slip out after the overseer pulled most of his men from the building.

"Don't worry, sir," the overseer said. "The boy took a hit from one of my men."

The breath caught in Ultan's throat. "He what?"

"Not enough to take him out immediately, sir."

Ultan took a moment to unclench his fists. "Overseer, do you recall the very specific instructions I gave you detailing the most fundamental requirement that this boy was *not to be killed*?"

"Ah, yes, well. We didn't kill him. But, ah," the overseer hesitated. "My men were using scattershot, sir."

Ultan didn't answer. His men had stopped working and were watching him, perhaps wondering if he would order them to drag the man here and execute him on the spot. But that wouldn't do—this man had friends, influence.

He took a deep breath. "Carry on, overseer," he said. His changed tone from shocked outrage to pure ice should have told the man that his days were numbered. Ultan's men glanced at each other and raised their eyebrows.

"Try to remember not to kill the boy," he finished.

Ultan blew out a long breath. That scattershot would be a problem, but Wild Card was on his own for now. Still, the boy had escaped tight situations before. As for Overseer Greene, he was incompetent and had to be eliminated. Anything he guarded was put at risk. In his report to his superiors, Ultan would throw suspicion on the overseer as a Defiance conspirator.

These tactics were what made Ultan effective, more effective than his superiors knew. He had an innate ability to solve multiple problems, put many forces into motion, and complete unrelated tasks while he carried out his primary mission. He thrived in situations like these. He would stop at nothing to destroy the last remaining threat to the security of the State.

"Sir, may I ask you something?"

Ultan replied to his lieutenant with a nod.

"I was reading up on all the files related to this mission. Including the ones on Student Meagan."

"What's your point, lieutenant?"

"Do you think it's dangerous bringing her along like this?" He glanced at the other men, and lowered his voice. "Do you think there could be a problem considering what you did fourteen years ago?"

Ultan shook his head. "She has no way of finding out."

Outside the Space Center, sheets of rain poured down, drenching the streets and blending the world into a single shade of black. The only light came from the occasional streetlight that created a small puddle of light in the wet darkness.

In the alley, Meagan retrieved the backpack from the dumpster and changed into her gray jumpsuit and the soft gray shoes she was accustomed to. She also took her own personal out of Jacob's backpack. It felt good to have it with her again. She waited, shivering.

More than thirty minutes later, Jacob staggered into the alley, breathing hard. His left arm hung limp at his side, and he clutched it near the shoulder.

"Where's my personal?" he asked.

Meagan handed it to him. "What happened back there?"

Jacob shook his head. "Not right now. We need to—" His personal buzzed. Jacob glanced down at his screen and cursed.

"What?" she asked.

"The hotel room I booked as a fallback hideout just canceled my reservation." He shoved his personal into his pocket. "Don't worry about it. You can go."

"Go where? You can't just leave me." She shivered in the rain.

"Back to your hotel. They don't know you're with me."

When Meagan hesitated, Jacob said, "Oh, right. You want to be paid." He reached for his personal.

Meagan shook her head. "Look, I think Public Security knows I helped you, so I can't go back. Forget the payment and let me stay with you instead. We can get out of this together."

"Okay." Jacob held out his hand. "Give me your personal."

Meagan took it out of her pocket, but didn't give it to Jacob. "What do you want it for?"

"We can't have anyone tracking you." He snatched the personal from her hand, dropped it on the ground, and smashed it with his heel. Meagan screamed.

"Quiet," Jacob said. "I'll get you a new one."

"That … that was my life!" Meagan shrieked. "You can't just get a new one. All my papers. My rations. My ticket to Chicago!"

"We'll talk about this later. Right now we need to hide." He hesitated and swayed a little on his feet. "We really need to hide," he repeated. "We need to hide and … I'm not sure where to go."

Despite her shock and fury, a location rose in Meagan's mind. She blew out a short breath.

"I know a place."

"Lead on then." Jacob shook his head, as if to clear it.

They hurried out of the alley, and this time, it was Jacob who followed Meagan. She walked quickly, staying out of the light of streetlamps, ears straining for any sound of danger. All she could hear was the pounding rain, broken occasionally by a crack of lightning and the roll of thunder.

She was reassured, in a way, hearing no sound of pursuit. Still, the Black Fists worked in silence. Would she hear them before they attacked? She doubted it. Meagan shuddered. Don't think about that, she told herself. Worry about one thing at a time.

"It will be safer if we stick to the river," Meagan said. Jacob nodded.

The rain pouring into the river was deafening, but Meagan hoped the noise would hide their movements from their hunters. The two fugitives jogged down the concrete walk that ran along the river. After about fifteen minutes, Meagan was out of breath. She wiped her wet hair out of her eyes.

"We follow the river just a little longer," she told Jacob. This time, he didn't even nod. He stumbled along behind her, breathing harder than before. Meagan realized that he didn't care where she was leading him. She could take him wherever she wanted.

Meagan shrugged. It didn't matter. She wasn't ready to give him to the Black Fists yet.

They left the river, heading into a part of the city broken down after more than a decade of neglect.

"Here we are."

There were no streetlights here, so they couldn't see more than a few yards in front of them, but Meagan knew this place. The two escapees stood on the edge of destruction.

"Stay close," Meagan said as she started forward. "This isn't the safest place to be in the dark."

Giant slabs of concrete jutted out at odd angles and rubble covered the ground. With no road, Meagan and Jacob slogged through mud that sucked at their shoes as they walked. Massive shadows rose up around them, mounds of earth piled up for reasons Meagan could only imagine. Rain ran down their slopes, forming streams in the low ground.

"Careful of the water," Meagan shouted to Jacob over the roar of the storm. In the dark and the mud, Meagan had no way of telling how deep the pools and streams were. One could be just an inch-deep rivulet, another, a death trap filled with mud and debris.

On hands and knees, Meagan started up one of the smaller mounds. She reached her destination and looked back.

"Here." She waited for Jacob to reach her.

Two slabs of concrete had fallen over a dip in the hill, forming a small shelter. Meagan shoved aside branches of a thorn bush that had grown over the opening, her hands so numb from the cold that she could hardly feel the thorns tearing at them.

Crawling through the opening, she moved to the concrete wall at the back to make room for Jacob. She felt him struggle in and crouch beside her. They jostled around a bit, situating themselves with their backs to the dirt of the hill, covered by a concrete roof and wall. In the small space, their heavy breathing sounded loud.

Outside rain poured down, enclosing them in a tiny world filled with the roar of falling water. At least now they were sheltered from the wind. Even so, Meagan would have given anything for a hot meal and some dry clothes.

"There … there's a lantern in the backpack," Jacob said. "It's marked with blue tape. Can you get it?"

Meagan pulled the backpack around in front of her and opened it, wondering how she would find the lantern in the pitch-black of their hideout. When she looked into the pack, she knew. Everything was marked with tape of a different color that glowed in the dark. She located the blue tape and pulled out the lantern.

She switched it on, and the space was filled with a pale blue light. Jacob had unzipped his server's jumpsuit and pulled his arms out of the sleeves. Meagan's breath caught in her throat. Jacob had torn a strip of cloth from the bottom of his white tee shirt and bound it tightly around his arm, just below the shoulder. The makeshift bandage was soaked with blood, and in the light of the lantern Jacob's face appeared drained of color.

"Are you okay?" Meagan asked. She felt short of breath. Why did the sight of blood always have that effect on her?

"Me and Security got into a bit of a shootout," Jacob answered. He began to unwrap the bandage. "Hurts like anything."

"What are you going to do?"

Jacob didn't answer for a moment. He inspected his bloody arm and fingered it carefully. "Well, that's not good," he said.

"What?" Meagan focused on the ground.

"There are fragments in here. They're not bone; it's just a graze."

"Um, is that not normal?"

Jacob took a deep breath. "I'll worry about that later. Just dump some water in it to try to flush some of this out. We can't leave the light on."

"All right."

Meagan took the metal canteen out of the backpack and did as Jacob instructed. When she poured the water over his arm, he gasped in pain. She was sure he was going to pass out, but he didn't.

When he'd caught his breath, he said, "There's a first aid kit in the pack. Grab a bandage."

Meagan passed him a bandage and watched as he clumsily taped it around his arm.

"I bet you wish you were back in your hotel room now," Jacob said with a humorless smile.

"I don't," Meagan answered. Her words surprised her, especially because she spoke the truth. Why did she prefer hiding out under war ruins with a desperate criminal, being cold and hungry and wet, when she could be curled in her assigned bed at the School of Information? She shrugged. If she were at school, she would still be hungry, and cold. Someone would probably be yelling at her for some imagined crime, and she would feel angry and humiliated and Alice would give her that wicked smile and—

"Shut the light off," Jacob said.

Meagan's face had grown hot and she took a deep breath to calm herself. Jacob popped two pills into his mouth and took a drink of water.

"What was that?" Meagan asked as he closed the first aid kit.

"Painkiller. Shut the light off."

Chapter 10
Questions

Transparency is a gift from the State to its people. The government wishes for all people to share in the collective knowledge and the innovations of the IAS.
— Fact 902, Citizen's Handbook

Meagan woke stiff all over. A slimy block of concrete loomed a few inches from her face, and she was curled on wet dirt.

The events of last night rushed back to her. She groaned and sat up. Gray light filtered into the hideout from a cloudy sky. She was hungry, but, to her surprise, not cold.

Meagan saw she was covered with a dark gray blanket. She could feel cool air on her face, but her body under the blanket was completely warm. She felt the fabric, and it almost didn't feel like cloth. It was thin, far thinner than it should have been for the amount of warmth it provided, but it had a rough, waxy feel to it.

Beside her, Jacob was awake. He had removed the bandage, and was probing his wound with tweezers. The area had swollen and turned a purple-gray. However, his face was less pale than it had been last night.

When Meagan sat up, he looked over and gave her a weak smile.

"Good morning." His tone suggested the opposite.

"Is there anything to eat around here?" Meagan asked.

"There's some food in the pack, some water too."

Meagan wasted no time digging into the backpack. What she found included several cans, some packets of nuts and dried fruit, some energy bars, and a plastic box of instant potato flakes. She pulled out an energy bar.

"Don't drink too much of our water," Jacob warned. He winced as the tweezers slipped.

"What are you doing?" Meagan asked.

"Trying to get most of these shards out," he said. "But I'm not sure why the bullet left fragments in the first place."

"Don't look at me," Meagan said with a mouth full of granola. Switching topics, she said, "This is the warmest blanket I've ever used. Is it made out of wool?"

She had never felt wool before, but she had heard it was warm.

"No. It's a fabric called Thermo. I know someone who is friends with the people who invented it."

"It isn't fair," Meagan pouted. "Why doesn't the Information Ministry get things like this?"

She hoped Jacob would slip up and tell her which ministry he belonged to.

"The IAS doesn't know it exists," Jacob said proudly.

"Oh."

Well, that was interesting to know at least.

"Who invented it?" Meagan pressed.

"How did an information girl like yourself find a hiding place like this in a completely different sector of the city?" Jacob asked.

Meagan's eyes narrowed. Jacob's question was a dodge, and a clumsy one at that.

"Answer my question first," she said.

"I can't tell you," Jacob replied. "Now, that was an answer, so answer mine."

Meagan tossed her head. "Well, I can't tell you either."

"Okay," Jacob said. "Compromise." He set down the tweezers and began to rebandage his arm. "We are both curious, and we both don't like taking no for an answer. We'll trade. Question for question. But I'm not going to start giving you names. There are some things it's best you don't know."

Meagan leaned forward. She felt a smile curl across her face. "Agreed. But if you don't answer, I don't have to answer."

"Of course."

"You can go first," Meagan said.

Jacob finished bandaging, and shifted slightly toward her.

"How did you find this hiding place?" he asked.

Meagan dug a second energy bar out of the backpack. "It wasn't by choice, I can assure you," she said. "I missed a train and ended up being out after curfew." Meagan looked down at the bar in her hand. "A Protector gang was chasing me."

Jacob muttered a few choice cuss words. Meagan took a bite of the bar.

"Luckily," Meagan continued with a grin, "I'm smaller than

they are, and fast when I need to be. I didn't even know this place existed before that."

"They were interstate ramps."

"What is that supposed to mean?"

"All this concrete. I looked around outside a little this morning while you were still asleep. These are ruins of several interstates that crossed each other. Three, I believe."

"And they were destroyed during the War?" Meagan asked.

"Is that your question?" Jacob said with a smile.

"No."

"Well, it's your turn to ask."

Meagan had some big questions she wanted to ask, but she didn't want to just come out and demand the information right away. She wanted Jacob to be in the habit of answering questions before she asked what she really needed to know. She thought a moment before she spoke.

"Last night you said you and Security were shooting at each other."

"Not much," Jacob said. "I came around a corner and there were three of them down at the other end of the hall. They hollered and raised their pistols. I fired off a shot and dove right back where I came from." He winced. "I just wasn't quite quick enough."

As far as Meagan knew, the only ministries allowed to use weapons were Defense, Public Security, and State Security. Since he had a gun, was Jacob from one of those?

"Well, here is my question." Meagan said. "We went through a full body scan before we entered the museum. How in the world did you get through with a gun?"

Jacob grinned. He shifted slightly, and drew a pistol from the waistband of his suit pants. It was small and matte black. It looked powerful and deadly.

"I have some new technology the IAS hasn't developed yet, let alone come up with a way to counter. There's a device in the pistol that, when the person is scanned for weapons, sends its own signal to the scanning computer. The signal sends the computer a picture of what it would see if the weapon were not present. It wouldn't fool a person physically searching you, but they hardly ever do that anymore."

Jacob's smile widened. "Even so, there are ways around that, as well. My turn to ask you a question."

"Go ahead."

"What made you decide to fight against the IAS? Like me, you're too young to remember the War."

Meagan said nothing for a moment. She hoped Jacob thought she was hesitant to talk about the traumatic events that led to her defection, but really her mind was racing frantically. Mix the lie with the truth, she recalled from her propaganda training. That makes it harder to tell one from the other.

"The IAS killed some people I was close to," Meagan said. It was repulsive to describe herself as close to her parents, but she ignored the feeling. She was mixing the truth with a lie, she reminded herself.

"Why were they killed?" Jacob asked.

"It's my turn for a question," Meagan retorted. She stuck her hands in her pockets to warm them, and was reminded that she still had the locator in her pocket. An idea began to form in her mind.

"What is the code for my locator?" Meagan asked. "I might need to know at some point."

Jacob smiled. "It changes."

"What do you mean?"

"Did you shut it off?"

Meagan nodded. "Actually, I turned it on and off and on and off again."

"Okay. Every time you turn it on, it resets with a new password. Even if someone were to break the old password, they could only have used it until the locator was turned off. When you turn it back on, new words will be required."

"How do you know what password to use?"

Jacob tapped his head. "Memory. It's my locator, and I come up with all the passwords. I might leave it with instructions somewhere for a contact to pick up. Like how I left it for you."

Like how he left it for the man who died in front of her. She swallowed. "Okay, so what's the next password?"

"'In such an angry sea.'"

"That's the password?"

"Yeah. It's from the poem 'The Wreck of the Hesperus.'" Jacob answered. "All the passwords are from poems I've memorized."

Meagan barely kept her jaw from dropping. Instead she smiled coyly at him. "What ministry lets you memorize poems all day?"

"It's not my job," he said. "But where I come from, boredom and depression can be real issues. People will organize events, like a poetry recitation, or a dance-off, or something, to help keep people's spirits up."

"A dance-off? That doesn't sound like the IAS I know."

Jacob smiled, but didn't answer. Instead, he said, "My turn for a question."

"Ask away."

"What happened to those people you were close to? Why were they killed?"

"I don't know, and that's the truth." Meagan shrugged. "Look, I really don't want to talk about this."

"Well, it's your turn."

"What is your favorite job you've ever done?" Meagan asked. She would get him to tell her who he worked for.

"Ever heard of Rails?" Jacob asked.

Meagan shook her head.

"It's short for Underground Railroad, which is a prewar term," Jacob explained. "Basically, I helped smuggle people."

"Smuggle them where?"

"Well, even though the IAS technically rules the world, they have a stronger influence in some places than in others. If a person were being hunted by the Region Nine government, I might get them to Region Twenty-five. Of course, I'm not with Rails anymore."

"What do you do now?"

"My turn for a question," Jacob said. "How did you get that cut on your face?"

"What?" Meagan raised her hand to her cheek. She felt her face grow hot. What would she say? The School of Information. Her Shaming. Alice.

"Nothing I couldn't handle," she said. She would not let Jacob think she was weak.

"That's not an answer," he retorted.

"I got in a fight." That was true enough.

Jacob laughed. "How do you get in a fight at propaganda training? You're at a school, right? It can't be that rough."

"You don't know anything," Meagan said, turning away. She had changed her mind. Jacob was probably the son of a high up official, a spoiled brat, who was rebelling out of boredom. He didn't know anything about what life was really like.

"Hey, I didn't mean to upset you," Jacob said. "I was surprised, that's all."

Meagan shook her head. She shouldn't be so sensitive. "It's nothing."

"Did you win?" Jacob asked.

"What?"

"Your fight. Did you win?"

"You already asked your question. It's my turn," Meagan said.

"Go ahead, ask."

"Who are you?"

Now it was Jacob who asked, "What?"

"Who are you?" Meagan repeated.

"I'm Jacob."

Meagan raised her eyebrows. "You will have to answer better than that."

"What more do you want to know?"

"What ministry are you from?"

"Not Information."

"Obviously." Meagan realized the double meaning of Jacob's words. She crossed her arms. "Fine, don't tell me. But you owe me an answer."

"Some other time." Jacob leaned back against the concrete slab. "Why did you want to go to Chicago?"

That question threw Meagan completely off guard. Then she remembered that, among other things, Jacob had paid for the code with plane tickets.

"It doesn't really matter now, does it?" she answered softly. That ought to make Jacob feel bad, and save her from having to come up with an answer.

"Try to rest," Jacob said. He turned to look out the opening of the hideout. "I'll get us out of this."

Meagan had not been asleep, not exactly. She was lying against the dirt with her eyes half closed. Beside her, Jacob was reading something on his personal, his eyebrows drawn together in concentration. One reason she couldn't sleep was that he kept muttering to himself and shaking his head as he read. Occasionally, he would type in something himself.

Without warning, he blurted out, "It's not a space program."

Meagan gave up trying to sleep and rolled over, propping herself up on one elbow.

"What?" she asked.

Jacob ignored her. "The technology is all wrong. The supplies don't match up, the equipment is wrong. Even the specialists are wrong."

Jacob continued scrolling through whatever information he was reading as if he wanted to be sure he understood it correctly.

"I didn't download everything I wanted before I had to run, but the information here seems to indicate that the New Worlds Space Program isn't really a space program."

"That's ridiculous. Why wouldn't it be a space program?"

"Beats me," Jacob said. He started typing rapidly. "There are plenty of SciTech people working at the facility, and a good number of SciTech specialists have been brought in from time to time, but you would expect more of them and less of these other specialists—from the Housing Division of Civil Affairs, for example. What in the world does where people live have to do with space exploration?"

Meagan shook her head. "I'm just trying to figure out your oh-so-mysterious background that lets you know all this."

"Furthermore," Jacob continued, "something is seriously wrong with the equipment. The facility is outfitted more like a hospital."

"Forgive me for seeming dense," Meagan said, "but what's the big deal? What use could the Defiance have for this information?"

"It's not that I don't trust you," Jacob began, "but—"

"I know, I know. You can't tell me."

Chapter 11
Scattershot

Universal access to equal healthcare is a basic human right.
— Fact 100, Citizen's Handbook

It was raining again that night, a slow drizzle, making the world seem miserable and depressed. Which made an interesting contrast to Jacob's mood, Meagan dryly observed. He was practically ecstatic.

"The rain will make us less visible," he told Meagan as he handed her some dinner, cold noodles out of a can.

"You have a place for us to go?" Meagan asked.

"Yeah, I'm going to try to take you to the house of one of the Defiance members." Jacob hesitated before adding, "I think she'll help us."

"You think? You're not sure?"

"No, sir. I guess you're right," Jacob said. His voice stiffened and became more formal. "We have to face things as they are."

Meagan cocked her head. "What are you talking about?"

"I'll handle things myself from now on," Jacob said. His face had gone pale again, and he was staring at the wall.

"Jacob, you're not making any sense."

Jacob shook his head. "What?"

"No, what to you. You're babbling."

His eyes returned to her. "Was I talking to you?" Jacob asked. "I thought you were … someone else. Never mind. What was the question?"

"Are you okay?" Meagan asked.

"Sure. I'm fine." He rubbed his wounded arm. "Arrow, the woman I'll take you to meet, should be able to get me in touch with the Manager of the Defiance. I want to tell him about the space program."

"No argument here. I'm ready to get away from this place as soon as possible." Meagan looked closely at Jacob. "You sure you're okay?"

"Meagan, I'm fine."

All was dark outside, except for some dim lights from the city.

A cold feeling of apprehension settled in Meagan's stomach.

Meagan and Jacob crawled out of their hiding place at about ten thirty that night. They crouched at the bottom of the pile of dirt and concrete and looked cautiously around. Then, moving as quietly as they could, they dashed from one cover to another. Like ghosts, the two fugitives hurried through the wasteland and farther into the city.

Meagan pressed herself against the cold bricks of a building. She watched as Jacob blended into the darkness of the next building. Meagan's eyes moved frantically, scanning the streets for the gleam of a security camera. Cameras were all over the city. She could only hope the rain would mask their movements, or that she would see a camera in time to avoid it.

Jacob turned his head, making sure they had not been spotted, and motioned for her to join him. She sprinted quietly to his side before he dashed to the next building. Meagan's muscles tensed as she prepared to follow, but her straining ears heard a voice farther down the street.

She froze, heart pounding. Chances were it was Road Patrol checking to make sure no citizens were breaking curfew.

The voice spoke again; this time she could make out his words.

"Yeah, I'm coming around. Be there in a minute."

He sounded like he was moving away. Still, Meagan waited a full sixty seconds before she peeked around the corner. The street was deserted. She ran to where Jacob crouched against a brick wall. He didn't move as she came up beside him.

"I think he's gone," she whispered.

"Meagan, everything is distorted. I … I feel like I'm going to throw up."

Meagan took the canteen out of the backpack and held it out. "Here, take a drink," she said. The softness of her own voice surprised her.

Jacob gulped down two mouthfuls and passed the canteen back to Meagan.

"That's a little better," he said. "Let's go."

As they hurried across the street, Meagan wondered how far away this Arrow woman lived. The longer they were out, the higher the chances they would be discovered. And something was definitely wrong with Jacob. She shook her head. She shouldn't worry about it. If they could only keep from being captured long enough for her to get some good information, nothing else would matter. Still, Meagan thought as she sprinted forward, they couldn't be caught just yet.

Nearly two dark hours passed before they reached the woman's street. The houses here were older, but well kept. Most were three or four stories and built very close to the road and to each other, with only a narrow alley between them. Meagan thought they were in the housing section for low-level financial workers.

Jacob ducked into one of the alleys that ran between the houses. Meagan was right behind him. The brick walls of the houses on either side of them loomed up, protecting them from the light of the streetlamps. Even so, Jacob crouched behind a dumpster, motioning for Meagan to do the same.

"Okay, just follow my lead," he whispered. "But be quiet. Arrow lives on the second floor, and there are other people above and below her."

Meagan nodded.

A ladder led up the side of the house next to Arrow's. Jacob began to climb it, somewhat clumsily. Meagan followed.

When Meagan was opposite a second-story window, Jacob whispered down to her. "Knock on the window."

Gripping the cold metal rung of the ladder with one hand, Meagan leaned out over the alley, trying to reach the window. The rain had made everything slick, and Meagan shot a quick glance at the ground below. Directly under the window was the dumpster, filled with bags of trash.

"At least the trash will break my fall," she muttered.

Meagan had a good head for heights and did not slip. She rapped sharply on the window. After waiting twenty seconds, she repeated the signal.

A curtain pulled back, and a pale face appeared in the window. The window opened and the face disappeared.

"All right, Jacob," Meagan said to herself. "How are we supposed to get in?" The alley, narrow though it was, was still too wide to climb across.

A thick board slid out the window, and Meagan got the idea. She settled the end of the board on one of the rungs of the ladder, and the woman leaned out the window, holding the board steady. Her shoulder-length brown hair, tousled from sleep, spilled around her face and began to stick to her forehead in the rain.

Meagan wasted no time crawling onto the board. The longer she waited the wetter and more slippery the board would become. She scurried across and slid through the window.

From what she could see by the tiny amount of light coming through the window, she assumed they were in the kitchen. Meagan moved aside to let Jacob crawl in after her. He breathed a sigh of relief when his feet were firmly planted on the wooden floor. Meagan guessed he was not as fond of heights as she was. She helped the woman pull the board back into the room. Jacob shut the window and the curtains. Now the room was completely dark, but after a moment, a dim glow from the built-in flashlight on the woman's personal illuminated their faces.

"Hold this a minute please," she said, handing her personal to Meagan.

When Meagan had taken it, the woman laid the board across two brackets screwed into the wall, then set a large pot on top of it. Meagan realized that the board was a kitchen shelf. It was a brilliant idea. No one would suspect the board's other use.

The woman took the light back from Meagan and led the two fugitives into an adjoining room. She set her personal on a low table in the middle of the room and from a drawer took out a candle and match. She lit the candle and the room was filled with a soft light.

"Please, sit," she said, motioning to a sofa along the far wall. Meagan and Jacob gratefully dropped onto the worn cushions. The woman smiled, and in the candlelight, Meagan noticed her brilliant blue eyes. Her hair fell in waves framing her round face. She wore a thin white tee shirt and shorts, but she wrapped herself in a blanket from several that were folded on a wooden chair in the corner. She took a seat on the edge of the table.

"You I know, Wild Card," she said, "but who's she?"

Jacob turned to Meagan, but hesitated, perhaps wondering what name Meagan wanted to give.

"I'm Meagan," she said.

The woman gave Jacob a look of mock disapproval. "Wild Card insists on using my call sign, Arrow, but you can call me Tina."

Tina turned to Jacob. "What are you doing here?" she asked. "I thought—"

"I know I'm not supposed to be here, but this is serious, Arrow."

"Relax," Tina said. "It's fine that you're here. You need a doctor, right?"

"No, actually I want to speak to the Manager."

Tina's eyebrows drew together. "That won't be so easy to arrange."

"Who is the Manager?" Meagan asked.

"He is the leader of this Defiance cell," Tina said. "We're the last real resistance in this city." Tina glanced sideways at Jacob. "He also told Wild Card—"

"I know what he said," Jacob interrupted. "Let me worry about that."

Tina gave him a slight smile.

"I wouldn't be here unless it was important," Jacob said. "Tell him Wild Card has information. He'll want to see me, even if he's not happy about it."

Tina shrugged. "I'll see what I can do. In the meantime, I'll get our doctor to take a look at your arm."

"I know how hard it is to get a doctor," Jacob said. Then he shouted. "But I'm not going to let you die! We'll get through this."

Tina looked sharply at him, then turned to Meagan. Meagan shook her head.

"This might hurt," Tina said. She leaned forward and tore the bandage off Jacob's wound. Jacob gasped and seemed to snap back to reality.

"You were hit with scattershot, weren't you?"

"There were fragments—" Jacob began. He gripped the arm of the couch, and closed his eyes.

Tina turned to Meagan. "When was he shot?"

"Last night. What's wrong?"

"Scattershot is designed so even a survivable wound will eventually kill the victim," Tina said. She stood and hurried into the kitchen.

"Kill the victim?" Meagan called after her. "But it might not be scattershot, right?" Meagan heard her open a cabinet.

"Has he been dizzy? Jumping from a present conversation into a remembered one?"

"Yes, but not too much," Meagan said. In the kitchen, a pot clanged.

"It's scattershot. You're lucky the wound was just a graze." Tina emerged from the kitchen holding an old ration box. "Has he taken pain medicine?"

"Yes," Jacob answered. He sat up straighter. The confusion was gone from his voice.

"That slowed it down," Tina said. She dumped the contents of the box on the table. Pills of various sizes and colors rolled out. She glanced up at Meagan. "My illegal stash."

Tina selected a pill and handed it to Jacob. "This will hold off the effects for a while."

Jacob swallowed the pill. Tina set about rebandaging his arm.

"You'll be good for twenty-four hours," Tina said. "I'll get you our doctor, and maybe—maybe—our Manager."

"How long will that take?" Jacob asked.

"Well, I think our doctor can be here tomorrow. His call sign is Deuce. As for the Manager, well, we'll see."

"Not too long."

Tina shook her head. "He's not going to be happy, you know."

When Jacob didn't answer, she said, "Well, you know your own business best, I suppose. In the meantime, you and Meagan can stay here. Just keep quiet. The people above and below us aren't Defiance."

"We understand."

"Bathroom's over there." She nodded over her shoulder. "The door in the kitchen leads downstairs; showers are in the basement."

"Thank you for everything," Jacob said.

"Everyone does their part, but for now, I'm going to bed. I have to be at work in a couple of hours."

"Good night," Jacob said.

"Night," Tina responded. "Good night, Meagan."

"What? Uh, night?"

Tina laughed and went into her bedroom, closing the door behind her. Jacob turned to Meagan.

"Have you never said good night before?" he asked.

Meagan shook her head. "At school, we have a completely different custom before bed."

Jacob stood up, swayed a little, and regained his balance.

"Well, you can sleep on the sofa, if you want."

"I'll be fine on the floor," Meagan said, standing. "You're the one who's wounded."

Jacob smiled gratefully and stretched himself out. Meagan grabbed a blanket and curled up on the floor.

As she closed her eyes, she breathed out a sigh of contentment. She was safe here. Here with Jacob and Tina she would be protected for the night. She smiled, but then pushed the feeling to the back of her mind. She needed to work out a plan. She had to get the information Ultan wanted. If things kept going like they were, she would be able to give him not only Jacob but also three other rebels: the Manager of this cell, the doctor, and Tina.

Meagan bit her lip. When she completed her mission, no one would ever trust her again. Not like these people had.

She felt a flash of annoyance. Since when had she cared about trust? When this was over she wouldn't need anything from anyone.

Meagan rolled over, suddenly uncomfortable. Could she trust Commander Ultan to keep his promise? How would he find her? The Black Fists didn't know where she was. Or did they? Sighing in frustration, Meagan shifted to her back. She stared up at the ceiling. She would have to contact the Black Fists herself. She couldn't count on them finding her.

Meagan flipped over onto her stomach, squeezed her eyes shut, and tried to push every thought and doubt out of her mind. Within moments, she was asleep.

Chapter 12
Getting Along

Harmony between ministries and between the individuals who make up those ministries should be foremost in the mind of every citizen.
— Fact 347, Citizen's Handbook

It was past midnight, but Ultan still sat in his office inside the Black Fist headquarters. The night shift had alerted him to a message they had received and decoded. He scanned the short message again and nodded to himself.

Already his work was bearing fruit. He had guessed Meagan and Wild Card would not remain hidden for long. They needed shelter and information. Now that he had pinpointed their location it was time to act. Meagan was loyal to him, but that was only because he was offering her something she wanted very badly. That in itself, however, was not enough. Using Meagan's desire for power to buy her loyalty would only work as long as there was nothing else she wanted more. He had dangled the carrot in front of her and she had willingly followed. Now he wanted to be sure she remembered that he also held the stick.

Ultan leaned back in his chair. He really wanted to use his own men for the job. He knew them and he knew exactly how well they would perform. They wouldn't have done something as stupid as shooting the invaluable prisoner. But he was already pushing the rules as it was. He sighed, picked up his personal and pulled up a contact.

The voice on the other end said, "Seriously? It's like two in the morning."

"I thought you liked to be out at night."

"Having some fun in the Reeducation Ward is one thing, listening to your voice is something else."

"Shut up," Ultan said. "I have work for you."

"Me and my men don't work until two in the afternoon. Call then."

"Keep in mind who you are speaking to, Warren."

"Oooh, the Black Fists. I'm terrified." His voice dropped to a hiss. "Our groups are allies, remember?"

"You will only remain that way if you do what we want."

Not for the first time, Ultan marveled at the way the Protectors' leader could annoy him so quickly.

"It must really get under your skin to know that you can't just pop a bullet in me," Warren said. "Not unless you wanted an all-out war between the Black Fists and the Protectors."

"Don't think I couldn't kill you," Ultan said. "No one would trace it back to me either."

"So why don't you? No real guts?"

"It's called duty, thug. Duty and an oath I swore. I don't expect trash like you to understand."

"You're not the only one who swore an oath. You don't get to be so high and mighty."

Ultan realized that the conversation was deteriorating quickly.

"I get to be whatever I want," he snapped. "You, however, will find your options severely limited if I don't see three of your people in my office in fifteen minutes."

"That's not enough time for them to get there."

"I'm sure you'll think of something."

"How about half an hour?"

"Let them take your car."

There was silence for a moment before Warren spoke. "No one will care when you die, Ultan."

Ultan laughed. "You're confusing popularity with impact. Maybe a few people will cry over whatever ditch you end up in, but when the final accounts are rendered, your life will have been wasted, with no accomplishment to your name."

"Whoa, preacher," Warren said. "You could get executed for a sermon like that."

Ultan's eyes narrowed. "I'll see your men in thirteen minutes."

When Warren began cussing, Ultan hung up.

Meagan woke with a cry. She threw out her hand to ward off an unseen attacker, and her arm connected with something solid. She gasped for a breath and opened her eyes.

The gray light of a cloudy dawn lit the room. She was on her knees. Her blanket had been hurled partway across the room. Her cheeks were wet with tears, and her arm hurt where she had banged it against the table. She wrapped her arms around herself to stop the shaking.

"It was just a nightmare," she said to calm her racing heart. "Just a stupid dream."

Meagan took a deep breath. She hadn't dreamed like that in a long time. Not for years. Hadn't she stopped for good? Meagan retrieved the blanket and wrapped it around her shoulders. Those kinds of dreams put a damper on the whole day.

"Hey, Jacob," Meagan said, turning to the couch. She faltered. The couch was empty.

"Jacob?" Meagan said, louder this time. No answer. Quickly, she checked the rest of the house as terror built in her. By the time she stood in the kitchen, she knew it was true. Jacob was gone.

Panic gripped her chest, constricting her lungs. Jacob had left her. But why? He was supposed to wait here for Deuce. Why leave now? Meagan took a deep breath, trying to work through this rationally. Perhaps Tina had been able to arrange that meeting with the Manager after all, and Jacob needed to go to him urgently. But why not take her with him? Why leave without even telling her where he was going?

Meagan's imagination supplied answers enough. He had only wanted her help getting out of the Space Center. Now that her usefulness was through, now that he was with his Defiance friends, he was ready to be rid of her. Ultan was wrong; she had not been able to get close to Jacob.

Meagan clasped her hands over her mouth. She had failed. She had failed the Black Fists. Her task had barely started and already she was stopped cold.

But what if that was it? What if Jacob knew, if he had found out?

Meagan shook her head. He couldn't know. He had no way of knowing she was a Black Fist spy. Unless … unless he had witnessed her conversation with Ultan. If he had, if Jacob knew she was a traitor, then bringing her here was a trap. He could be bringing the Defiance to come get her at this very moment.

She couldn't stay here. She couldn't wait for Jacob to move against her. Meagan checked her pocket to make sure she still had her personal. It was her only possession. She cursed when her hand came up empty. Jacob had stolen that from her as well.

Meagan choked down a sob. She had no information. No pass to the top. Not even an identity since Jacob had destroyed her personal. Meagan began to shake with fear and adrenaline. She had failed the Black Fists. Ultan would not take that lightly. Which would she rather face, the Black Fists or the Defiance? Both options would probably end in her death.

She'd worry about that eventually. Run first, think later. Meagan opened a cabinet and grabbed the first box of food she could. As she turned to the door, it swung open. Jacob stepped into the kitchen.

Meagan froze.

"You're finally awake, I see," Jacob said, closing the door behind him. "Don't eat Arrow's food."

"Where have you been?" Meagan asked carefully.

Jacob jerked a thumb back toward the door. "Checking our escape options in case we have to run. Familiarizing myself with the layout in case I have to fight."

Very slowly, Meagan took a deep breath.

Jacob cocked his head to one side. "Is there a problem?"

"Problem?" Meagan set the box down on the counter then whirled on Jacob. "How dare you leave like that?"

"Like what?" Jacob said.

"Just get up and leave without telling me." Meagan ran her hand through her hair. "I could've … could've … left and you wouldn't have cared."

"You were fine, Meagan. I was just out for a few minutes." He gave her a confident smile. "I do know what I'm doing."

"No, you don't," Meagan said. How dare he tell her she was fine? "You just left me there."

"You were sleeping."

"So that's your excuse?"

Jacob threw up a hand. "Yes. My sole purpose was to upset you."

"Well, don't feel like you have to lie to me. If you don't want me around, just say so."

"I never said anything about not wanting you. What's your problem here, Meagan?"

"You could have left a note," Meagan said. "Or woken me up."

"I chose not to," Jacob snapped. "I have things under control. You should trust me."

"How am I supposed to trust you if you're just going to leave me alone whenever you feel like it?"

"I've taken care of things fine so far."

"Hey, I was the one who saved us after the Space Center," Meagan said. "And I'm the one who had to deal with your delusions. You know, you're not as smart as you think you are, Jacob."

Jacob's face flushed red. "Fine," he said. "If that's the way you feel, then you should just leave. I'm not forcing you to stay here."

"I can't leave!" Meagan shrieked. "I have nowhere to go."

Jacob crossed his arms. "Well, I'm obviously incapable of protecting us here, so I wouldn't be qualified to help you."

"You don't care," Meagan cried. "You're just like everyone else. You don't care about me. You don't care about anyone other than yourself." Meagan shouldered past Jacob and yanked open the door to the stairs.

"You can't—" Jacob began.

Meagan whirled around. "Don't you dare tell me what I can and cannot do. I'll be back in a little bit."

"Oh, so you can leave whenever you want, but if I go out for our own safety, then I'm the horrible person here?"

Meagan didn't answer. She stepped onto the stairs and closed the door. Let Jacob have a taste of his own medicine. Besides, she wanted a shower.

Despite her seething anger, Meagan quietly descended the stairs. When she reached the last step, she froze and glanced about. She wasn't going to completely abandon caution. She was in a small room, apparently shared by all three floors of the building. Ahead of her was a door leading out to the street. Light came in from the window beside it.

A handwritten sign reading "To Basement" was taped to a door on her left. Meagan ran silently across the wooden floor. She paused for a moment when she heard voices. A curtain was hung across a doorway in the back wall. Meagan guessed it led to the rooms of the person who lived on this floor. The cloth swayed a little, betraying the movements on the other side. Meagan's eyebrows drew together. That was a little strange. Everyone should be gone. It didn't matter though, as long as no one saw her. She continued on through the basement door and down the steps.

On one side of the basement sat a washing machine and a dryer. Wedged between these and the white wall was a treadmill. A layer of dust coated it, attesting to the amount of use it had seen. Meagan assumed it must have been put there before the rationing had taken full effect, back when citizens were expected to maintain a proper body weight on their own. Now exercise was mostly unnecessary. Rationing ensured that the populace stayed under the weight standard.

A heavy curtain enclosed the other half of the room. Meagan shoved it aside. As she expected, there were shower stalls here. The three stalls had no doors but each had a curtain for some privacy. Towels sat on a small table. Meagan grabbed two. She undressed and, wrapping herself in a towel, put her clothes in the machine to wash. It would feel great to be clean with clean clothes. Jacob would be jealous.

Despite the rush of cool water, Meagan still felt hot. How could Jacob have been so insensitive? She had saved his life, after all. How hard could it be to leave a girl a note?

Three minutes later, when her teeth started chattering from the so-called warm water, Meagan decided that she was finished. She dried herself and again wrapped the towel around her, rubbing the second through her hair.

She waited while her clothes dried, and they warmed her after the cold shower. Meagan threw the towels into a labeled basket. Jacob was probably still furious with her. The feeling was mutual. Meagan slammed her hand into the wall and let out a frustrated sigh. As much as she hated the thought, she was going to have to make up with Jacob. Was it her lot in life to take blame for faults not her own?

Still, she had to keep the greater goal in mind, and that was to get Jacob to trust her, to talk to her. That obviously wasn't going to happen while he was mad at her.

Meagan's lips tightened as she reached the top of the basement stairs. She'd had plenty of practice faking apologies.

Carefully, she opened the door at the top of the stairs. No one was in sight and she didn't hear any noises coming from the adjacent room. She stepped into the room and turned to close the door silently behind her. When she turned back around, she found herself looking into the eyes of a tall, dark-haired man. His unshaven face was only inches from her own.

Chapter 13
Protectors

The Protectors, chosen from your own communities, are the first line of defense in maintaining social equality. They are your neighbors and friends. They hold the privilege of making sure no person or group ever rises above another. With their help, we will all rise, hand in hand, together.
— Fact 878, Citizen's Handbook

The man let out a short, barking laugh at the surprise that must have crossed her face. Meagan's eyes darted to the left and right. Two other men stood behind him. A red spider tattoo ran up the side of one man's neck, standing out against his dark skin. The other was shorter than Meagan, with blond hair that fell to his shoulders.

"I don't remember you living here," their leader said.

"Who are you?" Meagan demanded. She took a step forward so she was glaring up at the man. She could not let them know how afraid she was.

"Guess." The man waved a hand, indicating the jumpsuits he and his companions wore. Meagan had already noticed. The jumpsuits were black, the color of State Security, but they were jumpsuits, not the uniforms the Black Fists wore.

"You're Protectors," Meagan said, not letting the dismay she felt creep into her voice. "Let me through."

She tried to push past the leader, but he shoved her back against the wall and held her there with one hand on her shoulder.

"I have a message for you," he said, still in the same mocking tone. "From a mutual commander."

"How … ?" Meagan began.

"How does he know where you are?" The man's smile widened. "This is his message: 'Don't think you can double-cross the Black Fists. You will get what you want if you play your part well, but if you fail, you will suffer the consequences.'"

"I understand," Meagan said, trying to move away from the wall. She wasn't planning on betraying the Black Fists. If the Protectors would just go away—

"I don't think you do," the man said. "We're here to give you a taste of what happens when you fail the State."

He yanked her arm, wrenching her away from the wall. She stumbled forward. The two others pressed in around her. Meagan cursed under her breath. Why did she always end up like this? Without thinking, she raised her fists. All three Protectors started laughing. Meagan felt her arms twisted behind her by rough hands.

"Let go!" she shouted. She tried to pull away, but the short Protector only held on harder.

The leader slapped her. Meagan's head snapped back, and her eyes watered. Through the stinging in her face, she felt blood trickling from her lip.

"You cannot escape the detection of the Black Fists." He raised his hand again.

The door opened and someone stepped in off the street. Meagan was facing the other direction and only caught a glimpse out of the corner of her eye.

"Protector business, leave now!" the Protector with the tattoo shouted.

"I'm just looking for Joe," the man said. "Is he here?"

Meagan tried to twist around to see what was happening, but the short Protector held her firmly.

"Get out," their leader growled.

"Sure."

Behind her, Tattoo Protector let out a short, startled shout. All of the Protectors started yelling and cursing. The Protector holding Meagan let go of her arms and shoved her forward. She dropped to her knees.

A dull thud sounded from behind her. Meagan's head was spinning, but she pushed herself to her feet and tried to make sense of the scene.

Tattoo Protector wrestled with the new arrival. The short Protector was slumped at Jacob's feet, and blood flowed from a gash in his head. Jacob held his pistol by the barrel, and his face was dark with anger. He switched the pistol back to a normal grip and stepped over the fallen Protector toward the leader, who yanked a billy club from his belt.

Jacob stopped short, snapping the gun up to a ready position.

"Hands up," he said. "Now." He didn't shout, but Meagan's

blood turned to ice at the tone of his voice.

The leader glared at Jacob for a moment, then raised his hands, dropping the club. Jacob turned to the scuffle on the floor.

"You two. On your feet." The fight stopped, with both combatants raising their hands. Meagan was able to get a better view of the newcomer. His brown jumpsuit hung baggily on his tall, thin frame, and he wore thick black gloves. A ridiculous grin covered his face. What was most noticeable, however, was his bright red hair.

"You." Jacob indicated Tattoo Protector. "Get over there by your friend."

The Protector went reluctantly.

"You. Over here." That was directed at Meagan. Without a word, she moved quickly past the Protectors to stand behind Jacob.

"Turn around and face the wall," Jacob commanded the Protectors. "Now, on your knees."

"Are you going to shoot them?" the newcomer asked.

Jacob didn't move. He stood glaring down at the Protectors. His knuckles were turning white where he gripped his pistol.

Very slowly and deliberately, he asked Meagan, "Are you hurt?"

Meagan shook her head before she realized he wasn't looking at her. "No."

For another long moment Jacob didn't move. Finally, he shoved his pistol into his belt. "It'd draw too much attention, anyway," he muttered. He scooped the billy club off the floor and slammed it into the sides of the Protectors' heads. They both collapsed on the floor.

"Who are you?" Jacob demanded, turning to the newcomer.

The man crossed his arms and raised his eyebrows.

"Purple mountain majesties," he said.

"What?" Meagan said.

"Above the fruited plains," Jacob answered. He held out his hand. "You're the Defiance doctor?"

"Yeah, call me Deuce. And you're my patients?" He shook Jacob's hand. "Always a pleasure to meet fellow members of the Hate the Protectors Club."

"Yes." Jacob wasn't paying much attention. "Excuse me a moment."

Jacob turned to Meagan.

"In the future, maybe you could avoid just walking out of our hideout whenever you feel like it."

Meagan tossed her head. "I don't see why you're so upset, Wild Card. Everything turned out fine."

"I'm serious. What if I hadn't been here?"

"You're not listening to me," Meagan hissed. "I don't need your help."

"Lie to me after your mouth stops bleeding," Jacob snapped. He spun toward Deuce. "We can't stay here, and the Protectors won't be out much longer. I don't have the proper codes to warn Arrow."

"I can take care of that," Deuce said. "Did Arrow give you something for the scattershot?"

"Yeah. It'll last most of today."

"Okay, good. You both can come with me."

Jacob adjusted his backpack then opened the door and looked out.

"How will you send a message?" Meagan asked. "They are all read by Security."

"Streets are pretty deserted," Jacob said. Then, to answer Meagan's question he said, "The Defiance has some superior technology."

"Because Wild Card is nice enough to share," Deuce added. He turned to Jacob, glancing at his arm. All the movement must have caused it to start bleeding again; the bandage was turning red. "Can you manage?"

"I'm fine. Let's go."

The sky was overcast as they left the building, and the wind whistled down the gray streets.

"My car is a couple blocks away," Deuce said.

"Your what?" Meagan asked.

"I can shield our image from the cameras if we can make it in less than fifteen minutes," Jacob said.

Deuce nodded. Jacob unclipped a small device from his belt and hit several buttons.

"Okay, let's go."

As they hurried down the road, Meagan trotted beside Deuce.

"Is it standard for the Defiance to disguise as laborers?" she asked.

"It's convenient," he answered. "There are a lot of laborers, and it's not unusual for them to be on the street during the daytime since they don't have a desk job. Besides, you can't expect me to just go walking down the street in my doctor's blues, can you? Think of the attention it would draw."

"People don't associate with laborers," Jacob added. "And you can wear gloves."

"You don't wear gloves," Meagan said.

"I'm not in the system."

"That's ridiculous. Everyone is in the system. We're all fingerprinted and photographed every couple of years."

Jacob didn't answer. Meagan decided not to press the issue. Deuce was way more talkative than Jacob, and she had another question.

"You have a car?"

"Yes. Well, of course, it's not my car, but I'm allowed to use it."

"Doctors are allowed to have cars?" Was it easier to get luxury items as a doctor? It was too late to try to get into another profession, but the information might be useful.

"He makes house calls," Jacob said. "The State is trying to cut down on hospital overcrowding, right?"

"Well sort of," Deuce said. "The hospitals are not overcrowded, per se. Only so many people are admitted. However, there's a mile-long waiting list to get into a hospital, or doctor's office, or dentist. I try to eliminate some of the relatively minor complaints on the list so patients don't have to be admitted. And, as I'm sure you know, I am assigned patients by my superiors."

Meagan nodded. Apparently, she was more familiar with this than Jacob. No one ever said it was impossible to get treated by waiting your turn on the list, but she was not an idiot. Everyone knew that you had to be someone or know someone to receive medical care. There was a reason it was called a *waiting* list. As a student, and therefore the "future," Meagan had always received a complete medical and dental checkup every two years. In between, the unspoken rule was don't get sick. Or don't let anyone know.

Sickness meant quarantine, which was the worst punishment ever invented in Meagan's opinion. She had tried to get out of work once with an excuse that she was ill. She had been immediately sent to a building filled with other sick people waiting for treatment. Some of them had been waiting for weeks. Some were very sick. Luckily for Meagan, a preliminary check had called her bluff, and she was not admitted. If she had been, she had no idea when she would have been let out. Since then, when she really was sick, she kept it to herself.

"Of course, I don't always approve of my assignments," Deuce continued. "It's not that I mind helping people who are honestly sick, even if they are nasty bureaucrats. What frustrates me is the headaches and sniffles, things that shouldn't even qualify as illness, that I have to treat."

Deuce's face was drawn. "When I think about the people dying out there, who have been on the waiting list for years, it's just heartbreaking. Then some important guy gets a paper cut, and it's drop everything and rush over to his house and give him a bandage, because haven't you heard, those things haven't been sold in stores since I was a kid."

"And so you have your side business," Jacob concluded.

"Yes. I treat people who would never get treated otherwise. I may not be blowing up munitions and stealing supplies like the rest of the Defiance, but I have my own personal defiance against the International Administrative State."

"Well, I appreciate everything you are doing for us," Jacob said. "I will compensate you for the extra danger you have incurred by sheltering us."

Meagan raised her eyebrows in surprise. Jacob had used a word she had never heard before. She did not know what *incurred* meant, and she was intrigued. As a propagandist, whose life was words, she could think of few people who knew more words than she did. Once again, her mind turned to the question of who Jacob was.

Chapter 14
The Glory of Sons

Education is the security of the future. The right to educate is reserved by the State alone.
— Fact 205, Citizen's Handbook

Before they reached the car, Deuce pulled Jacob and Meagan into a sheltered space between two buildings.

"The car is parked in front of that house," he said, indicating a house up ahead. "I have a patient resting in there. I told him I had to walk back to the hospital to get something. I'm sorry, but you two are just going to have to wait until I can finish today's appointments."

"Oh, that's no problem," Meagan said, trying to conceal her grin. She would actually get to enter a car. Even better, she would get to be in it when it was moving.

Deuce stripped off his brown jumpsuit. Underneath was the crisp, blue and white uniform of the Health Ministry.

As Deuce departed, Jacob took Meagan's arm and said, "Follow my lead."

Meagan nodded. Jacob stepped around the corner and onto the sidewalk some distance behind Deuce.

The dingy green vehicle had seen better days. The paint was scratched in places, and there was a dent on the passenger door. Still, being permitted to use even a car like this was a status symbol. From the way pedestrians slowed as they passed and glanced at it out of the corner of their eyes, Meagan could tell that this was the closest about half of them had ever been to one.

Deuce approached the car and said loudly to the people walking past. "Out of my way or I'll have you reported. I have important business to attend to."

The people near the car rapidly dispersed and Deuce unlocked the car and dropped his brown jumpsuit inside before turning and walking into the house.

Jacob walked down the sidewalk as naturally as if he were just out for a stroll. When they neared the car, Meagan saw his head move ever so slightly, as he checked to make sure they were unobserved. Then, without hesitating, he dropped to a crouch behind the car, dragging Meagan down with him. She was startled by how quickly he had moved. They were almost completely sheltered from view by the large hedge that grew in front of the house and bulged out over the sidewalk. Jacob opened the back door about halfway. Meagan followed him into the car, crawling to stay out of sight.

The car was small; there was barely room for the two of them to hunker down on the floor between the front and back seats. The tinted windows would shield them from passersby as long as they stayed low.

Inside, they were sheltered from the crisp fall weather. Meagan leaned back against the door. Although his head was down, Meagan could see that Jacob's face was flushed. He was holding his injured arm. Meagan shook her head. She knew it was bothering him more than he would admit.

With a stab of guilt, she realized that if it had not been for her, they would have been safely hidden in Tina's house. Deuce would have examined Jacob's arm and administered the proper medical treatment, instead of the makeshift treatments they had been using so far.

Meagan didn't like to admit it, but she did feel a little bad about what had happened. Jacob had done nothing except protect her, and she had only made things worse.

Well, wasn't that what she was supposed to do? This boy was fighting against the State, and he deserved all the trouble he got. On the other hand, her mission was to get information, not cause trouble. Meagan told herself that she was completely in the right, but all she could think of was Jacob rushing to defend her from the Protectors. She bit her lip. The more she thought about it, the more she realized that she had overreacted back at Tina's house. It really wasn't all Jacob's fault.

Jacob was also the only person she could think of who had ever smiled at her, a real smile, not a threatening smile or the smile of a person who wanted something. Meagan could tell the difference. She could tell that Jacob genuinely liked being around her. At least, he had until she made a mess of things. He probably hated her now.

Without warning, another face filled her mind. This face was also smiling at her. It was a safe face—a face that cared for her. The weight of her memories was behind it, so she tried to focus, to remember, but the face was just a yellow blur.

It vanished into a scream and cold white. Meagan closed her eyes. Fear gripped her insides. She clenched her hands so hard her fingernails dug into her palms. The Black Fists knew where she and Jacob were hiding. They could never really escape them.

Meagan wished she were back at school, but Ultan was waiting for her to do her job. She exhaled, trying to erase her half memories. They were a distraction, and she had forced them down so far inside herself that she'd thought they were gone for good. She couldn't let anything stand in her way. She couldn't fail Ultan.

"Are you awake?" Meagan whispered to Jacob.

"Yeah," he answered without raising his head.

She had to apologize, regardless of her feelings. She couldn't afford to have Jacob mad at her.

"Look, I am sorry about the way things turned out back at Tina's place."

"You have to be more careful," Jacob said.

"And you should have told me you were leaving."

Jacob's face hardened, but after a moment, he spoke. "Meagan, I need you to accept the fact that I know what I'm doing. There may be times when I have to leave. It's part of the job."

Meagan looked down at her hands. She could still feel the rush of fear that had gripped her, the panic at Jacob's disappearance. But she could not argue her point; she must complete Ultan's task.

"Sure," she said softly, still looking at her hands. She met Jacob's eyes and gave him a small smile.

"Why were you so upset?"

Meagan shrugged. "You weren't there when I woke up. I guess I kind of freaked out."

"Maybe I should be pleased my absence caused you so much distress," Jacob said, returning the smile.

Meagan did some quick thinking. Jacob would dodge or refuse to answer her direct questions. Maybe he would be less defensive if he were talking about something unimportant.

"So," Meagan said, pulling her knees to her chest. "What does the Defiance do in situations like this to pass the time?"

"Sleep."

"I'm not tired. Know any good games?"

Jacob shook his head. "We don't even have a deck of cards."

"What about games without cards?"

Jacob thought for a moment.

"Well, there is this one game my grandpa and I would play." A slight smile touched Jacob's face. "He was teaching me to read."

"Wait, wait …" Meagan held up a hand. "Your grandpa would be your dad's dad, right?"

"Well, my mom's dad actually."

"Your grandpa taught you to *read*?" Meagan said. "That's illegal."

As soon as she said it, she knew it sounded silly.

"Yes."

Jacob's smile had grown wider. Meagan could tell he was pleased by her surprise. He was also proud of his family. It made Meagan feel sick. She was spared having to respond though, because Jacob continued.

"We would start with the letter A and name something the IAS has banned that starts with an A. We would go through the entire alphabet."

"You played this when you were how old?"

"About five. When I got a little older, we would play the same game, except I would have to explain why propaganda said an item was banned, and then give the real reason."

"What do you mean?" Meagan asked, brushing a strand of hair out of her face.

"Take blue jeans for example," Jacob said. "They were banned under the IAS supposedly because they were too big a drain on resources. The real reason was because, for one thing, the jeans were too durable. People didn't rely on the IAS for their clothing as much when the clothes were lasting years, and for another thing, the IAS was pushing for the colored jumpsuits for the different ministries. Jumpsuits made it easier to keep track of people, and made them more dependent on the IAS."

"That's a lot to remember for one game," Meagan said. "And it doesn't sound like much fun."

"I enjoyed it. It was more fun than just memorizing facts. Grandpa was teaching me about the history and purpose of the IAS, and he wanted to make it fun so I would remember."

"So J would be for jeans," Meagan said, wanting to keep this conversation going.

Jacob shook his head. "Nope, B for blue jeans. J was always the same word."

"Which was?"

"Jacob."

"Jacob?" Meagan raised her eyebrows. "I find it hard to believe you were specifically banned by the State."

Jacob looked down for a moment, then his eyes met hers. "I would not have been born under the IAS. My grandpa wanted to make sure I remembered that."

"What do you mean, you wouldn't have been born? You're here, aren't you?"

"I was born a month before IAS troops took over our city, about three months before the end of the War. My parents had an arrangement with our doctor to keep the birth off the record. They had a good idea of what was coming."

So that was why Jacob wasn't in the State's system.

"But you still could have been born under the IAS," Meagan protested. "It's not like they just said you couldn't exist."

Jacob shook his head.

"About a year after our city fell, my mom and dad were pressured into taking the PGT."

"What's that?"

"It stands for Physical and Genetic Test. Everyone has to take it. It's a test that determines if you are fit enough to have children." Jacob's face was dark with anger. "My dad didn't pass. They said his offspring would be inferior."

"Jacob—"

"After that, my mom deliberately flunked."

"Why?"

"If she had passed, she would have been assigned a new partner. She was also afraid they would discover she had been pregnant before. I was still at home with her at the time, and they were terrified that I would be discovered." He looked up at Meagan. "I'm grateful for the risks my parents took, but I blame the IAS personally for robbing me of the chance to have a brother or sister."

"Trust me, family's not all it's cracked up to be."

Jacob's eyebrows drew together. "I just assumed … Well, I—Do you have family?"

"Not anymore. I wish I never did."

"But why? I mean no family is perfect, but," he hesitated, "don't you miss them?"

"No," Meagan hissed. "I don't. I don't have a family, and I don't want a family. The State is my father and the Earth is my mother. That's how I want it."

"But—"

"I don't wish to discuss this."

"Okay."

Chapter 15
Strange Occurrences

The so-called family unit is the last and strongest bond of the Old World. If we are ever to truly know peace and equality in this New Order, we must uproot this unit, and destroy it more completely than any other trappings of the Old World.
— Charter of the International Administrative State

Meagan and Jacob stayed in the car as Deuce traveled to his appointments. The first time they started moving, Meagan had to keep herself from shrieking with excitement. Jacob laughed at the expression on her face, and she asked him if he had ever ridden in a car. He told her he'd been driving since he was nine. She felt like kicking him then, but didn't.

After about fifteen minutes though, Meagan got over her excitement and began to feel that waiting to get out of a car was a lot like waiting to get out of a bus, only now she wasn't even allowed to look out the window. Deuce finally finished as the setting sun broke through the clouds and turned the walls of the buildings to fire. He didn't speak as he climbed in and pulled away.

After driving a few minutes, he said, "I have one more stop to make tonight, but I'll get you both to my house first and we'll have a look at your arm. Are you doing okay, Wild Card?"

"I'm starting to feel a little dizzy again."

"I'll get you the antidote and bandage you up properly as soon as we get to my house. I have quite a stash of medical supplies. Things I have 'borrowed' from the hospital."

"You must have a lot of unauthorized work," Meagan said. She figured it would be a good idea to see what information she could get. Commander Ultan would appreciate it, and he might give her a bonus for her good work.

"There is enough work for ten doctors. So many people need help, and there isn't any way I can help them all."

"Are things any better in the Reeducation Ward?" Jacob asked.

"Wait," Meagan interrupted. "I don't know that place."

"It's the part of the city where the IAS dumps the people they dislike," Jacob answered. "The State brands them enemies and confines them to the Reeducation Ward. Trust me, it's not a place you want to go."

"Unless you are a doctor. Most of those people can't even get onto the waiting list for medical treatment. There is the work of a lifetime in that small section of the city. And things are getting worse, not better."

"Now what?" Jacob said.

Deuce hesitated. Then he spoke slowly, choosing his words carefully. "There's always the odd disappearance in the Reeducation Ward. Someone vanishes during the night and is never heard from again."

"And between the Black Fists and the Protector gangs there are plenty of people to blame," Jacob muttered.

"But the disappearances are more frequent now."

Jacob cursed.

"What?" Meagan asked.

"I thought something like this might happen sooner or later," Jacob said. "The IAS has finally decided that just killing the entire ward is easier than reeducating them."

"That's what the Defiance thought too," Deuce said. "We got in touch with some of our contacts in Re-ed, trying to work out some sort of plan, but from what they told us, something a little more strange is going on."

"What did they say?" Jacob asked.

"The increase in disappearances began about a year and a half ago. However, about four months ago this man named Albert vanished. From bitter experience, they assumed that they would never see him again. Then, five weeks later, he turned up. He acted like he was never gone, just sort of picked up where he left off. So they asked him what happened and found out that he had no memory of ever being away. Of course, what family he had was overjoyed that he was back."

Meagan opened her mouth, but Deuce noticed and answered before she could speak.

"Yes, they still have some family ties in the Reeducation Ward. One way they are luckier than the rest of us."

Sadness flickered across his face before he continued.

"However, after the first day, people started to realize that something was wrong. Albert was different. He wasn't acting normal. Sometimes, he would stare at the sky for hours. When he finally stopped, he would stare at the ground for several more hours. Then he went back to acting normal, as normal as possible."

"And no one had any idea why he was behaving that way?" Jacob pressed.

"Wait, it gets weirder. His wife told me that one time, as she was coming home with her work group, Albert was out on the street. He was just walking back and forth, up and down the street. One of the guards from their group ran over to him and started yelling at him for not going straight home after being let out of work. Albert just kept walking down the street, completely ignoring the guy. Another of the guards came over and they started hitting him. He still didn't stop. He didn't respond. Well, the second guard hit him in the head with the butt of his rifle. He knocked Albert to the ground, but he just got up and kept walking. By this time, everyone was a little nervous, if not completely disturbed. They left Albert to his walking. About half an hour later, he stopped, and started bleeding from his ears and nose. He collapsed. Even though it was against regulations, his wife went out and checked on him. He was dead."

"Why?" Meagan breathed. Despite herself, she was enjoying the story.

"No one knows. Later, more people began disappearing. But then they come back. They can be gone anywhere from a few days to a week or more, and they never have any memory of the time they were gone. Besides that, there is always something strange about them."

"Like with Albert?" Jacob asked.

"Well, it varies from person to person, but it mostly involves repeating the same task over and over again. Some of the people have lost memory of more than just the time they were gone, and a few don't even remember who they are. Something very strange is going on, but it hasn't become public knowledge. Especially since no one cares about the Re-ed Ward. I'm wondering if the IAS is trying to cover up an outbreak of some kind. Or trying to start one." Deuce fell silent.

"Well, I certainly want to know what's going on," Jacob said. "Do you have any more information?"

"I could get into specific details if you really want, but I doubt you'll be able to make any more sense out of them than I can."

Jacob frowned. "You said the disappearances noticeably increased a year and a half ago, yet the first person who returned came back about four months ago, right?"

"Yes. As you can imagine, I am very curious about this whole matter. One of my contacts, a lady who lives in the Re-ed Ward, told me that a man she knows disappeared about three weeks ago. He just returned yesterday. She was hoping that I could talk to him, check him, as a doctor, and see if I can discover what the problem is. That's the other stop I have to make tonight. Everyone in Re-ed is afraid it might be a disease."

"Has anyone who hasn't disappeared started acting like the returned ones?" Jacob asked.

"No. And that's what makes me wonder. The only ones who have the problems are the ones who have vanished and reappeared. So far." Deuce sighed. "My contact is letting the man stay with her right now since his room was given to another family when he disappeared. That will make it easier for me to examine him."

Deuce turned the car into the driveway of a small two-story house that gave the impression of having been built around the garage. From her vantage point, Meagan could see a window on the first floor that had duct tape around its edges.

Deuce pulled into the garage, and Meagan dislodged herself from between the two seats as the garage door closed. She climbed out of the car and Jacob followed, moving carefully. Meagan could tell that his arm was bothering him.

Deuce came around to help Jacob.

"Meagan, grab the backpack," Jacob said. Meagan hoisted it onto her shoulder and followed Jacob and Deuce into the house.

Deuce took them through a small kitchen into a living room. He dropped his bag into a faded yellow armchair and switched on a tall floor lamp. Heavy polka-dotted curtains were drawn across the window Meagan had noticed from outside, protecting the occupants from prying eyes. The three of them barely fit in the room.

"You can sit here in a minute," Deuce told Jacob, indicating the small sofa. "Take off your shirt."

Deuce pulled a long sheet of plastic from underneath the sofa and draped it over the cushions. "Just have to make sure we don't leave any blood for the Black Fists to find."

Jacob sat down. Deuce began carefully removing the bandage. Meagan drew her breath in sharply when she saw how bruised and swollen the arm was. The wound had reopened as the bandage came off, and fresh blood welled up from the multiple cuts in Jacob's arm. The entire area was sticky with blood. Meagan's stomach twisted and she felt faint.

"I'll be upstairs," she said. Neither Jacob nor Deuce answered.

Meagan made her way up the steps in the dark. When she reached the top, she took Esma Droncht's personal out of the side of Jacob's backpack and switched on the flashlight. From the bed in front of her, she guessed she was in Deuce's room. She also discovered a closet, a bathroom, and another room that contained nothing but a sofa and a lamp on the floor. There were no windows in this room.

An idea entered her mind, and she felt a small surge of adrenaline. She switched the lamp on, shut the door, and dropped the backpack to the floor. Unzipping it, she began searching through its contents. If there was information here, she would find it.

Nervous that the door would open at any moment, Meagan worked quickly. She laid out the backpack's contents neatly on the floor. First, there was the medical kit. She skipped this. She also skipped the food and water, and the Thermo blanket. She pulled out a rather large cloth bag held closed with two buttons. Opening this, Meagan discovered clothing of all kinds. Most were jumpsuits of various colors and levels. There was also a pair of dark pants, a belt, and several dress shirts. All of these were folded into tight rolls and fitted into the bag. Meagan tried to put them back the way she found them.

Next she picked up what appeared to be a makeup kit, which she could not help opening. Meagan expected the usual assortment of cosmetics, but was surprised to discover hair dye, paint, what appeared to be putty, false facial hair, and two small bottles containing what looked like glue and remover. Meagan was intrigued, but she knew she needed to hurry. She had no idea how long Deuce would be with Jacob. At the bottom of the pack was a plastic box containing ammunition and what Meagan assumed was equipment for Jacob's pistol.

Looking through side pouches that held even more equipment, she found multiple devices, computer chips, and high-tech looking gadgets, but had no clue as to their purpose. She also discovered three personals, but when she turned them on, they were empty. A deadly looking knife in a sheath was strapped to the inside of the backpack, and Meagan found three extra clips of ammunition in a front pouch.

Someone rapped sharply on the door. Meagan nearly jumped out of her skin.

"One minute," she gasped as she returned the things to the backpack. She dropped the first aid kit back on top of everything else. Then, Meagan took the locator out of her pocket. She pressed the button and made sure it flashed green before sliding the device between two pieces of lining in the side of the backpack. If she needed to, she could enter the password into her personal, or tell Ultan the password and they would be able to track Jacob. At least, that was possible as long as he stayed with his backpack. He wouldn't be able to just disappear on her again.

Again came the knock. Meagan sprang to her feet and opened the door. Deuce gave her a tight smile. Meagan could tell from his drawn face that he was worn-out.

"I'm finished with your friend," Deuce said. "He'll be okay as soon as the medicine I gave him takes effect." He ran his hand through his red hair. "I still need to visit that other patient."

He nodded toward the sofa. "That folds out into a bed. Make yourself at home. I'm sure you know this, but I'll say it again. Keep an eye on your water usage. My house is monitored as much as the next guy's. I don't want Black Fists showing up at my door because you two flushed the toilet too many times."

"Don't worry. I know how to conserve water."

"And electricity," he added.

"And electricity. We will be careful."

"All right. You can get something to eat if you like."

"I will."

Meagan slung the backpack over her shoulder and followed Deuce downstairs. Jacob was resting on the couch.

As Deuce passed, Jacob asked, "You're seeing your other patient?" He sounded groggy, probably from the medicine.

"Yes. I should be back before dawn."

Jacob nodded to Meagan. "Meagan'll go with you."

"What?" Meagan demanded, dropping the backpack on the floor with a thud of protest.

"I don't need either of you to go with me," Deuce said. "Neither of you should leave the house."

"Well, I can't go, so Meagan has to."

"She most certainly will not," Deuce answered.

Jacob sat up slightly. "Look, I'm not just saying this because I'm loopy on meds. I want to know what's going on in the Reeducation Ward. It might be relevant to my mission."

"I don't see what that—" Deuce started.

"It's all connected, all the strangeness, I think. I need more information."

"I could give you an eyewitness account, and that of a doctor, moreover."

"We might not be with you very long. We might be on the run again. I want someone with me who has seen the disease, if that's what it is."

"Well—"

"Maybe she'll see something you missed."

"Do I get a say?" Meagan interjected.

"This is really important," Jacob said. "Please."

Meagan sighed.

Deuce spoke. "I'm aware of your reputation, Wild Card. I'll trust your judgment."

As he headed for the back door, Meagan heard him mutter, "Even if you are loopy."

Chapter 16
Par

Upon the signing of the peace accords, all children between the ages of five and ten will be tested to determine the ministry into which they will be placed. All children under the age of five will be processed under the Ministry Allotment Act.
— IAS Charter for the North American Continent Regions

So Meagan was once again out on the streets at night, with another criminal, keeping out of sight and making her way across the city. She and Deuce had dressed in brown jumpsuits and they wore heavy black gloves.

Before she left, Jacob had given her one of his empty personals to be her own. He'd also loaded it with false papers.

"It won't stand up to a thorough check," he said, "but it should get you where you want to go tonight."

Now they stood at a train station waiting to be let through security, keeping their eyes down and their shoulders hunched just like everyone else. They were now mixing with the lower ranks. Like Deuce and herself, some of the people wore brown. More wore the blue and white jumpsuits of the Health Ministry, but the blue shade was so dark that Meagan knew they were only sanitation workers and janitors. Deuce seemed to know how to blend into a crowd, and they boarded the train unnoticed.

After taking her seat, Meagan leaned back and closed her eyes. Deuce would alert her when they'd reached their stop.

Meagan awoke with a start. For a moment, she had no idea where she was. The air was stale and smelled of unwashed bodies. Then she saw red hair and Deuce's grinning face.

"Time to go," he whispered.

Meagan pulled herself to her feet. Despite her nap, she did not feel any less tired. She gritted her teeth and told herself to deal with it. She had managed worse at the School of Information. She could handle this.

As they crouched in a muddy alley about half an hour later,

Meagan tried to remind herself of her resolve. She had never been in this part of the city before. They were hiding behind a dented trash can, pressed against the side door of a tiny house. Meagan wondered what would happen if someone inside decided to step out for a breath of air.

"Where are we?" Meagan whispered.

"Justice Ministry's section. Housing for aides and clerks and such."

"Why here?"

"Well, we're in Security's sector of the city. Reeducation is under the direction of Security, as is the Ministry of Justice."

"But we're in Justice. You want to go to Re-ed."

Deuce gave her a small smile. "You'll see."

He ran his hand along the doorframe.

"What are you doing?" Meagan asked.

"There's a buzzer hidden here," he answered. "It will get the attention of the people inside."

"Inside the house? Do you have a death wish?"

Deuce laughed. "Don't worry. The men who live here are friends of ours. One of them should be here soon. They're expecting me."

"Are they also Defiance members?"

Deuce nodded. "I've known them since they were little. Not that I was all that much older. The War ended before either of them had turned ten. They were, what? Seven? Eight? But they worked out their tests so they both ended up in the Justice Ministry. I don't know the details, but, when they graduated, they pulled some kind of trick on an administrator to get them assigned to this house."

"What's so special about this house?" Meagan asked.

"Well, back during the War—"

"Aw, Deuce, you'll ruin the surprise," said a voice behind them. Meagan and Deuce both turned. A man stood in the shadows of the darkened doorway. "Come in before someone sees you."

Meagan and Deuce ducked into the small house. Deuce closed the door behind them.

"How's it going, Par?" Deuce asked the man.

"Well as can be expected," he replied. "Lungs are still breathing, heart's still pumping blood. Can't ask for more than that."

"Then I will," said Deuce. "I want to get into Re-ed. Cynthia's place."

"Right." Par turned to Meagan. "Don't listen to Deuce. You'll see why we wanted this house soon enough."

Par switched on the flashlight on his personal. He led them away from the door and through a kitchen so small they could barely squeeze between the table and the cabinets.

"So what are you going to pay me for staying up late and taking you on your little sightseeing tour?" Par asked.

"I don't pay you." Deuce sounded slightly amused.

"It's a new rule I came up with," Par answered. "If the government can do it, why can't I?"

"You have an excellent point," Deuce said. Meagan glanced back at him. A wicked smile stretched across his face. "I'll remember that the next time I'm giving you stitches."

"On second thought, I think I can do without the dough," Par said hastily. "Man. Why does everyone but me end up with money?"

"It's okay," Deuce replied. "Not everyone can have your impressive brain."

Par sighed. "I'll choose to take that as a compliment."

"Take it in the spirit it was intended."

"That's exactly what I don't want to do."

Par led them down a short flight of steps, then across another darkened room.

He stopped at a metal cabinet that stood taller than Meagan. Par opened the rusting doors, then crouched down and put his personal in his mouth. He pulled a box off the bottom shelf and gestured for them to move forward, holding his personal so they could see. Deuce dropped to his hands and knees, clutched his bag to his chest, and crawled into the cabinet. As his thin legs vanished into the opening Meagan blinked in surprise. The cabinet wasn't that deep. She dropped to her knees like he had done and then she understood.

Part of the back of the cabinet had been cut out, leaving an opening big enough to crawl through. Beyond the opening was blackness.

Meagan crawled into the cabinet. The only light came from Par's personal behind her. She felt the floor change from metal cabinet to cold concrete. The room, at least she thought it was a room, was filled with a strong musty odor. Meagan considered standing, but she had no idea how high or low the ceiling was. She heard movement on her right.

"What is this place?" she asked Deuce.

"You'll see," he whispered back mysteriously.

Par switched off his personal and crawled through. In complete darkness, Meagan heard him enter the room. Then it sounded like he pulled the box back over the opening. Meagan heard a click and light filled the room.

Meagan blinked in the florescent glow. When her eyes adjusted, she saw that they were in a small, concrete room with a wooden ceiling just high enough for Meagan to stand comfortably. The room was about three paces across, and its width was only a little bigger. In the far wall, Meagan noticed a small metal door, secured by a padlock. Deuce was sitting on a dark green plastic tub.

Meagan was now able to see their host. Par wore the standard tee shirt and shorts, but over that he had strapped a wide belt with a holstered pistol. He was nearly as tall as Deuce but not as lanky. He was well muscled, but Meagan couldn't tell much more because he wore a black ski mask over his head. All Meagan could make out were green eyes.

"Hi, Deuce," he said, inclining his head slightly in Deuce's direction. "Is this lady one of your new trainees? And more importantly," he took Meagan's hand, "are you free for dinner?"

"What?" Meagan did not understand what dinner had to do with any of this.

Deuce rolled his eyes. "She is a friend of Wild Card's."

Par let go of her hand. "Oh. That means that all this mystery and sneaking around has been a walk in the park compared to what you've probably been through."

Meagan could not resist. She affected an air of boredom. "It is rather tame."

"Well, she seems okay to me, Deuce, and she's a friend of Wild Card's ..." He pulled off the mask.

Meagan couldn't help smiling at the way his sandy blond hair went in all directions. He noticed her look and grinned back. His wide smiled stretched his face and his green eyes shone. He ran his hand once through his hair to straighten it. It didn't really help.

Deuce laughed. "Meet Par. Or," he glanced slyly at Par, "the jester of the Defiance."

"Aside from yourself, you mean," Par shot back without missing a beat. He shooed Deuce off the tub and, opening it, pulled out a brown jumpsuit. He began to get dressed, buckling his belt and pistol over the jumpsuit. "You're regular comic relief, Deuce."

"No, what'll really be funny is when your friend comes down here and finds us talking instead of working."

"Only if you think murder is funny."

"Your murder," Deuce specified. "And Sword always describes what he is going to do so creatively. That fascinates me, as a doctor."

"That fascinates you as a sadistic person who happened to get a job sticking needles in people," Par corrected.

Deuce opened his mouth, and Meagan, afraid the banter would continue, cut in.

"I'm Meagan."

Par smiled at her. "Pleasure to meet you, Meagan." He turned to Deuce. "Ready?"

"We're waiting on you."

"Well then." Par took a ring of keys off a hook on the wall. "We should get started."

When he unlocked the door and swung it open, Meagan half expected the door to grind along the ground or squeak with age, but its hinges slid silently. Cold air blew into the room from the darkness beyond.

Chapter 17
The Reeducation Ward

Sedition runs deep in family lines. Therefore, those deemed an enemy of the State, their children, and their grandchildren, must be kept away from the people and reeducated. They will be taught how to live in peace under the IAS.
— IAS Charter for the North American Continent Regions

Par took a flashlight out of his pocket. It was one of the old-fashioned kinds, with a thin metal body and LED lights.

"Right outside the door is a drop," he warned Meagan as Deuce prepared to go through. "There is a metal ladder set against the wall. Climb down it." Deuce ducked through the door and Meagan watched him climb into the darkness. Then it was her turn. Par shone the light on the ladder so she could see what she was doing. She felt the first rung with her foot, making sure she had her balance before climbing quickly down. Par followed, closing the door behind him.

When he reached the ground, he edged past Meagan and Deuce to take the lead.

"Where are we?" Meagan whispered. They were walking on concrete and judging from the echoes and the feeling of openness, there was a lot of space.

"Subway tunnels," Par answered.

"The city doesn't have a subway," Meagan said.

"They never finished building them. Project was stopped even before the beginning of the War. That was before I was born, but I heard there were some pretty messed up things going on in the years leading up to the fighting."

"Anyway," Deuce broke in, "during the War, a thirteen-year-old girl found these blocked off tunnels. Her dad and some others connected some buildings and houses to the tunnels. They used them some during the War, but the tunnels were always kept secret. Most people from that old group are dead, but the girl's dad is now the Manager of our Defiance cell. So we get the tunnels."

"And they are really the only way to get into the Reeducation Ward," Par said. He was silent for a moment, then said, "We're actually quite lucky. The State hasn't been able to reform this city completely."

Deuce nodded. "We've all heard horror stories from people who have come from cities farther east. What they have to live with is unimaginable."

"Especially in Region Six." Par's voice was grim. "There are a lot of things we get away with here that would be impossible in a more reformed city. 'Course that won't last. The IAS will eventually bring the full force of their programs down on us. Don't know what we'll do then. Figure it out when the time comes, I guess."

"In the meantime," Deuce added cheerfully, "these people really put the underground in underground resistance."

Par let out a half laugh. "That joke was pathetic, Deuce."

"I'm tired," Deuce retorted.

"Oh, sure," Par answered. "I think you're losing your touch."

"Losing my— Don't make me spank you, young man."

Par laughed out loud. "That explains it. You're going senile. "

And they were right back into their banter and insults, although they kept their voices low. Meagan tuned it out. This dark, underground world fascinated her. She wished she could turn on a light. What did this place look like? Was it simply one long tunnel, or had the Defiance made it branch off into many different passages? Who all knew about this?

Meagan wondered what Commander Ultan would say when she told him about Defiance-controlled tunnels running under the city. She was not even a trained agent, and already she had so much information for him. Surely, he would reward her well.

Meagan felt a flash of annoyance that turned to fear in her stomach. She was still failing the mission the Black Fist leader had given her. Jacob was her goal, not the Defiance. What did she know about Jacob? Practically nothing! Meagan was sure that Commander Ultan would not be impressed with just any information. Not when he had asked for—demanded—specific information. She had to pry more, much more, information out of Jacob. She frowned. He wasn't the easiest person to get information from. Still, she could do it. She had to.

"And we arrive," Par said. He and Deuce had both grown more serious, their banter done. Par shone his light on a rusting stepladder leading up to a door with a black cloth tied around the handle.

Par climbed the ladder and took his ring of keys out of his pocket. While he was unlocking the door, Deuce took two white hospital masks out of his bag. He handed one to Meagan.

"Put this on."

Meagan covered her mouth and nose with the mask, and Deuce helped her tie it behind her head.

The door swung open silently. Par shone the light down the ladder and motioned them up. Par had again covered his face with the ski mask.

Deuce looked at Meagan.

"Don't speak louder than a whisper," he said. "Don't do anything crazy. Above all, do not take off your gloves or your mask, and do not tell anyone your name. Do you understand?"

Meagan nodded.

She followed Deuce up the ladder. Deuce heaved himself through the small door, then crawled farther in to make room for Meagan. She followed his lead, going into the darkness on hands and knees. The ground was soft under her gloved hands. Par switched off the light and closed the door.

He did not turn the light back on. Meagan felt him brush against her as he took the lead. His voice, barely audible, drifted back to them through the darkness.

"There's a plastic cord running along the ground. Grab ahold of it and just follow along."

Meagan reached her hand over what felt like dirt until she found the thin cord. It did not seem like much, but it was all she had to go by, and she wrapped her fingers around it tightly. She felt it tremble a little in her hand as Deuce also took hold.

Again, Meagan crawled through the dark. This time, however, she was not on concrete. Her knees became damp as the moisture in the ground soaked through the thin fabric of her jumpsuit. A strong smell of waste and decay permeated her mask and Meagan wrinkled her nose in disgust. She heard shuffling noises and low murmurings from above. The wood of the floor above them creaked and groaned continuously. Meagan jumped as a baby's wail sliced through the darkness. She clenched her teeth and moved on.

Even on her hands and knees her head kept brushing against the ceiling. A cobweb wrapped around her face. She tried to brush it off with her shoulder. Scratching and rustling nearby alerted Meagan to the presence of mice. She tried not to think about it, about any of the details of this place. She thought instead of how she would get back at Jacob for dropping her in this situation.

Meagan bumped into Deuce. He had stopped. Ahead of him, Meagan heard Par tapping on the floor above them. He tapped three times, and Meagan heard a return tapping. Par knocked again, in a different pattern. It sounded like something was dragged across the floor above them. A crack of light appeared overhead as a trapdoor opened. Par rose to a crouch, pushing it open the rest of the way.

Meagan could still hardly see anything. The light that filtered down was not electric, but flickered faintly like a candle or dim lantern.

Par climbed out. Deuce was next, then Meagan. She blinked and looked around. They stood in a square area partitioned off by sheets hung from the ceiling. The room wasn't more than a few paces across, and from the noise, Meagan guessed they were in quite a large building. She could see the silhouette of another person through the thin sheets. A baby continued to scream. To another side, someone was sobbing, and, farther away, a man yelled curses in a drunken voice. On the floor above, a man and woman argued.

Deuce wasted no time, but stepped up to the woman holding the candle. Her age could not have been more than thirty, but Meagan thought she looked much older. Her pale blond hair was limp and bedraggled and her face was lined. The clothing she wore was made for a man and was too big. She stood next to a thin mat on the floor. Meagan guessed she had removed it to reveal the trapdoor. The only other furniture in the room was a plastic lawn chair, in which a man sat. His arms rested on the arms of the chair and his eyes were half closed. His pale skin, stretched tight over his bones, looked eerie in the dim candlelight. Meagan's eyes narrowed. From the coarse stubble on his head, it appeared that his hair had been recently shaved off.

"Hello, Cynthia," Deuce greeted the woman. His voice was muffled a little by the mask.

She tilted her head toward the man in the chair. "That's Mack." Her voice was soft with no trace of emotion in it.

"Thanks." Deuce took some paper bills out of his pocket and handed them to her. Meagan felt a thrill of excitement in spite of herself. Paper money! Only criminals and spies used paper money. Deuce brushed past her to stand in front of Mack. Mack did not move.

"Hi Mack," Deuce said gently. "How are you feeling?"

Mack looked up at him. To Meagan he looked lost and despairing.

"Who you are?" His voice was cracked and dry.

"A friend," Deuce replied. Mack turned his head away and stared at the wall.

"You'll notice that his head's shaved," Cynthia said, counting her money. "It was longer when he came back, but he kept scratching at it. I didn't want lice or nothing, so I took care of it." Cynthia slipped the money into a pocket, set the candle on the ground, and lay down on the mat. Immediately, she began to snore.

"I'll keep watch," Par whispered. He slipped out past one of the curtains. Deuce pulled off his thick black gloves and put on thin latex ones.

"Aren't you afraid one of these people will turn you in?" Meagan asked as Deuce began to examine Mack.

"Terrified," Deuce answered. "Still, I am the only way these people will ever get medical treatment. So they have a vested interest in making sure nothing happens to me."

"But the person who sold you out would be rewarded," Meagan persisted. "*They* wouldn't have to worry about medical help."

"True, and I don't doubt that some would betray me to the Black Fists. That's who runs things here." He shook his head. "However, you shouldn't be so quick to judge these people. There's more loyalty and honor among the people of the Reeducation Ward than you will find just about anywhere else under the IAS."

"But why?"

"What do they have, if not loyalty to each other and hatred of the State?" Deuce took a stethoscope out of his bag. "Some people here are the children and grandchildren of powerful people, businessmen, politicians, and the like. And some had parents who were ordinary people, completely normal, with boring, everyday lives. But these families, powerful or not, risked it all. They dared to stand against the might of the International Administrative State. They refused to be afraid. They refused to do the smart thing and keep their heads down. The people here are the children of a stubborn people."

"And look where that got them," Meagan muttered under her breath. She was going to say something more, but she stopped mid-breath. Mack had turned in his chair and Meagan noticed several scars, like small x's, running across his head.

Deuce also noticed. He leaned forward for a closer look. As he did so, Mack turned and looked at him. The movement was more natural this time, and his eyes seemed clearer.

"You're Deuce, right?" he said.

"Yes. Do you remember anything that has happened the past few days?"

"What about the last few days? I've been working just like always. I haven't done anything wrong."

Deuce put out a hand to calm him. "I know. I was just wondering where you were. Can you tell me anything?"

Marc's eyes clouded. "I was working," he answered dully. Deuce nodded and leaned over to examine the scars more carefully. Mack's body jerked clumsily. He pushed himself out of the chair and stood. Deuce stepped back, a frown creasing his face.

Mack spun his body to the right, then froze, raising his head to look at the ceiling. Meagan took a step back, eyes wide. Mack turned in a circle, still staring at the ceiling. His head jerked back down so he was looking at Meagan. He took two steps in her direction. Meagan felt the sheet behind her. She prepared to step to the side to avoid him, but she didn't have to move. Mack's head dropped so he was staring at the floor, and he pivoted back around. He brought his head back up to look directly at Deuce, walking clumsily toward him until his face was inches from Deuce's. He stood like that for several seconds. No one moved. He dropped back into his chair.

"That was interesting," Deuce commented.

"That's one word for it," Meagan said.

"Mack?" Deuce asked.

"What?" Mack gasped. He sounded more like a person waking up than a person answering a question.

"What are you doing?" Deuce asked.

"I haven't done anything. I've been working."

Deuce heaved a sigh of frustration and rubbed his eyes. "They've done something to his head, but I don't know what."

Meagan sat down on the floor and closed her eyes. She didn't think she could fall asleep. Her heart was still racing from Mack's freaky actions. But she was tired, and she didn't have to watch every little thing Deuce did. He would tell her if he figured something out.

The next thing she knew, she was being prompted to climb down into the dark hole in the floor. She had a vague memory of being half encouraged, half dragged through the foul-smelling place under the building. After that, she remembered nothing.

Chapter 18
The Security Breach

The might of the State is the ultimate security.
— Fact 699, Citizen's Handbook

"I'm glad you're here, Commander," Jorn Belwir said, holding open the door to the New Worlds Space Center and letting Ultan in.

"What's the problem?" Ultan asked.

The small man glanced around. The back hallway where they stood was deserted, as it should be at half past midnight. Still, Belwir didn't answer, but said, "Come with me," and started down the hallway.

Ultan had been looking forward to going home and getting some sleep. It had been a long day at the office, made even longer by the fact that Warren, the Protector boss, was annoyed about the damage his men had suffered. But when the Project's supervisor called Ultan and informed him that they had a serious problem at the Space Center, Ultan had put his plans on hold and prepared to give the situation his full attention. The Project and its scientists were under Belwir's direction, and technically Ultan was as well. Sort of. Belwir could not actually command the Black Fists, but he held the ultimate say in the Project's security. Ultan's orders were to provide that security. It was a delicate situation.

Now, Ultan watched the smaller man with interest. He held his pass key in one hand, and the other hand fluttered from the edge of his uniform jacket to his belt, and from his belt to his pocket and back, like it was searching for a place to comfortably settle. His gray hair was slightly frazzled and his jaw worked back and forth. Ultan raised his eyebrows. Something was clearly disturbing the man. Normally, he was composed and absolutely on top of things.

"What is it, Belwir?" he asked again.

"I'll show you," he answered. The supervisor stopped in a hallway and turned to face a blank wall. He swiped his pass key in front of it and it slid open, revealing a concealed elevator. Only a handful people knew about this elevator that ran the entire height of the Space Center. People with higher security clearance used it, allowing them to move quickly and access the more restricted parts of the Space Center. Belwir pressed a button to send them to one of the underground levels.

The elevator doors opened and the two men stepped into the Project's data storage room. Squat pillars, the servers, sat in orderly rows. The darkened room emitted a low hum.

Belwir strode quickly through this room and then down a long white hallway. He swiped his pass key at a door, but this time he also punched in a code at the keypad beside it before the door opened. The two men entered.

Here, low florescent lights stretched the length of the room and illuminated a long table. Computers lined both sides of the table, a chair in front of each one, eighteen in all. The room was deserted at this hour. Belwir strode quickly, heading for the station at the end of the room.

He stopped beneath a large screen that filled a good portion of the wall. A desk faced this wall, and Belwir leaned toward the computer there and began to type rapidly.

"I was called in by our late shift," he said. He gestured to the big screen. "Watch this." Ultan crossed his arms and looked up.

A video began to play. The view was blurry and jerked around, so he wasn't sure what he was seeing at first. It was dark. A flickering orange light suggested fire and not electricity was being used for illumination. The video shook and a voice spoke, garbled and hardly intelligible, almost lost in static and background noise.

"How are you feeling?"

"Who are you?" This voice came through loudly and perfectly clear. Ultan winced and Belwir turned down the volume a little. He had to turn it right back up.

"A friend," the garbled voice spoke again. The camera jerked around, and Ultan saw what looked like someone's leg. The only sound now was static and noise and a horrific hissing that might have been talking. Ultan was beginning to see what had Belwir worried. Ultan had seen videos like this before, and he knew where Belwir had gotten it.

"What's the trouble?" Ultan asked smoothly.

"What's the trouble?" Belwir echoed. He paused the video and turned to face Ultan. "Oh, nothing really. Mack Ginh, from the Reeducation Ward is just getting checked by a doctor, that's all."

"Calm yourself. Take a seat." Ultan gestured to the chair in front of the computer. "How do you know this is a doctor?"

Belwir did not sit down. He reached over and started the video, then paused it again. A face filled the screen. Ultan recognized him immediately, even with the mask, but he let nothing show on his face.

"Well?" he said.

Belwir crossed his arms. "I ran this picture through face recognition. Jasper Rodman, Health Ministry. Doctor."

"I believe I am in charge of security for this Project," Ultan said.

"I want him arrested."

"I have the situation under control."

Belwir jabbed a finger at the screen. "This is not under control. I want this man dead."

"You are not in a position to give me orders." Ultan's voice was low and dangerous. Usually after he spoke like that, people let him have his way.

But Belwir wasn't budging.

"I have given you leeway because of the respect I have for the Black Fists. However, you have already allowed information to be stolen from me, and now this." Belwir pointed to the screen, but kept his eyes locked with Ultan's.

"Kill Rodman or I will report you to my superior, who will talk to your superior, who will make you regret ever joining the Black Fists."

A mocking smile curled Ultan's lips and his ice blue eyes returned the small man's glare. Belwir's face paled a little. Threatening a Black Fist, even one under his control, was never a good career move. Black Fists were never really under control.

"Thank you, Belwir, for your *suggestions* regarding security. I will put my men to work."

Belwir nodded and stepped back. Ultan knew it had not escaped Belwir's notice that Ultan had not specified what his men would be doing, but he also knew Belwir was not ready to press the issue. Belwir had made his position clear. They both understood that Ultan could not let a gross breach of security such as this slide.

"Thank you for your time," Belwir said with a curt nod.

Outside the Space Center, Ultan sat back in his car. He had caught sight of another person in the video, whom Belwir had apparently overlooked. He sighed. He'd wanted to give Meagan more time, but that wasn't going to work now. Maybe, despite the short time, she had some information for him. Or not. It would be a shame to waste a talented girl, but she knew too much. If she had no information, or if she wasn't ready to fully commit herself to assisting him, she would have to be killed. A pity, really; if he had a few more days, things might have been different. But, then again, she might surprise him and be ready for the role he had for her. He'd know soon enough.

Ultan pulled out his personal and contacted his lieutenant.

"Meagan and Wild Card are hiding at Jasper Rodman's house," Ultan said. "Bring Meagan and Wild Card to headquarters for interrogation. Do what you have to to take Wild Card, but under no circumstances is he to be killed."

Ultan knew he didn't have to stress the importance of that order. Unlike Public Security, his men knew the value of taking live prisoners. He continued, "Don't worry, your boys can still have some fun. I want Rodman dead."

Over six thousand miles away, an old man straightened from the gauge he was checking. A strange unease filled him. His eyes traveled over the bleak landscape, eerily lit by the blue aurora that twisted across the dark sky. The light of his headlamp caught the wisps of swirling snow, and farther away he could hear the slow grind of the icy sea. Closer were the calls of the birds. The wind whistled past, as it always did, tearing at his clothing. Nothing seemed to be amiss. There was no sign of immediate trouble.

The old man's lips turned down in a frown. This was more a feeling that someone else was in danger, a friend perhaps.

Jacob filled his mind.

The old man hurried inside, closing the door against the draining cold. He dropped to his knees and began to pray.

Meagan woke suddenly. As fragmented dreams faded from her mind, she took a deep, shuddering breath. Where was she? She lifted her head. She was lying on a couch in a dark room. A little light filtered in from the half-open door. Was it from a streetlight? Meagan sat up.

Her heart pounded in her chest and a strange feeling of dread filled her. She was back in Deuce's spare room. She took another deep breath to quiet her nerves.

The feeling of dread did not subside. If anything it got stronger. Meagan turned her head slowly. Nothing appeared to be out of place, so why this feeling? Had she heard something?

Holding her shoes in her hand, Meagan got up and crept quietly to the door. Something was wrong, she knew. She couldn't explain it. She just felt it, like a snake coiling in her stomach.

She pushed the door open and peered out. The light was indeed from a streetlight shining through a window across from her. On her right, Deuce was asleep in his bed. Meagan took out her personal. The time was 5:47. After her late night, she should still be asleep.

She crept down the steps. The heavily curtained windows made it darker below. Even so, enough light filtered in for Meagan to make out the armchair, the lamp. Jacob was still asleep on the sofa. Meagan walked through the kitchen and back around to the foot of the stairs. She sat down on the lowest one and looked enviously at Jacob soundly sleeping.

Being the only one awake in the dark house gave Meagan an eerie feeling all its own. She took several deep breaths and tried to think rationally. Even though she could not have had more than a couple hours of sleep, she felt wide awake. Her heart was still racing. What was she afraid of? Everything seemed fine in the house, yet she felt that she must act quickly.

Meagan made her decision. She would wake Jacob. A few quick steps brought her to his side, and she laid her hand on his shoulder. The next thing she knew, her arm was twisted behind her. Jacob was on his feet holding both her arms in a vise-like grip. She was pressed against him, her back to his chest.

"Jacob," she gasped, "it's me. Meagan." He released her slowly, breathing hard.

"Don't do that," he said.

"Sorry."

"What's wrong?"

Meagan turned to face him. "I don't know. I have a sick

feeling in my stomach."

"Are you hungry?"

"No. Something bad is going to happen, or is happening. I don't know what. I just have this awful feeling. We need to leave. I know it sounds crazy, but—"

Jacob slung his backpack over his shoulders. "Okay. Put your shoes on. I'll go wake Deuce."

He ran up the steps. Meagan slipped on her shoes and waited. Only seconds passed before Jacob again descended the stairs, Deuce on his heels. Deuce also wore a small backpack.

"Go out the back door," Deuce said as he led them into the kitchen. He stopped to open a cabinet and shove some cans and small boxes into his backpack. "We can go to the park over in Development's sector. I know how to get in. We'll hide there until we decide what we want to do."

Jacob hurried past Deuce, then paused at the back door. He pulled his pistol from his belt. Meagan was so tense that she jumped when he cocked it. Jacob opened the door and looked both directions before ducking out to the left. Meagan followed him into the alley, with Deuce a few steps behind.

The light from the streetlamp cast a long shadow over the small alley. Only a few steps from the door, Meagan tripped over a clump of grass. Deuce leaned forward to steady her.

At that moment, a crack split the air. Meagan let out a startled yelp and Jacob flattened himself to the ground. Deuce's eyes widened at the hole gouged in the wall above his head.

"Run!" Jacob shouted.

Chapter 19
Better Dead Than Captured

The State has proven, on more than one occasion, perfectly willing to torture and execute prisoners of war. We ask all Militias and Defiance to remember: BETTER DEAD THAN CAPTURED.
— Midwestern Free Press, wartime news

Jacob rose to a crouch. He opened fire, and the gunshots cracked and echoed in the quiet. Across the alley, a figure on a roof ducked out of sight. Meagan and Deuce wasted no time sprinting down the alley. When Meagan reached the end, a chain link fence enclosing a house and yard rose up to block her path. The gunshots had ceased, and Meagan looked back over her shoulder.

"Don't stop," Jacob said, coming up behind her. He moved into the lead.

Jacob brushed past the weeds that twisted through the metal of the fence and skirted the small yard. When the fence ended against the side of the house, Jacob paused and crouched in the shadows. A narrow street separated them from the next alley. Jacob turned back to Meagan and Deuce and whispered, "Meagan across first, then you, Deuce. I'll cover you."

Meagan nodded once, vaguely wondering why she had to go first. She took a deep breath and hurled herself forward, running as hard as she could. She was expecting to hear a gunshot at any moment, to feel burning pain as a bullet ripped through her. Had the Black Fists changed their minds? Why were they shooting at them? She dropped into the shadows on the other side of the street.

Meagan looked back across the road and watched a figure rise and begin to run. She knew it must be Deuce, but it could have been either one of them in the dark. Still, no shots fired. Deuce squatted down beside her. Jacob came soon behind him.

"Have they fired at all since that first shot?" Deuce asked.

Jacob shook his head. "No."

"Jacob..." Meagan began softly. Jacob turned to see what she was looking at. Meagan had noticed the front of small white car poking out from behind a house.

"Meagan, you're brilliant."

The three of them quickly surrounded the car. Meagan tried the passenger door handle. It was locked.

"Jacob, can you pick a—" Meagan began, looking up in time to see Jacob smash in the driver window with his jacket-wrapped fist.

"Never mind," she finished, as he stuck his hand through and unlocked the doors.

The three of them slid into the car, Meagan and Jacob in the front, Deuce in the back. Jacob detached a flat metal device from the outside of his backpack and jammed it into the ignition. When he turned it, the engine clanked to life.

"Down!" Jacob suddenly screamed. Meagan and Deuce ducked. The back windows shattered as a bullet flew through one side and out the other. Jacob threw the car into reverse and backed down the alley. Meagan was thrown back as he slammed on the brakes and shifted into drive.

As they raced down the street, Meagan sat up and grabbed the sides of her seat. Jacob swung the car around a corner, and the road stretched ahead of them. The car began picking up speed and Meagan took a deep breath. They were going to make it. They were going to escape.

With a screech of tires, a black van pulled up at the end of the street, blocking their flight. Meagan slammed against the door as Jacob jerked the car to the left without slowing. They raced down a side street, the edges of the small car scraping the walls of the houses on either side. Meagan pushed herself upright just in time to be thrown in the opposite direction as the car whipped around another corner. Meagan twisted in her seat to look behind them. The black van was not in sight.

"We lost them," Meagan said.

"No we didn't," Jacob snapped. His mouth was set in a tight line, and sweat covered his forehead.

"The IAS can track all vehicles," Deuce added. "At least, that's what I heard."

"They'll get ahead of us and block us off." Meagan tried to keep the panic she felt out of her voice. Why did the Black Fists want to kill them now?

Jacob jerked the car around a building and slammed on the brakes. Meagan's body snapped forward, and she flung out her arm to prevent her head from hitting the dashboard.

"Out. Now," Jacob commanded. Meagan and Deuce tumbled onto the road.

"Run and don't stop," Jacob shouted. He came around the front of the car, sliding his backpack to the ground. Meagan stumbled forward, Deuce two steps ahead of her. They reached a T in the road and Meagan looked back. Jacob was crouched by the car, messing with something near the tire.

"Come on," she shouted. He did not reply. Meagan ran a few more feet and stopped. She heard screeching tires, and as the sound grew louder, Jacob stood and ran toward her. The Black Fist van rounded the corner.

"Go!" Jacob shouted, grabbing Meagan's arm and dragging her down a street to their right.

With a flash of orange light, an explosion tore through the air. A roar filled Meagan's ears. Jacob let go of her arm, and all three of them ran faster.

Meagan had no idea where they were going, or if they were going anyplace at all. They had no other choice. If they stopped, they would die. Meagan's heart pounded out a drumming thud in her ears, and her breath came in gasps, but she did not stop. They could hear no sound of pursuit, but none of them thought the Black Fists had been killed or given up. The fugitives had to keep moving.

They ran until they reached the National Resources sector, near the river. There were no houses here; these were old buildings, some still showing scars of the War. This was a place of peeling paint and bullet holes. A thin fog drifted in from the river and above them the sky grew lighter.

A newer warehouse sometimes interrupted the dreary neglect, and it was to one of the warehouses that Jacob led the fugitives. He tried the dark brick building's side door and found it locked. Jacob did not seem surprised. Meagan saw the small scanner next to the door that indicated a pass key was needed for entry. Jacob held his personal up to the scanner. There was a click, and the door unlocked. Meagan raised an eyebrow. Apparently, Jacob had just picked the lock with his personal.

The three of them hurried inside and the door locked behind them. Jacob switched on his personal's small light and led them through the darkened warehouse at a run.

"I hope you have a plan," Meagan said to Jacob.

"I always have a plan," Jacob answered as he led them past rows of shelves.

"Where are we going?" Deuce asked.

"The office."

They dashed through a wide doorway into another section of the warehouse. Jacob turned right and they stopped at another door. The doorknob turned under Jacob's hand.

"Come on," he said, swinging the door open.

Meagan and Deuce followed Jacob into the small office. Without hesitation, Jacob dove around the desk and started typing rapidly on the computer there. He didn't even bother to sit down. Seeing only one other chair in the room, Meagan dropped into it. Meagan saw Deuce turn up the collar of his blue uniform. She watched curiously as he tore open the seam. Something small fell out into his waiting hand. He closed his fingers around it.

"What is that?" Meagan asked.

Deuce opened his hand to reveal two pills of different sizes and colors. "Together, these two pills are fatal," he said grimly. "The Black Fists seem to want us dead, but I'm not taking any chances. Better dead than captured." He closed his hand again. Meagan bit her lip.

"We aren't dead yet," Jacob said, switching off the computer and rounding the desk. "We do, however, need to get out of here."

"Why?" Meagan asked. "Why can't we just hide here?"

"They know where we are," Jacob answered as he led them out of the office at a dead run. "Or they'll figure it out soon enough. They'll surround the building. Then things will get really unpleasant. We've got to get out before we are trapped entirely."

Meagan wondered what he meant by "really unpleasant," but she did not ask. Jacob didn't go back the way they had come, but sprinted deeper into the warehouse, passing crates taller than they were. Light was starting to filter in through windows high above them. As they ran, Jacob removed the partially used magazine from his pistol, and, from a pouch in his backpack, exchanged it for a full one.

They reached the far wall. Meagan glanced around. To their left was a huge door used for loading and unloading trucks.

"We're leaving out that side door, there," Jacob said, running toward a door farther down the wall. At the door, he turned to Meagan and his brown eyes met hers. "Don't stop for anything. If Deuce or I get tied down in a firefight, keep running. Head north on Handigen Street if you can."

He took a deep breath and threw open the door. After the darkness of the warehouse, Meagan was temporarily blinded by the bright morning sunlight. The three rushed out onto the street together. Meagan glanced around at the now bright streets and sides of buildings. Where were the Black Fists? Maybe Jacob really had lost them.

Unconsciously, Meagan slowed.

"Keep moving," Jacob gasped, as both he and Deuce ran past her. Meagan stayed close behind. They turned down one street and dashed across another. Where was Handigen Street? Meagan didn't know. She glanced behind her. Nothing. Smack. She slammed into Deuce who had slammed into Jacob. Jacob had stopped. Ahead of them, a Black Fist van had rounded the corner. It braked hard, cutting off their escape.

The van door opened and three figures in black jumped out. All wore masks and leveled weapons at them.

"Hands up. Now!" one of the men shouted. Meagan was already raising her hands.

"Drop your weapons," the Black Fist shouted again. "Keep your hands up."

"We're done," Jacob said, slowly setting his pistol on the ground. He stood, keeping his hands visible. "Don't shoot."

The three Black Fists surrounded them. Deuce still had the pills clutched in his hand. Out of the corner of her eye, Meagan saw him jerk his hand to his mouth. Jacob reached across Meagan and grabbed his wrist. The pills flew out of his hand and onto the street. Deuce and Meagan both turned to Jacob. Deuce shot him a betrayed look before the Black Fists threw hoods over their heads. As blackness engulfed her, Meagan took a deep breath, trying to calm herself. A cord was slid around her wrists and tightened.

Suddenly, a gunshot cracked across the air, and Meagan was spattered by warm liquid. Two voices screamed. Meagan realized one was her own.

"Go. Go now!" a Black Fist shouted.

One of the Black Fists grabbed Meagan and dragged her forward. She was lifted and thrown to the floor of the van. Someone moved behind her. She heard a thump close to her head, and someone stepped on her hand, then quickly stepped off. She heard another thump. Who was shot? Were they all going to be executed?

"Meagan!" Jacob shouted.

He was okay. Deuce, then? Had they shot Deuce?

"Keep still and keep quiet," a different male voice commanded.

"Here. Back here. Quickly." Another voice she didn't recognize. Someone was shoved against her. Meagan heard the door of the van slide closed.

"Go," the Black Fist shouted. Meagan was thrown back as the van pulled away.

Chapter 20
Rescue?

The IAS has called for “a peaceful end to all this defiance.” We will show them how Midwesterners take foreign orders. We will show them Defiance.
— Midwestern Free Press, wartime news

Meagan tried one of the calming breathing exercises they were taught at school. It didn’t help. She was still on the floor of the van, crushed between the seat in front of her and the one behind her. Someone was pressed against her right side. Around her, people were still shouting. Their voices hammered into Meagan’s brain without creating any meaning.

She was going to be killed. She was agent for the Black Fists and they were going to kill her in cold blood. Panic gripped her. She had to find a way to convince them she was on their side. Her breath came short and ragged. The person beside her squeezed her arm.

“It will be okay.” The whispered voice belonged to Jacob. Meagan could hear the fear in his voice. He sounded taut, like a string pulled too tight and ready to break. Things were not going to be okay, they really weren’t. Meagan managed to take a deep breath. Why was she afraid? She shouldn’t be. She wasn’t really part of the Defiance. The Black Fists hadn’t killed her yet, so they shouldn’t kill her before she had a chance to explain who she was. It was Jacob who should be afraid.

Jacob shifted, and Meagan became aware of his body close to hers. For a moment, she was grateful for his solidness, a fixed point in a world spinning wildly out of control. Meagan shoved the thought away angrily, and cursed herself for her weakness. Eradicate her emotions, that’s what she had to do, what she had spent years doing. No fear and no love. Being away from school was making her soft. Stupid emotions, probably inherited from her criminal parents. She had to fight them, fight for her future. And there was no point in fighting unless she was willing to give everything to achieve her goals.

Meagan took another deep breath and clenched her fists. She

would have to use all her wits to get the best deal she could out of this situation.

The van stopped and Meagan was completely ignored. Shouting washed over her. Sharp commands were issued. The voices receded, and then Meagan felt her arm caught in an iron grip. She was yanked to her feet. Her captor hauled her out of the van and hurried her along. From the sound and feel, she guessed they were in a narrow corridor with a wooden floor. After several turns they stopped. A knife cut through her bonds, and the hood was whisked off.

Meagan blinked. She stood in a low tunnel, lit by florescent lights. The walls were metal, and the whole area smelled damp. Ahead, four wooden slabs served as steps up to a small door that stood slightly ajar. Meagan heard lowered voices coming from the other side. She'd thought they had been captured by Black Fists, but now she wasn't sure. The tunnels seemed more in keeping with what she knew of the Defiance.

"Go on," the man beside her said. He let go of her arm, giving her a slight push toward the stairs.

Meagan looked back at him. He was not very tall, but with his dark hair and eyes and the large pistol strapped to his hip, Meagan could tell he was not someone to mess with. He looked only about twenty-three, but already there was a quiet, competent, deadly air about him. He certainly could have convinced Meagan that he was a Black Fist. But Jacob stood behind him, neither bound nor blindfolded, and Meagan thought she knew what was going on.

"You're with the Defiance?" she asked.

"No, I'm with the Auditing Ministry," he said. "Of course I'm with the Defiance. Now move."

Meagan started up the steps. When she was halfway up, he said, "Keep quiet and stay out of the way."

Meagan went up the two remaining steps and pushed open the door. The Defiance man and Jacob came up behind her. Jacob closed the door.

Meagan had the impression that, under ordinary circumstances, the room would have been a calming place. Various paintings, mostly of ships on the ocean or of outdoor scenes, hung on the walls of the small, carpeted room. A large armchair sat in a corner, a small table next to it. The table had books on it! Not just words on a screen, but five real books, ordered from tallest to shortest, stood on it. Meagan wanted to touch them, to see their names, but that would have to wait for better circumstances.

Right now a plastic tarp covered the white carpet. Deuce lay on his back in the middle of it. Part of his jumpsuit had been cut away and blood pooled on the tarp. A woman knelt beside him. Her slender hands pressed thick gauze onto the right side of Deuce's chest. Meagan noticed a string of numbers tattooed on her wrist. The woman's lined face was drawn and sweat plastered her thin black hair to her forehead.

"Just hang on," she kept repeating. "Hang on."

An older man, with white hair and a weathered face that suggested a life outdoors, crouched on the other side of Deuce. Deuce appeared semi-conscious and mumbled something to the older man, who leaned closer and gave an answer.

Meagan heard a beep, and the man behind her checked a message on his personal.

"Manager," he said. The older man raised his head. "Ace is on his way."

"Thank you, Sword," the Manager said. "Par is upstairs waiting to let him in." He nodded at Meagan and Jacob. "Take those two into the other room. As soon as Ace gets here, you and Par can leave."

"We should have enough time before we're missed at work," Sword answered. He turned to Meagan and Jacob. "You two, come with me."

He led Jacob and Meagan around the others and out a door on the far side of the room. They went through a short hallway and into a larger room. There was no furniture here, but a staircase on the back wall led up. Meagan guessed they were in a basement.

"Got here fast as I could manage," said a voice from above them. The voice had a drawl to it, a trace of an accent that Meagan didn't recognize. A small, wiry, man hurried down the stairs. He wore a yellow suit with the blue trim of the Agriculture Ministry, although he was removing the jacket. His pale hair fell in wisps over his dark-rimmed glasses. He caught sight of Jacob, and his blue eyes showed surprise, but he jogged past them and disappeared into the other room.

"Wait here," Sword said. He hurried up the stairs. The door

down the hall opened, and the Manager came out. Jacob stood.

"Sir, I—" he began.

"Not now, Ja—Wild Card," the Manager interrupted. He started up the stairs. "We'll talk later." He did not sound happy.

Jacob shifted uncomfortably.

"Did you call the Defiance to help us?" Meagan asked.

"Yeah." Jacob sat down on the floor and slid his backpack off his shoulders. Meagan dropped down beside him.

"So what's our plan now?"

Jacob stared at the carpet. "I don't know. I hope Deuce is okay."

"Yeah."

They both sat in silence. Meagan stared at a door in the far wall, wondering briefly what was behind it. She felt dry inside. She couldn't cry, and she wasn't sure she even wanted to. Deuce was a member of the Defiance after all. He had it coming. So why did she feel so hollow? She hadn't even known him that long. Why had the Black Fists tried to kill him? Was this another message to her, to illustrate the price of failure?

"So, this is the Defiance," Meagan said.

"Not all of it. Some of them are at their jobs. That's why Sword and Par had to leave so quick."

"What about Ace?" Meagan asked.

"Maybe it's his day off."

"Oh."

Everyone received one day off a week, but those were allotted so only about a seventh of the workforce was off on any given day. Even then, Meagan and her fellow students had only been allowed to do State approved activities. Still, it was better than school.

Meagan and Jacob both fell silent, lost in their own thoughts. Meagan actually dozed off. She had had a long and rather terrifying night. At least here she had a little safety, though the Defiance's Manager did not seem very pleased with Jacob.

Meagan woke to the sound of someone coming down the stairs. The Manager went past them and into the room where Deuce was. After a few moments he returned, followed by the woman with dark hair. She had changed from her Black Fist disguise into a purple jumpsuit, the color of the Supervision Ministry.

"You," the Manager said to Jacob. "Come, now."

Jacob, the Manager, and the woman all disappeared into the room across from Meagan and closed the door behind them.

Meagan waited three seconds, glanced around to make sure she was unobserved, then crossed the room and listened at the door.

The first voice she heard was Jacob's.

"Is Jasper ...?"

"He will live. You are lucky we got there when we did." This deep voice belonged to the Manager. Meagan was confused for a second, but realized that Jasper must be Deuce's name.

"We ..." Jacob began, but stopped.

"I wasn't very happy about you contacting me over a nonsecure line," the Manager said, "but it's a good thing you did."

"Why would the IAS want to kill Jasper?" Jacob asked.

"Why wouldn't they?" said the woman. "He's part of the Defiance."

Meagan moved closer.

"I think the Black Fists were only trying to kill Jasper," Jacob said. "I don't think they ever shot at me."

"That doesn't matter right now. Why are you here?" the Manager asked.

"Um, I was trying to escape the Black Fists."

"That's not what I meant. Jacob, why are you here, in this city?"

"I thought we talked about this before. I can't tell you."

"Yes," the Manager said. "We did discuss this. You were also not supposed to involve the Defiance."

The room was silent. Finally, Jacob said, "I know I'm putting you in danger."

"You nearly killed our doctor."

The Manager wasn't shouting. And, although Meagan could detect the anger in it, his voice was low and even. Strangely similar to Jacob's, she thought.

"And the only reason Tina isn't also hiding here," the Manager continued, "is that Public Security accused and arrested the man who lived downstairs from her after your antics at her place. We have no obligation to help you."

"Jacob," the woman said softly, "you have to understand. It's not the same as if you were a member of the Defiance. The Manager is responsible for our group. He can't give assistance to every anti-State person who needs us."

"I'm not just some person."

The woman sighed. "I'm not faulting you for hiding with our members, but this has gone too far."

"I understand the situation, Mother," Jacob answered. "I don't think you and Grandpa do."

Chapter 21
Intentions

Those who do not actively support the IAS are considered enemies.
— Fact 837, Citizen's Handbook

Meagan's mouth dropped. This was Jacob's family? She shouldn't be so surprised. She had known he had family. Still, her heart started racing. A mother and grandfather in the Defiance, and his grandfather was the Manager, no less. This was exactly the kind of information that would make her a hero to the Black Fist commander.

Jacob's grandfather spoke. "And what understanding do you have that I do not?"

"The New Worlds Space Center is a fake."

The room fell silent. Then the Manager said, "What proof do you have of this?"

"I broke in and downloaded this information. Look it over; I've highlighted the pertinent parts."

Again the room became quiet. This time Jacob's mother broke the silence.

"Jacob, who is the girl with you?"

"Her name is Meagan. She helped me break into the Space Center."

"And?"

"She and I are both on the run. She's pretty handy to have around, Mom."

Meagan crossed her arms. She wasn't sure if she should be insulted or not.

"Jacob," the Manager said, "while this information is interesting, it doesn't automatically mean the Space Center is a front."

"Can't you just believe me?" Jacob said.

"You don't have enough evidence to make a case."

"You could help me get more."

"My decision stands. The Defiance won't help you."

"I am certain it is not a space program."

"Are you?"

"I know what a space program looks like, and this is not it," Jacob snapped.

"*If* you are right," the Manager said, "it will need to be looked into. If it's not a space program, then it's something the State wants to keep hidden."

"We don't have the ability or resources to worry about that, especially after what's happened to Jasper," Jacob's mother said.

"I'm not asking you to investigate," Jacob said. "I just need some help, a place for Meagan and me to hide."

"And I'm saying no," the Manager said. "Your investigation threatens to unravel the entire Defiance."

"I understand, sir. I'll do something else."

Meagan could hear the disappointment in Jacob's voice. After a moment, he said, "Could Irena reestablish Meagan with a new identity?"

"Jacob—" his mother began.

"Reestablishing someone is not easy," the Manager broke in. "It's not something she can just do."

"I know it's asking a lot, but Meagan saved our lives. She never complains, but it's only a matter of time before she gets hurt. She can't go back to wherever she came from. I'm the reason she is on the run."

Now Meagan was insulted. Did Jacob think she was just some waif who needed protection? She would show him.

The Manager sighed. "I'll see what I can do."

"Dad, wait," Jacob's mother broke in. "I have an idea. Do you remember that job your friend contacted you about?"

Meagan held her breath, waiting for the Manager to speak.

"Jacob, I think we can get a place for you to hide after all."

"What's the job?"

"A friend of mine contacted me two days ago. He wanted to see about getting some people to do a job for him."

"And?"

"He didn't give me the details because I told him the Defiance was not out for hire. What he did tell me was that he needs two people for a risky mission. One of them needs to be a young woman, brave, able to stay cool and keep her head in a tense situation. The other person would have to be able to provide backup. Be able to drive and shoot well."

Jacob's mother spoke. "He said he knew it was asking a great deal, but he could reward well. My thought was, you and Meagan could do this job for him in exchange for him hiding you."

"And he can deliver what he promises," the Manager assured Jacob. "He is probably more capable of helping you than I would be if I were inclined to do so."

"You said he contacted you two days ago?" Jacob said. "That was the day after Meagan and I broke into the Space Center."

"You think it might be a trap?" Jacob's mother asked.

"Well, the timing is interesting, and the kind of people he wants. Do you think it's a coincidence that the people he asked for fit Meagan and me so well?"

"I think it's good that you're being cautious," the Manager said, "but I've worked with this person before. He's trustworthy."

"Dad, are you sure?" Jacob's mother asked.

"Yes. If it would make you feel better, Jacob, I'll arrange a meeting in person for you with my friend. Though he will probably insist on wearing a mask. He is very protective of his identity."

"I—"

"Arrange the meeting," Jacob's mother said. "And, Jacob, be careful."

There was so much compassion and worry in her voice. Meagan felt a stab of bitterness in her chest, bitterness and envy. She clenched her hands into fists. She would have left, except her mind overruled her emotions and demanded that she stay and listen. Information was the only thing that would protect her when the Black Fist commander came for her.

"I'm always careful, Mom."

"Then what happened to your arm?"

"Nothing. It doesn't even bother me."

Jacob's mother sighed. "You know I sent you away to protect you."

No one spoke. Then Jacob said, "The Exiles are good people, Mom. What I do for them is important."

"I just wish it didn't have to be you."

Meagan's heart started racing. That was it. That was the information she needed. She had no idea who the Exiles were, but Commander Ultan surely would. She would have laughed out loud had she not been crouched outside a door eavesdropping. Her future was secure. She was safe. She had done it. She, Meagan, had accomplished the job of a Black Fist. Nothing could stand in her way now.

"You hearin' everything okay, darlin'?"

Meagan whirled at the voice, fear crawling up and trying to choke down the triumph that had risen in her.

Ace stood behind her. His hands were at his sides, and his words were nonthreatening, but there was a hint of steel in his voice.

"I …" she began.

Ace crossed his arms, waiting.

Meagan clamped her mouth shut. Saying nothing was better than babbling while she tried to think of an answer.

Ace glared into her eyes as if he could read all her intentions there. Meagan wanted desperately to look away, but she did not. Then Ace moved quicker than Meagan would have thought possible. She found herself gently but firmly pushed against the wall, one of his hands on her shoulder.

"What was that you were doin'?" he demanded.

Meagan pushed his hand off and crossed her arms. "What's your name?"

"Don't try to change the subject."

"I'm not. What's your name?"

"You can call me Ace."

"That's the point, isn't it?" Meagan took a step forward, forcing Ace to either step back or leave them uncomfortably close. He moved back.

"I don't know you," Meagan continued. "I don't know your Manager. I don't know his intentions."

She gestured to the closed door.

"I was brought here without my consent. Don't get me wrong, I'm grateful I'm not a guest of the Black Fists, but your Manager didn't seem too happy with my friend. I'm not going to let him face who-knows-what from all of you while I just sit quietly and wait. I'm his partner in this, and you're just going to have to accept that."

Ace pushed his glasses farther up his nose. "Well," he said slowly, "I certainly can respect that loyalty to your friend. How long have you known Wild Card?"

Meagan shrugged. "Four days."

Ace laughed. "He's got that effect, don't he?"

Meagan's eyebrows drew together. "You know him well?"

Ace shook his head. "I used to. But today is the first time I've seen him in eleven years."

"That's a long time."

"Yeah, well, things happen. You know how it is. Still, for near three years I helped raise him, taught him a lot of what he knows. He was a good kid."

"Why did you let him go?" Meagan asked.

"It weren't my choice, if that's what you mean. Kid never could stay in one place for long. Circumstances kept detonating whatever sort of stability he had." Ace gave Meagan a wry smile. "'Course the point of this is, you don't have to worry about our intentions. You and Wild Card are among friends here. The Manager will get things sorted out."

Meagan smiled. "Thanks for getting us out of that mess back there."

"My pleasure." Ace adjusted his glasses. "I've treated you rather rudely. I hope you understand; I have to be suspicious. Of everyone. And I didn't know you and all."

"It's forgotten. I'm Meagan."

The door opened. Jacob and his family came out.

"You might as well stay here," the Manager said to Ace. "I'm calling a Defiance meeting tonight. After what has happened, I want the team aware and on high alert."

"Fine by me, sir; it's my day off. Deuce seems to be stable and he is resting. He lost a lot of blood."

"Will we need a transfusion?"

Ace shrugged. "I don't think so. But you should really ask Deuce when he's more coherent."

Jacob pulled Meagan aside.

"Ready for a new mission against the State?"

Chapter 22
A Deck of Cards

The State encourages all relationships. However, Humans, as a species, are known to falter, to hurt one another both emotionally and physically. When these relationships fail, turn to the steady and unchanging arms of the IAS.
— Fact 99, Citizen's Handbook

Ultan watched Belwir watch the video. Ultan had already seen it twice, and had debriefed his lieutenant.

He waited until he heard the final gunshot.

"As you requested," he said smoothly.

"Are these your men?" Belwir asked, pointing to the screen.

"No. That is the Defiance. They have worked closely with this boy in the past."

"Are you sure he is dead?" Belwir pressed. "The Defiance takes him into the van."

"Yes," Ultan replied. "He was not yet dead in this video, but by now he should be gone, and your problems with him."

Belwir was nodding. "Good work."

When he left the room, Ultan's lieutenant turned to him.

"Sir, I thought I made it clear in my report. If the Defiance can provide competent medical aid, as we know they can, then Rodman's wound is not fatal."

Ultan glanced up at the man. He was a good lieutenant, if still a little by the book.

"You made it clear," Ultan said. "Did you receive the message we've been waiting for?"

"Yes, sir. Meagan and Wild Card are at the house of Marcus Zekelman, the Defiance's Manager. Rodman is there as well."

Ultan nodded.

"They won't be expecting an attack now," the lieutenant said. "Would you like me to send in a team and have Rodman killed?"

Ultan waved a dismissive hand. "No, forget Rodman. And forget capturing Wild Card and Meagan. We'll wait for an update on what Wild Card's next move is."

Meagan sat beside Deuce in the basement. She wrapped her arms around her legs and rested her chin on her knees. She looked at Deuce. His eyes were closed and his breathing shallow. She was tired, and she was very alone. But she had done it. With no training, she had achieved what Commander Ultan had demanded of her. Now, all she had to do was get the information to the Black Fists. Commander Ultan had said not to try to contact him, but Meagan doubted the Black Fists actually knew where she was. She couldn't wait for them to find her.

Especially now. Now Jacob had decided she would play a central role in this mission against the IAS. Meagan didn't really want to be involved in something like that. Even with her information, would the Black Fist Commander forgive her for the part she had played in helping the Defiance? Still, she didn't really have a choice. Her other option was to let the Defiance craft a false identity for her and reestablish her into a new life. Then she really would be branded a traitor, hunted down, and killed.

Meagan's heartbeat quickened. She knew what she had to do. She would go on the mission, but she would not make it a success. In the midst of the mission, she would turn Jacob over to the Black Fists. The task was daunting, but she could do it. She was brave. She would stay cool, keep her head, and wait for the right moment.

"That's the left," Jacob said for what seemed like the tenth time.

Meagan muttered a curse under her breath.

"Well, Meagan takes the trick," Ace said.

"And loses the hand," Jacob retorted.

"Go easy on her," Tina said. "It's only the second game."

Meagan sighed. Tina, Ace, and Jacob had taken it upon themselves to teach Meagan how to play euchre while they waited for the other Defiance members to arrive for the meeting. The Manager was upstairs working. Meagan had learned that he'd reached a high enough level in the Agriculture Ministry that he was allowed to work from his house. Jacob's mom was on watch upstairs. Meagan and the others waited in the small room where Jacob and his relatives had been talking. It contained only one couch, and no windows, so they did not have to worry about light leaking out into the streets. Even so, they were keeping their voices low, and Tina and Ace seemed a little on edge. Meagan got the impression that even hidden in the basement of the Manager's house, they didn't feel completely safe.

Meagan, however, was feeling much better. She had been able to take a shower of sorts using some wipes and a very little water. Most of the Manager's ration had been used during the initial crisis with Deuce, and more was used getting Deuce's blood off her jumpsuit, so there was little to spare. She had also been given food, enough to take the edge off her hunger. She really didn't have much to complain about. Except for this stupid euchre game.

Ace shuffled the deck. "My deal."

All four of them jumped at a knock on the door. A man entered. He was tall, with dark skin and hair. He wore the purple jumpsuit of the Supervision Ministry and a large rifle was slung over his shoulder.

The man said something to Ace and the two of them went into a corner to talk quietly.

"That's Jack," Jacob told Meagan.

Almost immediately, there was another knock on the door. Par and Sword entered followed by a woman dressed in a silver suit to match their own. Justice Ministry, Meagan noted. She was small, with light brown skin. Her hair, dark with red highlights, was cut in a geometric block around her narrow face. She caught sight of Meagan and appeared to be sizing her up. Meagan could see the fire of a sharp intelligence in her eyes.

"You already met Sword and Par," Jacob said, scooping up the cards and returning them to their box. Jacob nodded to the woman in silver. "She's Diamond."

Diamond walked over to Jack and wrapped her arms around his neck. She whispered something in his ear.

"Excuse me," Tina said. She stood, gave Par a brief smile, then turned to Sword.

"I missed you," he said. Then they were full-out kissing. Meagan watched, wondering what it would be like to kiss someone like that.

To kiss Jacob like that.

Jacob noticed what she was looking at. "They're engaged," he whispered. He pointed to Jack and Diamond. "They're married."

Meagan snorted.

"What?" Jacob asked.

Meagan shook her head. "Forming attachments is just about as stupid as walking into Black Fist Headquarters and saying 'Hi, I'm a Defiance member!'"

Jacob's face became carefully blank. "Why do you say that?"

"Because people die," Meagan said. "Or they … they leave when you can no longer give them what they want." She noticed the weird look on Jacob's face, but didn't stop. "Or they only pretend to care about you. But they really don't. They care more about going off and doing whatever criminal acts are so important to them. And … and they abandon you. And then you have nothing."

Meagan stopped. Her face had grown hot. Jacob put his hand on her shoulder.

"Look, Meagan, I know relationships aren't always easy."

"Like you would know."

"I do know," Jacob said. "I really do understand what you mean by … well, feeling abandoned."

He glanced away, then back to Meagan. "My mother, well, when I was much younger, my mother had to choose between me and the Defiance. She couldn't have both." Jacob gave Meagan a half smile. "I happen to think she picked the wrong one."

The Manager came into the room and walked over to them.

"I want you two to step out for a bit," he said, laying a hand on Jacob's shoulder. "You're not the most popular person with the group after what happened to Deuce. Give me some time to talk to them and let them vent a little. I'll call you in when I want you."

"Yes, sir," Jacob said. "You want me to take watch?"

"No, Queen has that covered."

"As usual," Jacob said.

Meagan followed Jacob out of the room, and the Manager closed the door behind them. Meagan stretched out on her back on the floor. Jacob unloaded his gun and sat beside her. He dug through his backpack and took out the black plastic box that held his pistol's equipment. From the box he removed a rag and what looked like a stick with a loop on each end.

"So," Meagan said, this time out of genuine curiosity, "the Manager is in charge of this cell of the Defiance. What do the others do?"

"Sword has some talent in disguise and infiltration," Jacob said. He ripped a strip off the rag and threaded it through one of the loops. "Tina has similar talents, so they usually work together. Par is the person who normally makes contact with outsiders. Jack is the marksman. He's been with the cell longer than most of the others. Diamond is the forger. She actually works in the forgery detection division of the Justice Ministry, so she can be useful to have around."

Jacob ran the stick in and out of the barrel of his gun, cleaning it.

"Ace does demolitions," he continued. "He may look like a retired geek, but he was part of the Old Military. I'm not sure what he did while with them, but he's good with a bunch of different firearms, knives, and even unarmed combat. I wouldn't want to go up against him in a fight. Queen is good with logistics. She also isn't a bad shot, and I think she killed someone with a knife once."

"Queen is?"

"Dark haired woman. Purple jumpsuit."

Meagan realized he was talking about his mother.

"It sounds like you know them well."

Jacob shrugged. "Better than other outsiders do."

Something clicked in Meagan's mind. "Playing cards," she said, sitting up.

Jacob looked up from wiping down his pistol with an oily cloth. "What?"

"Some of their call signs are playing cards."

"Yeah. I know."

"Let's see. You have an Ace, Queen, Jack, and Diamond."

"I know," Jacob repeated.

Meagan laughed. "All you're missing is a King."

Jacob scrubbed his pistol harder.

"I mean," Meagan continued, "don't you think it's a little silly to have a Queen without a—" She stopped as the realization hit her.

"Oh," she said.

"Yeah, he was my dad," Jacob said.

"Jacob, I—"

"It's okay." Jacob shrugged. "I didn't really know him. He died when I was four."

"Yeah. Mine's dead too." Meagan sounded a little more disgusted than she meant to. Jacob glanced up sharply.

"You knew your dad?"

"Ha. No. And I'm glad I didn't. The State is my father, remember?"

Jacob's eyebrows drew together, and he smiled. "If the State is your father, you are one rebellious little brat."

"Why, you …" Meagan growled, drawing back her hand.

Jacob laughed and pushed it down. "Relax. I was joking."

Meagan let out a deep breath. She realized that she needed to be more careful throwing around that quote, given the role she was playing.

"So that's why your call sign is Wild Card?" she asked, moving to safer territory. "Because it's a family name thing?"

Jacob took out a box of ammunition and started to reload one of his magazines. "Sort of."

He seemed reluctant to talk about it, which made Meagan all the more curious.

"So why did you choose it?"

"A Wild Card is unpredictable," Jacob said, keeping his eyes on his work. "It could change the game in any direction. And—" He hesitated. "And it doesn't belong with anything else."

Jacob had tried to keep his voice light, but Meagan could hear the bitter mocking in it. It seemed Jacob was not so different from her after all. They were both outsiders; they both had nothing and no one but themselves against the world. Maybe Jacob did understand her better than she thought.

But no, that wasn't true. Jacob had the mysterious Exiles; he was with them. And Meagan was truly alone.

Chapter 23
Providence

Religion is a drug—more addicting and dangerous than marijuana or caffeine—and shall be treated as such.
— Fact 428, Citizen's Handbook

The Manager stuck his head out the door and motioned for Jacob and Meagan to come into the meeting. Meagan followed Jacob into the room. Defiance members sat on the couch and floor. Sword stood leaning back against the wall. Meagan raised her eyebrows. The room had a sharp smell to it that burned her nose. Sword and Jack were smoking cigarettes. That wasn't too surprising; even though smoking was illegal, cigarettes were rather easy to acquire on the black market. Meagan knew that several students had gotten them on occasion. What was more surprising was the cigar held by the Manager.

All of the Defiance members were looking at Jacob. He smiled. "Hello, everyone." He sat down on the floor. Meagan took a seat beside him. The room was quiet. The members wore grim expressions.

The Manager spoke. "I want the Defiance to be on high alert. Several incidents have come to my attention that make me believe the IAS is up to things we won't like."

He nodded to Jacob, who stood.

"While I can't prove it to you," Jacob began, with a glance in his grandfather's direction, "I have reason to believe the New Worlds Space Center is merely a front for something else."

"That's nothing new," Sword said. "It's practically standard operating procedure for the IAS to hide projects within other projects."

Jacob continued. "Deuce was also telling my partner and me about the increase in disappearances in the Reeducation Ward."

"He mentioned something to me about that, too," Ace said.

"I don't know if these are connected, or if the IAS has multiple covert projects—"

"Or if they're trying to cover something up in Re-ed," Par said.

While they were speaking, Meagan let her eyes travel over the faces in the room. Par and Jack seemed to be genuinely interested in what Jacob was saying. Ace appeared to be thinking. A scowl covered Sword's face. Tina's eyes were narrowed. Diamond's face was unreadable.

"You want to investigate this further?" Tina asked Jacob.

"Yes. I plan to."

"Then I think we should help him," she said to the Manager.

The Manager opened his mouth.

"No way," Sword said. "We have enough problems of our own."

"Especially since Deuce is out of commission," Diamond said. The way she said it left no doubt who she believed was at fault.

"I think it's in our own interests to—" Tina began, but Sword interrupted.

"Who is this Wild Card anyway, that we owe him allegiance? Do we really want to start giving aid to just any dissident who comes along and tells us the State is up to something?"

"You don't know everything," Jack said to the room in general. He kept his eyes on Jacob.

"This discussion is pointless," the Manager said. "I have already told Wild Card that we will not be assisting him at this time. Perhaps we will later, if he discovers something that merits our attention, but for now, he will be leaving tonight."

"Where does the Defiance get so many explosives?" Meagan asked Jacob as they crouched in the shadow of the wall that ran around the south end of the park. She put one foot into his waiting hands and he boosted her up the wall. Grabbing the top, she pulled herself over and landed on the other side. She heard Jacob's boots scrape the wall before he dropped down beside her.

"I supply some of them," he said, with a note of pride in his voice.

"Really?" Meagan was impressed.

Jacob and Meagan had left the Manager's house shortly after the Defiance meeting. Now, they would meet with the friend of the Manager. Jacob was planning to try to work out a deal with the man, if he was able to convince Jacob that this wasn't a Black Fist trap.

This wasn't a trap. She was the trap. He was going to go on this mission, and she would betray him. She thought of Black Fists arresting Jacob. Forcing him to the ground. Handcuffing him. While she watched. The image made her queasy. She closed her eyes and thought of her reward. She would have real power. Real opportunity. Jacob should know better than to underestimate her, to think of her as some waif who needed protection, who needed the sympathy of the Defiance. She was her own master. Her fate was in her own hands. She had good information, and the Black Fists would be pleased.

"The Defiance mostly steals supplies and disrupts things, and generally tries to help people," Jacob was saying. "But sometimes it's nice to just be able to blow things up."

As they'd left the Manager's house, Meagan had noticed several wooden boxes stored in the tunnel that connected his house to the old subway. Jacob had told her that was where the Defiance stored their explosives. Meagan wanted to ask what they used explosives for, but she was afraid Jacob would become suspicious. After all, shouldn't she already know the answer?

Meagan blew on her hands to warm them. The night air was like ice. She crossed her arms, grateful for the jacket Jacob's mom had given her. If she were wearing her gray jumpsuit, she would probably be freezing to death. Most jumpsuits weren't designed to be worn outside at night. They were thin and flimsy, and didn't stand up to the elements. Meagan rolled her eyes. Good citizens were supposed to stay inside after curfew.

Which was why she was wearing Jacob's extra pair of jeans and a cotton shirt, plus the dark blue jacket. Anyone who saw her would know she was up to no good, but at least she was mostly warm.

Jacob stopped. "There's the oak tree."

They had arranged to meet the man under a certain oak tree off the fourth hiking trail. The nearest light was a quarter of a mile away, but the moon shone brightly in the clear fall sky and covered the park in silver white light. Meagan started toward the tree, but Jacob grabbed her arm. He pointed to a low hedge running parallel to their meeting place.

"We'll wait there. It will hide us, and I'll have a good view of anyone approaching."

Meagan nodded. They settled down on the ground to wait. The dirt around the hedge was cold and damp. Meagan drew her knees to her chest and looked out over the landscape, strange in the moonlight. Her stomach twisted with anticipation. She didn't want to think about what she would soon have to do.

"Jacob?" she asked, to keep her mind off her impending betrayal.

"Yes?"

"That night at Deuce's, when I said I knew something was wrong."

"Yes?"

"Why did you believe me so quickly? I mean, it wasn't like I had anything concrete to go on."

Jacob gave a short laugh. "I've lost count of the times my life has been saved by following my hunches."

"Hunches?"

"Yeah, you know, a feeling you can't explain and you have no logical reason for."

"Humph," Meagan grunted.

"What?"

"Well, it's weird. That's all."

"What do you mean?" Jacob asked.

"I'm not doubting the existence of hunches, but it seems like there should be some sort of scientific explanation for them."

"I haven't heard a good one yet, and, believe me, I've lived with scientists."

"I just think science should be able to explain it," Meagan persisted. She hadn't had a good rational argument in forever. She had memorized all the facts in the Citizen's Handbook, but when she tried to use them to argue with the students or teachers it didn't go well. Their jealousy of her mastery was stronger than even their belief in the State.

"Science is the only thing we have to understand the world," she said, quoting almost exactly.

Jacob stared off into space for a moment. "I have friends who would call your hunch Divine Providence," he said slowly.

"What's that mean?"

"That God was watching out for us."

Meagan turned and looked at him. Oh, sure, Jacob, just throw rationality out the window.

"You don't believe there's a god, do you?"

Again, Jacob hesitated before he answered. "I don't know."

Meagan laughed, a small nervous laugh. "Well, that's a start. You had me worried."

"Why worried?"

"Well, I don't want to be partners with someone who is deluded."

Jacob shifted uneasily. "I don't think just believing in God makes you deluded," he said. "I've known Christians who seem to have it pretty well together."

Meagan's entire body went cold, and she glanced around quickly. Jacob was taking this way beyond rational discussion.

"You want to be killed?" she hissed. "Don't ever say that name again. I was speaking generally; you don't have to get into details. I'm not even going to ask how you formed that opinion, since supposedly there aren't any more of them left."

Now Jacob looked around cautiously. "Not so loud, Meagan," he said, putting a hand on her arm to calm her.

Meagan realized she was only inches from his face.

He smiled. "No need to get worked up about it. I'm just sharing, you know, things I think about."

"You shouldn't," Meagan said, settling back down against the hedge. "That kind of thinking is dangerous."

"I just start to worry when my personal beliefs are even remotely similar to the State's propaganda."

Meagan had to give him that. Propaganda was about as worthless as a used ration card. Still …

"Religion is a drug," she said, again quoting the Handbook, "and shall be treated as such." She looked Jacob in the eyes and whispered, "You could be killed for a lot less."

Jacob's face broke into a smile. "Or a lot more. Like Treason, Conspiracy, and Espionage. Speaking of Conspiracy, here comes our mystery man."

A shadowy figure stepped onto the path and approached the tree. The figure stopped beneath the oak. Jacob put his hand on Meagan's shoulder.

"Wait here."

He stood and walked toward the man. The man started when

Jacob materialized out of the shadows, but waited while he approached. Meagan watched as the two figures greeted each other. She knew they would give a sign and countersign as prearranged. Meagan wondered if she would get a bonus for discovering this man's identity as well. Jacob spoke to him for a moment, then motioned for her to come over.

Meagan joined the two under the tree. Curious, she looked over their potential employer. He was about six feet tall and wore a leather jacket and jeans, both of which were gray. A mask hid his face; all Meagan could see were penetrating green eyes.

"So you'll do the job for me?" he said.

Jacob crossed his arms. "I don't typically work for people who wear a mask."

"I don't typically work with children."

"If age is a problem, you should have specified in your request," Jacob responded.

"I care about results, not the age of the people getting them."

"What do you want us to do?"

"I want the girl to enter the Child Processing Center under a false identity, which I will supply."

"And why would you need her to do that?"

"Are you in?"

"Maybe."

"If you are concerned about the pay—" he began, but Meagan could tell that wasn't what he thought the problem was.

"I'm more interested in making sure this isn't a Black Fist trap," Jacob said.

"Do you trust the Defiance's Manager? He will vouch for me."

"Why now?" Jacob demanded.

The man nodded, "I see your point. I practically asked for you by name after what happened at the Space Center."

"How are you familiar with what we did?"

"I won't answer that. But you are correct. I did contact the Manager hoping to get you two for the job. I don't work with other people often, but when I do I like to have an idea of who I'm hiring."

He smiled at Meagan. "This lady is perfect for what I have in mind."

Meagan wasn't really listening. She was watching him

carefully. He was hiding something. Meagan could feel it. His eyes revealed nothing, and his voice was smooth. But there was something Meagan couldn't place. Maybe it was the way he subtly shifted his weight from foot to foot. Maybe it was the way his green eyes kept slipping away from Jacob to look at her. Meagan sensed half-truths, and she sensed fear.

"Is that so?" Jacob sounded unconvinced.

"I understand your concern," the man said. "The danger the Black Fists present is not to be taken lightly. I too must be … prudent, in my dealings. I will not fault you if you don't take the job, but I was pleased with your work, and I am willing to pay well for your talent."

"All right. I believe you," Jacob said. "What do you want us to do?"

"I wish for a certain child to be removed from the Child Processing Center. The girl will go inside. I have provided a cover and the proper papers. Get the child and get out. You will be the driver and wait outside in the car. You may have to get away from the center quickly."

Jacob thought for a moment before responding. "Sounds good. Do you have all the props necessary to pull this off?"

The man took out his personal. "I'll transmit your authorizations and identities to you. There are two sets. Your first identity will be mechanics. That will get you to the house that will serve as your home base. There is a repair shop down the street. An official car from the center is there, waiting to be picked up. You will, in your second identity as officials of the center, claim the car and drive it to the center. The uniforms are in the house."

"And in return, my associate and I need a place to hide. It will be no more than six days," Jacob said.

"That won't be hard to arrange."

"Then we're in." Jacob stuck out his hand, which the man shook. Jacob took a personal out of his pocket. The man transmitted the information from his personal to Jacob's, then loaded Meagan's identities into hers.

"Oh, two more things," the man said. "I loaded instructions for getting rid of the car into your personal. When you finish the job, return to the house. I'll meet you there to pick up the child."

"Understood."

"Any other necessary instructions are in the file I sent you."

He shook both of their hands, then departed between the trees. Jacob also walked away, but only a few paces. When the man was completely out of sight, Jacob ducked into the shadow of a tree and began to look over the information on his personal. Meagan leaned against the tree, watching him.

"Okay," he said. "We are going to the mechanics' neighborhood, so we'd better dress the part."

Jacob dug through his backpack and pulled out something marked with yellow glow-in-the-dark tape. He switched on his personal's light for a moment. Meagan saw that he was holding the cloth bag full of disguises. He took out two pink jumpsuits.

"They're not the right shade of pink, but that won't matter tonight."

He handed her one. Meagan took the tightly rolled outfit and shook it out. It was a little big, but that would be a welcome change from her usual jumpsuit size, which was too small.

Jacob stepped behind a wide oak tree.

"Just let me know when you're done," he said.

Meagan pulled off her clothes and stepped into the jumpsuit. She laughed.

"What's so funny?" Jacob asked.

"You," Meagan answered. "You're the first person I know who changes privately."

"Well, I assumed … I mean, you are …"

"A girl?" Meagan burst into another fit of laughter. "You're so old-fashioned, Jacob."

"Pardon me if my thoughtfulness amuses you," Jacob said, stepping out from behind the tree. He sounded annoyed.

Meagan hadn't meant to upset him. His ways just surprised her.

"I'm sorry," she said. "You're just so different sometimes."

Then, although she didn't know why, she leaned forward and kissed him on the cheek. "Don't ever change."

Chapter 24
Memories and Nightmares

A single child, improperly indoctrinated at the earliest stages, could spoil an entire class of students. A division must be established for these high-risk children.
— IAS Charter for the North American Continent Regions

By the time they arrived at the house, Meagan was feeling miserable. She knew that kissing Jacob had been a good move; it would deepen his trust in her and keep him off guard. It was a great plan—if that had been what she was thinking. Meagan could admit that she had reacted to a brief flash of emotion. Jacob was the first person who had ever shown her consideration, even respect. But she also knew it couldn't last. Her salvation meant his destruction. And she was honest enough to know that she would rather have the security of power than Jacob's respect.

The address they'd been given belonged to a small blue house with a neatly trimmed lawn and concrete steps leading to a covered porch. Meagan was surprised that they were in a nicer neighborhood and would have the house to themselves. She had always thought of mechanics as being in a lower station, manual laborers who fixed appliances.

"How come these mechanics have nicer houses?" she asked as they walked around to the back of the house. "They're not that high a class."

"These mechanics repair cars," Jacob explained. "The higher classes like having car mechanics nearby for when vehicles need repairs."

"Oh."

Jacob worked his hand deep into the branches of a decorative bush and came up with a key on a string. He unlocked the back door and they entered a small kitchen.

Neither Meagan nor Jacob turned on a light. Using the few silver beams from the streetlight outside, they felt their way past a table and into the living room. In the uncertain light, Meagan could see the vague outline of a sofa. When she dropped onto it, it creaked so violently that she almost jumped back up. She shook her head. She was lucky it hadn't broken.

Jacob, with more caution, sat beside her. "I'm going to check all the codes he gave us," he said. "Make sure we have all the proper authorizations. You might want to get some sleep. We will get ready to leave for the center in about three hours."

"I have a question first," Meagan said. She had been thinking over Jacob's conversation with their employer, and a gnawing fear had begun to grow in her mind.

"Yes?"

"What exactly is the Child Processing Center?"

Good, she had kept her voice from trembling.

Jacob leaned back into the couch. It groaned in protest.

"Well, as the name suggests, the CPC is under the Minors Division. After babies are born, they are sent to the center to be evaluated. Those that pass the examinations are sent to tier one of the Minors Division. You're aware of that part, right? Tier one raises the babies and sends them to the second tier when they are two years old."

Meagan felt a sinking feeling in her stomach. She thought she knew where this was going, but she had to be sure. Very carefully, she asked, "Which ministry is the Minors Division under?"

Jacob looked at her like she was being ridiculous. "The Ministry of Population. That's kinda duh, Meagan."

Even though she had been expecting the answer, she could do little to lessen her reaction. The sick feeling in her stomach erupted into a gasping fear that clenched her throat. The room spun. She stood up, short of breath, and, before an astonished Jacob could ask what was wrong, dashed out of the room.

Breathing hard, Meagan stumbled down the hall and into the bedroom. The door clicked loudly as she locked it behind her. She wrapped her arms around herself as a violent trembling shook her body.

In the total darkness of the windowless room, memories and nightmares came rushing back. She ran her hand up and down the wall, fumbling for a light switch. Her fingers found the switch and cold light flooded the room. She curled herself onto the bed, trying to stop shaking. She couldn't do the job, she wouldn't. No way could she walk into a building filled with Population workers. She buried her face in the thin blanket, trying to shut out the images that clawed their way into her mind. Images of uniforms. She couldn't remember faces, only uniforms.

A horrible thought crashed into her brain. She pulled herself off the bed and staggered to the closet. She hesitated, but then yanked the door open. Hanging there was the uniform she was to wear. Her own Ministry of Population uniform, dark blue, so dark it was almost black, with the red trim gleaming at her like so many stains of fresh blood.

Meagan fell to her knees sobbing, her face in her hands. How could she remember so little, and yet still too much? Once again, she was a little girl, crying on a cold concrete floor, alone and afraid.

Tears ran through her fingers. She was wrong. She could remember more than the uniform. Parts of faces came to her. A mouth, wide, laughing, mocking. Eyes like ice. A hand raised to hit her.

Meagan recoiled instinctively, sobbing harder. She shuddered as endless nights of hunger and pain and fear wrapped themselves around her. Always fear. Not a day in her life had she not felt fear. But there would be, she thought as her sobs of despair turned to anger. She would make them all afraid, and they would pay. They would all pay for what they had done to her. Even the Ministry of Population's Reform Division had to respect the State's head propagandist. The thought was almost enough to make her stop crying.

Meagan became aware of a pounding on the door and remembered that she had left Jacob sitting on the couch. How long had he been knocking?

"Meagan?" His voice was half command, half plea. "Meagan. What's wrong?"

Meagan stood and took a deep, shuddering breath. Jacob sounded more worried than she had ever heard before. She dried her eyes on her sleeve and swallowed her feelings. When she opened the door, she was careful to keep her face blank.

Concern and confusion covered Jacob's face.

"I'm all right," Meagan said, forcing a little half smile.

"What was that about?" Jacob demanded.

"I lost my head," she said apologetically.

"I'd say you did a little more than that. You've been crying."

"So?" Meagan snapped. "It's not against the law."

"Are you sick or something?"

"Okay, look, I've never had to do something this big before." The lies came easily once she started. "I'm nervous, okay?"

Jacob crossed his arms. "You sure there isn't a problem?"

"It's just nerves." That was probably the biggest understatement of her life.

Jacob did not look convinced. "Meagan," he said. His voice was low and deadly serious. "That can't happen again. If you are not able to do this job, you need to let me know now. Once we get started, we have to see it through."

Meagan tossed her head, if only to break away from his penetrating stare. "I'll be fine." She hoped she wasn't lying.

Chapter 25
Crying Alone

The population must be carefully controlled. We must not only protect the crowded Earth, but also support the strongest and most mutation-free genes available in order to defend our species from genetic disaster.
— Fact 413, Citizen's Handbook

"Did we receive the update on Wild Card's actions?" The words were out as soon as Ultan stepped into his office. He was feeling good this morning; the night had been free from immediate problems, angry coworkers, and panicked underlings.

"Yes, sir," his lieutenant said. "And no, sir."

Ultan's good mood wavered. He really despised answers like this. He would rather have bad information than worthless information.

"Lieutenant ..." he began warningly.

"We received the update," his lieutenant said. "But it informed us that the location and actions of Wild Card have been lost."

"Where is Meagan?" Ultan asked.

"As far as we know, she is still with him."

"Good. This is a good time to try to make contact with her."

"But we don't know where she is."

"I'll handle it."

Ultan wouldn't admit it, but he wasn't happy about his informer losing the boy. Still, there were many ways of locating a person. Wild Card wouldn't remain hidden for long.

"There's something else, sir," his lieutenant said.

"Yes?"

"It's about the space program."

Soon after sunrise, Meagan found herself sitting in the passenger seat of the car they'd "borrowed," trying not to be sick. Jacob was talking, almost cheerfully, running over their plan, explaining what could go wrong and how to react. Meagan wasn't really listening. The Child Processing Center was a little ways outside the city, and she had been miserable the entire ride. Things would have been hard enough under normal circumstances. She needed to think clearly, to plan her next moves, but that was nearly impossible when her stomach clenched every time she looked at Jacob. Like her, he was dressed in the blue and red uniform of the Population Ministry. She was having trouble getting past the uniform.

Meagan tried not to think about the identical uniform that she wore. She didn't want to think of it touching her skin. In her mind, it smothered her.

"Stop touching your hair," Jacob said. "You'll mess up the dye."

Meagan realized she had been twisting a strand around her finger. She cursed. It shouldn't be so hard to remember. Her hair was dyed black, her face shape changed by Jacob's talent with putty, and her name was Suzanne Vicks. Her stomach twisted again, and she shook her head.

She had to focus. She had a job to do. Once the mission got started, it would be relatively easy to turn Jacob over to the authorities. The center was bound to have some security. It couldn't all be Population workers. Only mostly Population workers. She would have to go into the building alone, and face them. That was the plan anyway.

"Jacob, could you …" She stopped herself. She was not going to ask Jacob to go in with her. She wasn't that weak.

"Could you get there any faster?" she finished.

"Not really," he answered. "Get ready. It's almost time."

Meagan clenched her hands in her lap and focused on breathing. For some time, they had been driving past old houses with wide lawns. Most of the houses seemed to have been converted into government offices of one kind or another. Jacob turned onto a long tree-lined drive that ended in a parking lot half-full of cars. The building that rose up in front of them was not a converted house. With no windows and bright white walls, its minimalistic design looked more like a hospital. But with only three stories, it was too small for a hospital.

Jacob backed the car into a parking space only one row of cars away from the front doors, positioning them to pull out onto the road as quickly as possible.

Meagan took a deep, shuddering breath. Jacob gave her a

reassuring smile, which only made things worse. A smile from a Population worker meant that she had lost, that she had finally given in and done what they wanted.

"You're up," Jacob said.

Meagan jumped out of the car, closed her eyes, and took another deep breath. The image of Jacob as a Population worker had disturbed her enough to get her out of the car, but now her legs were refusing to move. She forced one step, then another in the direction of the doors. She walked up a sidewalk that gleamed in the early morning sun and stopped at the glass doors leading to the dark interior of the building. Her stomach twisted into knots and her legs felt weak. She tried to summon the exceptional daring that had served her well on so many occasions, but she only felt the need to throw up. She took a personal out of her pocket and scanned it at the doors. Her current identity was Suzanne Vicks and the personal was loaded with information to match. She heard the doors unlock and, pushing one open, stepped inside.

The air was cold and smelled like fresh paint and disinfectant. In front of Meagan sat a large desk. The lady behind the desk glanced up. Meagan's eyes darted around the room. There was a door behind the desk, and an elevator on her left.

"Can I help you?" the receptionist asked. She leaned forward with her chin on her fist and raised one graceful blond eyebrow. It took all of Meagan's willpower not to turn and run out the door.

"Y—yes," she managed to stammer, stepping forward. "I am here to transfer child 30175 40 586."

"I need to see a pass before I can let you in."

"Of course." Meagan fumbled with her personal, finally hitting the button that would send her pass to the lady's computer. The receptionist looked it over and pressed a button on her desk that unlocked the door behind her.

"You will need to speak to Mr. Arthur Rand. He is in charge of this facility and handles all our distribution. He will verify your authorization and complete the transaction."

She pointed a slender finger toward the door behind her. "Go straight ahead through there. His office is the second on the left."

Meagan nodded and did as the lady instructed. As she stepped through the door, the sounds overwhelmed her. Glass-walled cubicles filled the room, and each contained a person typing or talking on the phone. Most of them glanced up as she entered and Meagan felt the blood drain from her face. Every one of them wore the colors of the Population Ministry. She wasn't surprised, just so scared she could hardly move.

To her left were the offices, enclosed by solid gray walls. All of the doors were shut. She took a step forward. The faint scent of disinfectant in the air brought memories rushing back, memories that she couldn't deal with right now. She jerked herself forward and put one foot in front of the other until she reached the second door on the left.

She raised her hand, knocked, and tried to regain a little of her composure as Mr. Rand said, "Come in."

Meagan stepped into the room, and whatever composure she had mustered vanished in an instant. There, sitting behind a desk, looking up at her expectantly, was the man from the party; the man who had dropped his glass and stared at her like he had seen a ghost. He did not seem surprised to see her now, indeed he did not give any sign that he recognized her. Well, of course he didn't; she wasn't Esma Dronch anymore.

"I—I am," Meagan hesitated, took a gulp of air, and drew herself up, ignoring the churning in her stomach. "I am," she said, louder and stronger this time, "here to transfer 30175 40 586. My authorization."

She sent the documents from her personal to his computer. He leaned forward in his chair, checking the documents.

"I believe the query for pickup has already been processed," Meagan blurted out. She hoped that was right; Jacob had said something like that while they were in the car. Mr. Rand didn't answer, but her personal beeped as he sent the documents back to Meagan. He had digitally approved them.

"Everything is in order," he finally said. "Go to the second floor and wait in station number two. It's not in use right now. I will send someone to retrieve the child for you."

Meagan nodded her thanks and practically fled the office. She hurried out past the stares of the people in the main room, willing herself not to break into a run.

"I'm almost done," she told herself, although she knew it wasn't true. She made it to the elevator and stepped inside, stabbing the button to send her to the second floor. She would have liked to let her guard down, to curl up in a corner and cry while she rode alone in the elevator, but she was sure that cameras were watching her. The whole building was filled with cameras. Why did they have to have all those lifeless eyes staring at her? Meagan realized that she was shaking all over. How long had she been doing that? Had she been shaking when she talked to Mr. Rand? Had he noticed?

The elevator pinged and Meagan nearly jumped out of her skin. When the doors slid open, she covered her fright by striding forward into a lounge area.

A trim, young woman was waiting for her. "Ms. Vicks," she greeted Meagan, thrusting out her hand.

Meagan recoiled instantly, stepping back and bringing up her arms to protect herself. Her mind kicked in as she saw the look of confusion on the woman's face. Recovering quickly, she shoved her hand into the woman's and shook it. Meagan smiled nervously. The woman looked at her with a mixture of confusion and suspicion. Meagan realized she was still shaking the woman's hand and promptly released it.

"You can wait in here," the woman said, gesturing to a door marked Station #2. Her tone left no doubt that she thought Meagan was a complete nutcase. She swiped her pass key over the scanner and the door unlocked. The woman spun on her heels and walked down a hall. Meagan turned and hurried into the room, closing the door behind her. Had she gone out of her mind? She was going to get herself caught. Why couldn't she stop shaking?

Meagan released her grip on the door handle and lifted her head. The room was small and square and looked like a room where she would get her physical checkup, which made her stomach churn even more. She wasn't a fan of doctors. But she was alone. Finally, she was alone. Still, in every wall there was a closed door. At any moment, a blue and red uniform could step into the room. What if they discovered she was an imposter? What if they caught her? What would they do? Her head spun, and she gripped the smooth edge of the counter beside the door.

A metal table sat in the middle of the room, with two chairs behind it and a trash can under it. Various charts and clipboards full of papers hung on the walls or lay on the counter and table. Meagan stepped forward, thinking she could sit down and try to calm herself while she waited, but she froze mid-stride.

A noise filled the room. She didn't recognize the sound at first; it blurred together into an indistinguishable roar. She listened carefully, trying to place the many sounds that made up the larger sound. It was … crying? Babies crying. There must have been hundreds.

Meagan's throat clenched as she realized that at least two of the adjacent rooms were filled with the babies the center processed. Their hundreds of tiny little screams echoed around her, filling her ears and head. Memories flooded her mind. Memories of a little girl, crying alone. The sound bore down on her.

Meagan fell to her knees, shaking uncontrollably, and stared at the white tile floor without really seeing it.

"It's not real," she whispered, as tears filled her eyes. She was trapped in a nightmare. She had to wake up. She pinched her arm so hard she gasped in pain, but nothing happened. She still knelt on the cold floor, wearing a dark blue uniform, tears rolling down her cheeks. No. She had to stop. She had to pull herself together before she messed up her disguise.

Meagan reached for the edge of the table and tried to pull herself to her feet. Her hand slipped. Loose sheets of paper and two clipboards tumbled down around her. Meagan cursed and reached again for the table. Then she hesitated as her gaze traveled over the papers she had scattered on the floor.

Rows of numbers that represented children ran before her eyes. Beside them were the sections where they would be sent and the ministries they would be tested for. But that was not what caught her eye. Meagan brushed these aside, closing her fingers around a sheet poking out from behind the others.

More rows of numbers. And after them, words.

Unfit — termination.

Unfit — termination.

Unfit — termination.

The words ran on and on down the rows, each one a stab into her conscious mind. The screams echoed around her and her stomach turned. Meagan grabbed the trash can and threw up. She vomited again, and, to her surprise, felt a little better. She gasped in a deep breath of air.

A paper had landed under the desk. She shouldn't look

anymore. Hadn't she read enough? She looked anyway. What she saw sent a chill up her spine. She stood, clutching the paper in her hands. Her eyes raced over the paper again, making sure she hadn't misread. She hadn't. A feeling of cold spread throughout her body.

Chapter 26
Deidre

Every life belongs to the IAS. Every child is a son or daughter of the State.
— Fact 203, Citizen's Handbook

The click of the door handle turning sent a jolt of adrenaline through Meagan. It drove the last shred of illness from her and replaced it with something like outright terror. She scooped the papers off the ground and dropped them onto the table as the door opened.

It was the same woman, and this time she had a clear plastic box, like a little bed, tucked under one arm. A tiny bundle in a white blanket filled the box.

"Sign here," the woman told Meagan, thrusting a personal at her. Meagan scrawled her alias on the screen with her finger and took the box from the woman.

"The child is sedated," the woman explained. "That will wear off in about half an hour."

Meagan nodded. The woman spun on her heels and headed out of the room. Meagan tucked the box under her left arm and followed.

She breathed a sigh of relief when the woman led her into the elevator and pressed the button for reception. She was almost done with this nightmare. When they stepped out of the elevator, the woman nodded to the receptionist.

"Just sign out with Lanice here, and you can be on your way," the woman told Meagan. But before Meagan could move, a thin young man with a sharp face came out of the back room and spoke quietly to the woman. The woman shot a startled glance in Meagan's direction, then her chin bobbed up and down as she nodded to the man. Meagan's muscles tensed.

"I'm terribly sorry," the woman said to Meagan. Her face had gone white. "I'll have to ask you to wait here."

Meagan glanced over the woman's shoulder as the man went back through the door. Before the door swung shut, Meagan caught a glimpse of white uniforms. Public Security. She had to get out of here. Meagan took a step toward the glass front doors.

"I have other appointments," she said.

"I'm afraid that's impossible." The woman grabbed her arm, the one holding the baby. Meagan spun, slamming her fist into the woman's jaw. The woman released her hold on Meagan and staggered back. The receptionist behind the desk started screaming. Meagan lunged against the doors, but they didn't open. Meagan felt like screaming herself. Why did they lock the doors from the inside?

Now that she was in actual danger, Meagan's thinking became crystal clear. She set the baby on the floor beside the doors. Dashing back across the room, she dove over the desk, and grabbed the receptionist by the collar. Before the screaming woman could react, Meagan had her pinned against the wall.

"Unlock the doors," Meagan yelled, her face inches from the receptionist's. Even as the words left her mouth, Meagan heard a slam as the door to the back room flew open. Meagan saw Public Security white and knew she was trapped.

The sharp crack of a gunshot and shattering glass sounded behind her. The gunshots continued and the Public Security men staggered back. Meagan looked over her shoulder and saw Jacob firing through the glass doors, or what was left of them. She released the terrified receptionist, rolled over the top of the desk, and dashed for the exit, snatching up the box with its precious cargo on her way. Jacob stopped shooting and slammed another magazine into his pistol. Meagan stepped through the doorframe, broken glass crunching under her feet.

She sprinted toward the car, Jacob right beside her. The car was already running. Meagan yanked open the door and threw herself in. Jacob slid into the driver's seat and hit the gas before she even shut the door. The small car shot out of the parking space. Meagan clutched the box in her lap as Jacob swerved around the few other cars in the parking lot. Gunshots sounded behind them and bullets slammed into the car, ripping through the metal. Jacob sped out of the parking lot and thrust his pistol into her hands.

"Make them keep their heads down," he shouted.

Was he insane? Holding onto the baby in her lap with her left arm, Meagan twisted around with her right hand, holding the gun out the window. She couldn't turn far enough to actually see what she was shooting at, but she didn't think it mattered. She shut her eyes and jerked back on the trigger. Nothing happened. The trigger hadn't budged. Meagan clenched her teeth and squeezed it as hard as she could. The recoil startled her so much that she almost dropped the gun. Did it kick that much when Jacob shot it? She took a deep breath and fired again. It was easier this time. By now they were out of sight of the building. Meagan heard sirens. They didn't sound very far away. Panicked, Meagan looked over at Jacob. He was laughing! He really was crazy.

As a sharp turn slammed her into the side of the car, Meagan tried to get a better grip on the baby and the gun. She almost felt like laughing herself. Every foot of space she put between herself and that horrible building made her feel lighter.

"Okay, here's the plan," Jacob said. "I'm going to drive through the park. I'll drop you off there. There should be plenty of places to hide."

He braked sharply, reversed, and turned down a side street.

"Make your way back to the house. I'll lead them away, ditch the car, and meet you there. Understand?"

Meagan nodded. Jacob swung into the park entrance.

"Do you want a weapon?" he asked. "I have a knife if you want it."

"No thanks," Meagan answered.

The park was mostly deserted. Jacob started to slow down as they reached a small spread of woods.

"And out," he said.

Meagan left the gun on the seat, opened the door, and, clutching the baby's box in her arms, jumped. She landed on her feet, but then tumbled forward to her knees, almost losing her grip on the box. Jacob was already speeding up and pulling around the next bend in the road. Meagan didn't wait, but plunged into the bushes.

About an hour later, Meagan arrived back at the house, dirty, tired, and miserable. A smile crossed her face as she slipped in the back door. It was good to be home. Well, not home exactly; she didn't have a home, but after what she'd been through, the house felt … safe.

The baby, whom Meagan had taken the liberty of naming

Deidre, had woken up, and it was all Meagan could do to keep her from screaming. She had had to make do with muffling the sound as best she could while she made her way back to the house.

Now, as they entered the kitchen, Deidre started to wail.

"Shh," Meagan whispered as she took Deidre out of the box and held her in her arms. She had to keep her quiet. If anyone heard the sound of a baby, she would be reported and arrested for sure. Meagan had never seen a baby in real life before, let alone held one. She vaguely remembered reading something about supporting the baby's neck, so she tried to keep her hand under Deidre's head.

Deidre calmed down a little once Meagan picked her up. Meagan figured Deidre was hungry—that was usually Meagan's problem—so she started looking for something to feed her. Meagan wrinkled her nose.

"You smell," she whispered to Deidre. Meagan wondered if it was just Deidre or if all babies smelled that way. If they all smelled like that, she could see why people wouldn't want them.

Luckily, the kitchen was fully stocked. After looking through cabinets and the refrigerator, Meagan finally settled on giving Deidre some apple juice. She poured a little into a glass and, sitting in one of the chairs around a small folding table, held the glass to Deidre's tiny lips. The baby's mouth started moving and Meagan tilted the cup. Juice spilled down Deidre's face and neck. Meagan muttered a string of curses. She tried again with the same result. Deidre's blanket was now wet with apple juice.

Meagan thought for a moment, then dipped her finger in the glass and let Deidre suck the juice off it. Meagan laughed as Deidre's tiny tongue tickled her finger.

After about twenty minutes of feeding her this way, Meagan decided to try to clean her up a little and get some of the juice off her. Deidre needed a bath.

There was only a shower in the bathroom, so Meagan used the kitchen sink. She undressed Deidre and discovered why she smelled so bad. Meagan cleaned her up and gave her a warm bath. She found two extra diapers in the box and took her best guess as to the right way to put one on Deidre. After that, to Meagan's relief, the baby fell asleep in her arms.

Meagan tiptoed to the couch and let herself sink down onto it, being careful not to wake her. Meagan looked down at the tiny being in her arms and felt a strange warmth fill her heart. She could feel the weight Deidre's small body pressed against her chest, and the rise and fall of her peaceful little breaths. Meagan smiled, leaned back, and closed her eyes.

She woke to the sound of the doorknob turning. Instantly, she was on her feet. Someone was coming in the back door. She held Deidre against her chest and ducked down between the arm of the couch and the wall. She peered over the top just enough to watch the door open. A familiar figure stepped inside.

"Jacob," Meagan said, breathing a sigh of relief. "I'm glad you're back."

She was also pleased that he again wore his mechanic's jumpsuit and not the Ministry of Population uniform.

"The car is taken care of," Jacob said. "I also made sure I wasn't followed here."

"Good. Take Deidre, okay? I'm not wearing this uniform one minute longer."

"Deidre?"

"Well, I'm not calling her 30175 40 586."

"Yeah, sure. I'll take her."

Meagan handed Deidre to Jacob.

"Make sure you support her head," Meagan cautioned.

"I have done this before," Jacob answered.

Meagan went into the bedroom and changed into her jumpsuit. Then she went into the bathroom and scrubbed her face until all the makeup of her disguise ran down the drain. As she wiped the last traces of foundation from her now pink face, she ran through the conversation with Jacob in her head. What had he meant by he had done this before? He had taken care of a baby before? Was there nothing he hadn't done?

A small cry escaped her lips and she raced out of the bathroom.

Jacob was in the kitchen sitting at the table. He was holding Deidre, soaking a rag in a bowl of milk and letting her suck on it. Meagan snatched Deidre away and stepped back.

"Hey." Jacob stood up.

Meagan could tell he was annoyed, but she didn't care.

"Jacob," she said, staring into his eyes, "tell me the truth. Were you ever a part of the Ministry of Population?"

"Why would you ask me that?" he snapped. "Give me Deidre."

Meagan backed away. "Not until you answer me."

Jacob opened his mouth to respond, but his face changed when he saw that Meagan was close to tears. His brown eyes met hers.

"No," he answered. "I was never involved with them. Today was the closest I have ever been."

Meagan let out her pent up breath. She passed Deidre back to Jacob.

"Sorry," she mumbled. She turned to leave the room.

"Why does the Ministry of Population scare you so much?"

"I'm not afraid."

Jacob took her arm and turned her around to face him.

"Don't lie to me. Ever since we got this mission, you've been acting irrational. Obviously something is wrong."

Meagan lowered her eyes.

"Ever heard of the Ministry of Population's Reform Division?" Meagan said, her voice barely a whisper.

"Of course I have. I've been warned about it my entire life. That's where I would have ended up if—" He stopped and shoved his free hand into his pocket. "Yeah, I've heard of it."

"I was sent there."

Jacob's eyes widened. "You were?"

Meagan nodded. "I don't know why. It had something to do with my parents. They were criminals."

Jacob's eyebrows drew together. Meagan shrugged. "I never knew them. But I got sent to the Reform Division. I still remember a lot, even though I was really little. It was the worst thing that ever happened to me."

Meagan looked up at Jacob. She couldn't read his expression.

"Even now," she continued, "I really can't stand Population people, or buildings, or anything that has to do with them. I—" her voice broke, and she cursed herself for her stupid emotion. She turned around so Jacob wouldn't see the tears that welled up in her eyes.

"You went in anyway," Jacob said. "Meagan, you should have told me. I wouldn't have sent you in alone."

“Am I that weak?” Meagan asked. “Do you have to help me with everything?”

Jacob shrugged. “Everyone’s afraid of something. But friends help each other. I mean, you’ve saved me from the Black Fists, what? Twice?”

“I don’t—” Meagan began, but Deidre started fussing. Meagan turned, and Jacob must have seen something in her expression, because he passed the baby to her without a word. She took the tiny child in her arms and cuddled her close. Then she burst into tears. Tears of terror and relief and pain and love and a whole host of emotions that she didn’t understand.

Jacob looked startled and confused for a moment, and then he carefully wrapped his arms around her and held her close to him.

“You never have to go back there again,” he whispered. “I’ll make sure nothing happens to you.”

Chapter 27
Choosing Sides

There is no middle ground. Everyone must commit themselves to the cause they believe in.
— Midwestern Free Press, wartime news

They were interrupted by a soft tapping on the back door.

"Stay out of sight," Jacob said, letting go of Meagan and taking his gun from his belt. He looked out the window before opening the door.

"It's our employer, Meagan," Jacob said.

It was a good thing he told her. Since the man had worn a mask and it had been night at their last meeting, Meagan had no idea what he really looked like. He was not wearing a mask now. Meagan studied him with some interest as he greeted her and Jacob.

He was dressed as a sanitation worker in a dark blue and white jumpsuit. He looked about fifty, with hands and face creased from hard labor. Sandy blond hair fell to his shoulders and a large mustache drooped around his mouth.

"You have done good work," he said to Meagan. He looked at Deidre, fussing in her arms. "May I hold her?"

Meagan passed the baby to him. As her took her, Meagan looked up into his eyes. With a jolt, she noticed they were brown. The man they had met before had green eyes.

Meagan leaned over and whispered to Jacob. "This isn't the same man we met before. His eyes are a different color."

"Sure he is," Jacob whispered back. "He's disguised, that's all."

Meagan blushed. It made perfect sense. The man was the same height and build as the one they had met in the park, even though he was standing with his shoulders hunched now, which made him look smaller.

"I have your identities prepared," he said. He gave Deidre back to Meagan and knelt down. He took two personals out of secret compartments, one in the side of each boot.

"These personals are very special," he explained. "Right now they show your identity as low level Civil Affairs workers."

"We are going to need to disguise ourselves," Jacob said. "The authorities are after us."

"Don't worry. I haven't loaded your pictures into the personals yet. When you have disguised yourselves, enter this code." He handed Jacob a slip of paper. "Then take a picture of yourself. It will load the picture into your profile."

"And that will stand up to a security check?" Jacob asked.

The man nodded. "Not a careful analysis, but for the usual security checks it will be sufficient."

Jacob looked impressed. "This is good tech."

"It gets better. When you reach the car—I'll explain that to you in a minute—you will enter the second code on that paper. The first identity will be destroyed and your second, and more important identity, will already be loaded into the personal."

"And what will that identity be?" Jacob asked.

"You are both Supervision Ministry workers. There are openings for promotion and you two were given some time off to study for the exams. As such, you will be spending a lot of time in your hotel rooms: The First Official Hotel, downtown."

Jacob nodded. "I know the place."

"When you leave here, proceed to Train Station Eight," he continued. "Circle around to the Development sector. After that—"

Deidre let out a scream. All three of them jumped.

"Give her to me," Jacob said. "I'll settle her."

He left the room, bouncing the baby gently. Meagan and the man were left standing in awkward silence.

Something was gnawing at the back of Meagan's mind. This man seemed familiar, and not just as their employer. Ever since he had started talking, she felt that she knew him from somewhere. Was it his voice, smooth and controlled and out of place with his rough appearance? And why did he not let them see his undisguised face? Would she recognize him?

"Who are you?" Meagan asked. The words were out of her mouth before she realized that she had decided to say them. She was shocked by her own daring, but she did want to know and asking was as good a way of finding out as any.

The man looked at her. Surprise, fear, and excitement all passed across his features in an instant, but these were quickly hidden by a face that exuded artificial confidence.

"Why do you want to know?" he asked carefully.

"It's just … you seem familiar. Like I know you from somewhere."

The man did not answer, but gazed at her steadily. Meagan blushed and looked away. Had she gone too far? Did he know that her motives weren't altogether pure?

"Keep quiet. I just got the baby to sleep," Jacob said, walking back into the room. He glanced from the man to Meagan and back again. "Did I miss something?"

"Nothing much." The man gave a tight smile. "Your partner has suggested a better plan to me than my original one."

Jacob glanced at Meagan, eyebrows raised. Meagan kept her mouth shut.

The man continued. "The reason I did not choose this plan before was because it involves you two knowing who I really am. I must protect my identity carefully. However," he glanced from Jacob to Meagan, "I believe that both of you can be trustworthy."

He took a personal out of his pocket and hit several buttons. Then he gave it to Meagan.

"Does that answer your question?"

Meagan looked at the personal and her eyes widened. The picture was the man from the party, the man from the CPC, Arthur Rand. She looked up and realized that beneath the makeup, beneath the hair, it really was him. Wordlessly, she passed the personal to Jacob.

Arthur smiled at her warmly. "You seem surprised."

"Rand?" Jacob blurted out. "You're Arthur Rand. I can't believe this." He ran his hand through his hair. "You're a big man in the IAS. You're what? A Level Two? One of the Privileged levels?"

The man seemed genuinely pleased by Jacob's surprise and enthusiasm. Meagan rolled her eyes. Jacob could act so weird sometimes.

"You are correct. I am a Level Two."

"I don't see why you'd want to rebel," Meagan said. "That high up you wouldn't have to worry about anything."

Arthur's face darkened. "The IAS is an evil that must be destroyed."

Meagan looked at him sharply. He was a Level Two. He had no right to think like that.

"Well, I'm impressed," Jacob said. "Even the Black Fists have to show you respect."

"We've had our share of power struggles," Arthur said grimly. "The Black Fists are not to be underestimated. I believe it would be best if you both hid at my house until you can leave."

"Would that be safe? I mean, I'd be more worried about your safety than ours," Jacob said.

Arthur gave him a humorless smile. "I've done things that were much more dangerous for causes less worthy. Besides, my house is hardly ever subject to random searches."

"In that case, thank you, sir." Jacob shook his hand.

"Now, as I was saying," Arthur said. "You will go to Train Station Eight disguised as Civil Affairs workers. When you reach Development's sector, go to the Natural History Museum. There will be a car waiting for you. Don't worry about the driver. He knows what I'm involved in. You can trust him." Arthur pursed his lips, thinking. "What name do you want me to give my people?"

"Wild Card," Jacob said.

"I'm Meagan."

Arthur nodded and folded his hands behind his back. "Very good. Now, if I could take the child, I need to be going. I must get her to a safe place before my presence at work is missed. I have a meeting this afternoon, and, although I make a point of always being late, I do actually have to show up."

"I'll get her," Jacob said, and ducked out of the room.

Meagan turned to Arthur. "If you're in charge of the CPC, why didn't you just transfer the baby yourself, instead of getting us shot at?" she demanded.

"This wasn't an ordinary transfer, and I can't be connected to any trouble," Arthur answered. "The Black Fists would be all over me at the slightest hint of disloyalty. As for Public Security attacking you, well, I am sorry for that."

At least he had the decency to sound contrite.

"I didn't realize how hard the mission would actually be for you," he added.

Meagan wanted to ask him what he meant by that, but Jacob returned with Deidre fussing in his arms. He passed the baby to

Arthur.

"What do you want Deidre for?" Meagan asked, suddenly afraid for a reason she did not understand.

For a moment Arthur was quiet as he laid Deidre in her box.

"I'm taking her to her mother," he said without looking up. "When a woman wants to keep her child, I do my best to make it happen. The mother and child will, of course, have to be hidden, but at least they can be together. Or when a mother discovers that her child didn't pass the tests and will be killed, I try to get the child however I can, then hide and relocate it."

He took a small syringe out of his pocket and gave Deidre a shot in her leg. She calmed down and stopped crying almost instantly. Meagan took one last look at the tiny little girl she had come to care so much for.

"Bye Deidre," she whispered. She imagined Deidre having a nice life far away from the city, someplace safe. Arthur took Deidre and opened the door.

A thought entered Meagan's mind. "One more thing," she said. Arthur stopped and half turned in the doorway.

Meagan took a deep breath. "Why were you so surprised to see me that night at the party? As far as I know, we had never met."

Arthur hesitated. He opened his mouth, then shut it again. He looked at the ground before lifting his eyes to meet hers.

"You reminded me of someone," he said. It was a simple sentence, and yet there was so much pain behind the words. Meagan was too startled to reply. Arthur Rand stepped out the door and was gone.

Standing on the stone steps of the Natural History Museum, Meagan breathed a sigh of relief. They had had no problems getting this far. A shiny black car was waiting for them, just like Arthur said it would be. After showing the driver their personals, Jacob and Meagan climbed into the car. It was almost too easy. They were immediately whisked off down the city streets.

Meagan closed her eyes and sank into the seat, breathing in the rich smell of leather. Rubbing her hands over the upholstery, she felt a smile spreading across her face. This was how she was meant to live.

"Mr. Rand wants you to wait to enter your new identity into the personal," the driver told them. "You won't need a disguise at his house and when you decide to leave, you can do what you want in the way of concealing your identities."

"Good idea," Jacob said.

Meagan rested her chin on her hand and watched the buildings rushing by outside the tinted windows. Her mind wandered over the events that had led to this moment. Was it only this morning that she had broken into the Child Processing Center? It seemed like so long ago.

Suddenly she remembered. She had to tell Jacob about the discovery she made while she was waiting in that awful room. She turned to him.

"I found something in the CPC that you might find interesting."

"What?"

"Some files had children marked for termination." Meagan shuddered remembering it. "But there was this one page that had a list of numbers of children. I only got a glimpse of it, but it appeared that these children were to be sent to the New Worlds Space Center."

"The Space Center? How sure are you?"

"I'm almost completely sure."

"Was there anything else? About the babies or the Space Center?"

Meagan shook her head. "I only got a brief glance."

Jacob's eyebrows drew together and he stared out the window. "What are they up to in there?" he said to himself.

Meagan opened her mouth to ask what he meant, but she caught herself and closed it again. What was she doing? Had she lost her mind completely? Had she forgotten who she was? She had been planning to sabotage the CPC job, not actually complete it. She had planned on turning Jacob in. What had happened? The minute she had stepped out of the car this morning she'd forgotten that her real mission was not to help Jacob and the Defiance, but to destroy them. How could she have forgotten?

She had been thinking and acting like a full-fledged member of the Defiance all day, and she hadn't even noticed. Meagan was incredulous and a little frightened. She had slipped easily enough into her role as double agent for the Black Fists, and now she felt like she was tumbling head first into a new role, one she was pretty sure she didn't want to play.

Meagan was suddenly very afraid that she was losing her grip on herself, who she was. She had her own dreams. Her own plans. Dreams and plans that would never be realized unless she stayed focused. She also had very dire obligations. She had just assisted Jacob in breaking into a government building. Commander Ultan would not be pleased. She did not know what the Black Fists would do to her if she failed, but she didn't want to find out.

Meagan felt like she was waking from a deep sleep. She had enough information. More than enough. She had more than even the most demanding Black Fist could expect. No excitement accompanied this realization, none of the fierce elation she had envisioned herself feeling. There was only the grim reality that she had a job to do; the consequences of failure were too high. She couldn't risk losing herself again. It was time to expose Jacob, and she needed to do it quickly.

She glanced over at him, still staring thoughtfully out the window. What would happen when she turned him in? Would they torture him? Shoot him? An image flashed into her mind of Jacob on his knees, Commander Ultan standing behind him with a pistol to his head. Meagan turned away. It wasn't her choice. She belonged to the State and the State would reward her well for her loyalty. She had picked her side; Jacob should have chosen his more carefully.

Chapter 28
Loyal Service

The IAS will not give respect based on wealth or power. Honor is given to those who serve most loyally.
— Charter of the International Administrative State

Well, Ultan thought wryly, no one could accuse him of being wrong. He rubbed his temples. Wild Card had turned up, Meagan too. They had broken into the CPC and stolen an infant. What were they doing with an infant? Now, of course, he had lost them again. The boy wasn't working for the Defiance anymore—if he ever had been. He was playing some larger game, and he knew the space program was a front. That meant his target was the Space Center. But what had first drawn his interest to the Space Center? And why steal a baby?

Now Wild Card and Meagan had vanished again, despite his efforts to find them. Someone was very good at remaining hidden.

Ultan left his office and ran up the stairs to the roof of the Black Fist building. The September wind whipped his hair back and tugged at the edges of his crisp uniform. He breathed deeply, letting the icy air fill his lungs. He wasn't made for desk work. Standing here, above the city, this was where he felt truly powerful. This was where he also felt truly responsible. He could sit in an office and plan and connive and scheme. But up here the full weight of his responsibility washed over him. There were people in this city who would stop at nothing to destroy the very project he was tasked to protect.

His eyes narrowed. So the boy had broken into the CPC. That was Rand's territory.

Rand.

Ultan blew out a short breath, feeling his blood pressure rise just thinking about that spoiled, rich, half-drunk idiot. Could Rand be a part of all this? It wasn't the first time Ultan had suspected him of treason. But somehow Rand was never involved, always had a solid alibi, had no idea what Ultan was talking about. No one, not Ultan's superiors, no one, would believe his assertions that Rand was a threat. And Ultan could never connect him to anything.

Furthermore, since Rand was a level above him, every time Ultan accused or suspected him but could not prove it, Ultan got into trouble with his superiors. Still, his gut and his general revulsion told him there was more to Rand than anyone else suspected.

The houses in the elite administrative center of the city were few. Reserved for only the most important citizens, they rose above the streets, freshly painted and well kept. Meagan craned her neck, looking up at their sloping roofs as the car rolled past. She tried to peer through the tall windows to imagine what life was like inside. She would live this way someday. Not here. Here was nowhere. In Chicago, or maybe the capital, New York. She was a good enough propagandist. She could do it.

And now was as decent a time as any to start getting used to a life of luxury. Meagan straightened her back, crossed her legs, and stuck her nose in the air. She tried to forget that she was a nobody, here only by trickery, lies, and deceit.

The car slowed and Arthur Rand's house rose up before them. Meagan's pulse quickened. Three stories of warm brown brick sat atop a tiny lawn, still green even in September. The driver parked and stepped out, coming around to open the door for Meagan.

She could hardly contain her excitement as they walked up the short stone pathway to the huge oak doors set within a covered archway. Jacob rapped sharply on the wood. After a moment, the left door opened halfway, and a petite girl in a short yellow dress looked over the visitors with raised eyebrows. Her dirty-blond hair was pulled back into a bun, but half her curls had escaped and corkscrewed around her face. Judging from her stylish apron, Meagan guessed that she was one of Arthur's maids.

"Can I help you?" she asked.

Jacob nodded. "Our IDs," he answered, passing his personal to the girl. Meagan followed suit.

The maid looked them over carefully. "I was told you'd be arriving. Come in."

Meagan and Jacob followed the girl into the house. Meagan's eyes widened. A high ceiling arched three stories overhead and a huge golden chandelier lit the room with dazzling yellow light. Smooth wood floors stretched out underfoot and in front of them, a wide staircase led to the next floor; to Meagan, everything seemed polished and gleaming.

"My name's Kalyn," the maid said. "If you need anything, call me or Jenni, or anyone else you can find."

She tucked a strand of hair behind her ear and continued. "Mr. Rand is at work, of course. I can't tell you when he will be back. He never really sticks to a schedule." She bobbed her head, making her curls bounce. "I'll show you your rooms."

"Thank you," Jacob said.

Kalyn led them up the stairs. Meagan tried to keep from gaping at the luxury around her. Paintings of geometric shapes and blobs of color hung on the walls. Lavender scented the air, which was delightfully warm. Meagan sighed. Apparently, Arthur Rand was allowed to heat his house as much as he wanted.

When they reached the top of the steps, Kalyn started down a hallway. Meagan saw another maid watching them as they passed. Like Kalyn, this girl couldn't have been much older than Meagan. She stood with arms crossed, watching them suspiciously from under dark bangs.

"That's Jenni," Kalyn said as they passed. Meagan looked quickly away from the girl's penetrating stare.

"There's your room," Kalyn said to Jacob, gesturing to a closed door on the left. "And Meagan, yours is the one at the end of the hall."

Meagan did not wait. She hurried past Kalyn and pushed open the door to her room. The bedroom was right out of a dream. It was as large as the dining room back at the School of Information, with carpet that was soft and deep. The afternoon sun poured in through two floor-to-ceiling windows, its warm light complemented by the pale yellow blanket that lay across the large bed.

Meagan also discovered a large bathroom lit with warm yellow lights. Inside was a device that Meagan was not completely sure of. It looked like a tub, yet it was larger than any she had ever seen and had strange knobs and vents, making it look vaguely dangerous.

"That's a luxury tub," Kalyn said, coming up behind her.

"A what?"

"Trust me. It's the best of the best in bathing experiences."

"It looks more like a place to put someone you want to hurt."

Kalyn laughed. "Get settled in your room. After dinner, I

promise I'll come back and show you how to use it. After all, you're a hero."

Meagan's eyebrows drew together. "What?"

"Didn't you know? There was another maid here for a few weeks. The baby girl was hers." Kalyn took Meagan's hand. "She and the baby—Mr. Rand said you called her Deidre, right?—she and the baby left today with one of Mr. Rand's contacts. And I'm just so grateful to you and Wild Card. Do you do things like this often?"

"We like to keep things interesting," Meagan muttered. She shooed the overly appreciative maid out as quickly as she could.

Meagan ate dinner alone. She sat at a table that could hold twenty people, poking her barbequed steak with the end of her gleaming silver fork. Raised lettering along the fork read *15 yrs of loyal service to the IAS.*

Meagan stabbed the steak and began to saw it furiously with her knife. It was just as well that Jacob was eating in his room, busy concocting some new plot to investigate the Space Center. She really didn't want company. Not while she planned how to betray people who trusted her with their lives.

Despite her glorious surroundings, Meagan wasn't enjoying dinner. The woman serving her kept urging her to eat more, something she never thought anyone would have to do. Meagan drew swirls in the meat sauce with her fork. She sat alone at the long table, chewing the spicy steak and contemplating how to inform the Black Fist leader of her location.

Her first thought was to use the anonymous tip line that people could call to report lawbreakers, although Meagan doubted that anyone's identity remained anonymous. But the real problem with the tip line was that she would probably be reporting to some Public Security underling, not the Black Fist commander. If Ultan wasn't involved how would she get the credit and her reward? She might even end up being arrested herself. No, that would not work.

Meagan finished her steak and started on the baked potato. She would have to find some other way. Maybe she could send an e-mail from Arthur's computer. Everyone knew that all messages were read by security. Her classmates had always speculated that it was Public Security forces who read the e-mails. Although Megan had never shared her own suspicions, she believed it was actually the Black Fists who checked messages for rebel communications. The Black Fists could track the message back to the computer it originated from, leading them here, and she could indicate that she was the one sending the e-mail, assuring Ultan of her cooperation. She pushed some green beans around on her plate absently. Yes, sending an e-mail from the house was probably her best course of action.

Meagan finished her meal and trudged back upstairs to her room. She decided to look for a computer in the morning. While she didn't like the thought of waiting any longer to complete her mission, Arthur could be coming home at any time. If she were caught, it would be hard to explain why she was wandering around the house at night. People would be less suspicious of the same actions if she were discovered during the day. Arthur should be gone, so there was less chance of her getting caught, and even if she were, she could always say she was just exploring the house.

Meagan smiled wryly; since she was going to stay here overnight, she might as well enjoy herself. It was time to try out that luxury tub and see if it was everything Kalyn had promised.

"Sir," Ultan's secretary said, "Alfmarin is on the line, as requested."

Ultan picked up the phone and greeted the city's Head of Public Security.

"I want you to conduct a search of Arthur Rand's house," Ultan said. "Do it tomorrow afternoon, while he is at work downtown."

"I don't have the authority to search his house," the man answered. "Not unless you have some concrete evidence."

"I have the authority. I'm taking the responsibility. The signed orders were already sent to you. I'm also attaching a man, well, actually, a woman to your team. I want her dressed as Public Security."

"Any chance you can tell me what it is we're looking for?"

"No," Ultan answered.

"We will proceed as you have commanded."

Chapter 29
"Do You Remember Your Parents?"

Careless words endanger both peace and security. Never speak against the IAS. Every word is perceived and remembered.
— Fact 805, Citizen's Handbook

Meagan stripped off her gray jumpsuit, which desperately needed to be washed, and which she was beginning to despise. She wrapped herself in the fluffy white robe she'd found in her closet. The robe was too big, but that just made it better. She pushed the button that Kalyn had shown her to call for service and started toward the bathroom. As she passed the bed she noticed a slip of creamy white paper folded neatly in half lying on the yellow blankets. Had someone put it there while she was at dinner, or had she just not seen it when she first arrived?

Curious, Meagan sat down on the soft mattress and opened the paper. A single question was written in black ink:

Do you remember your parents?

Meagan felt the breath catch in her throat, felt the paper slip from her fingers. No, she couldn't remember her parents. She didn't know her parents. Even as she had the thought, an image, more feeling than picture, formed in her mind, but as soon as she reached for it, it was gone. Meagan stared blankly down at the paper in her lap. Who had left this note and why? What did the author know about her parents? Hot anger built inside her. Whoever it was should mind their own business.

Meagan stood abruptly and crossed the room, fuming. Why did this person care if she remembered her parents? She had spent most of her life trying to forget. They had been involved in criminal activity, that much she knew. It was because of their crimes that she had spent four years of her life in the living nightmare that was the Reform Division. Meagan clenched her hands so hard that her fingernails dug into her palms. She hated her parents. Hated them. She wanted desperately to forget that she ever had anything to do with them. They were not her parents. The State was her father and the Earth was her mother. Fact 1. Meagan tore the crinkled paper in half and hurled it away from her. The two halves fluttered down and landed at her feet.

Meagan turned at the sound of a knock on the door. "Come in," she said flatly.

Kalyn's curly head peeked around the door. "Ready for a bath?" she asked.

Meagan nodded mutely and followed her into the bathroom. She watched without really seeing as Kalyn explained the workings of the tub. Meagan couldn't concentrate on the words coming from Kalyn's mouth. After the maid finally left, Meagan settled into the warm water. It soothed her stiff muscles, but she couldn't relax. She felt sick and miserable. She was ready to go back to being normal Meagan and just wanted this all to end. She was tired of playing the double agent; tired and sick of it. Not even the thought of the promised reward could cheer her up. Something had changed. Power and a high station had lost some of its glamour. Meagan didn't like that. She didn't like feeling the way she did, dirty and all twisted around. Things had been so much simpler before.

But, no, that wasn't true. Things were simplest now. She could not fail the Black Fists. Who was she if not Meagan, Daughter of the State? She had a job to do, and she would do it. That was all.

With this resolution in mind, Meagan finished her bath and again wrapped herself in the robe. As she tied the robe's cord loosely, she glanced over at the mirror. It was steamed over from her bath so she could not see herself, but her eyes were drawn to something in the corner. Meagan's heart started racing and she felt herself grow hot. Tucked between the frame and the mirror was a small, cream-colored paper, folded in half.

Meagan snatched it up and dropped it into the trash can. She strode out of the bathroom and picked the softest, most elegant pajamas she could find in the closet, trying not to think about the note. She made herself sigh with pleasure as the silk fabric slipped over her head. She'd never had pajamas before. Meagan forced herself not to look at the bathroom door as she stretched out on the bed. She sank into the mattress and closed her eyes. But her teeth really needed to be brushed. Meagan opened her eyes and glanced over at the bathroom door. Did she really want to go back in there? Meagan got out of bed, put her nose in the air, and strode back to the bathroom. She wasn't afraid of anything.

As she brushed her teeth, she looked anywhere but at the trash can. She told herself that she didn't care what the note said. She didn't want to know. She finished and turned to leave, flicking off the light and stepping out the door. Then she hesitated. Sighing in exasperation, she switched the light back on, went to the trash can, and lifted out the note.

Meagan walked back to her bed and sat down. Slowly, she opened the paper.

I knew your parents. If you would like, I will tell you anything you want to know about them.

A.R.

A.R. That was Arthur Rand. How had Arthur Rand known her parents? Was he a friend, a coworker? Had her parents been important people like Arthur? Meagan felt like she had been hit in the side of the head with a board. How did Arthur know that much about her? And he knew her parents. She could find out anything she wanted about them.

So many questions about them bounced around in her brain. She had never known how many questions she had until this moment. She tried to tell herself that she didn't care, but she knew it was a lie. She did care. Meagan knew two facts about her parents, only two. One was that they were killed for being involved in criminal activity, and the second was that they had her. Meagan had not forgiven them for either.

She tore the paper to shreds. She didn't care. She couldn't care. She was turning Jacob and Arthur Rand over to the Black Fists tomorrow and nothing was going to stop her.

She stood in front of her bed like she had done so many times at the School of Information.

"The State is my father, and the Earth is my mother," she recited, trying to drive unwanted half-memories from her brain. With Fact 1 burning in her mind, she flopped down on the bed. Her jaw clenched. This was her first and last night in this house, and tomorrow she was going to make Arthur sorry he had dared to put her through this.

The sun was already streaming through the window when Meagan woke the next morning. She glanced at her personal. It read 11:48. Meagan groaned. She had slept most of the morning and she still didn't feel rested. Despite her exhaustion, she had tossed and turned all night, finally falling into a deep sleep in the early morning hours.

Meagan swung her legs over the side of the bed and stretched her tight muscles. She ran her hand through her short hair. Not bothering to change, she pulled her robe over her pajamas, grabbed her gray jumpsuit from the floor, and headed for the door.

On her way to the dining room, she ran into the dark haired maid. What was her name? Jenna? Jenni?

"I'd like some breakfast," Meagan said, stifling a yawn.

Jenni raised her eyebrows. "I believe there are some eggs and bacon being kept warm for you in the kitchen."

"Can you take care of this?" Meagan held out her jumpsuit.

"Of course. I'll incinerate it right away."

"No. I want it washed." She couldn't tell if the girl was joking or not, but Meagan was in no mood for games.

"I'll get it back to you." Jenni took the jumpsuit between her forefinger and thumb.

Meagan turned and shuffled off toward the kitchen. She forced herself not to think about last night's events before she had eaten. She didn't want to spoil her appetite.

After breakfast though, she began to wander around the house, looking for an office. She walked through a large room that appeared to be for entertaining guests, and then came to a small sitting room with a piano in it. After that, she arrived at a more open room in the middle of the house. Meagan would have called it the living room, but it was the nicest living room she had ever seen. The ceiling was two stories up and a huge television hung on one wall.

She turned as footsteps approached behind her.

"Here is the jumpsuit you wanted washed," Jenni said. Her eyes traveled over the robe and pajamas that Meagan still wore. "You do know there are other clothes in your closet, don't you?"

"I'm not blind," Meagan snapped, taking her jumpsuit.

"Blind, no. Rude, yes," the girl said. She turned on her heels and left the room.

Meagan ignored her.

Off the living room Meagan found a set of stairs that led down to the basement. It was unlikely that the office was in the basement, but it wouldn't hurt to check it out. Besides, she thought she heard a faint noise coming from below.

Downstairs several floor lamps placed strategically around the room provided dim light. Above the back of a large couch, Meagan could see a person's head and shoulders silhouetted against the light from a wide television mounted on the wall. The sounds she'd heard upstairs were louder now, music and gunshots.

"Jacob?" Meagan said, moving around so she could see his face. Jacob was holding a black object in his hands. He hit a button on it and the image on the TV froze.

"Hi, Meagan."

"What are you doing?"

Meagan now saw that the object in his hand was connected by a cord to a black box that sat under the television.

"Well, I had been working," Jacob answered. "But when I saw that Rand had some video games down here, I had to try one."

"What are video games?"

"They don't make them anymore, but before the War, they were a popular form of entertainment." He held up the object in his hand. "I had always wondered what playing them was like. These must have cost Rand a fortune."

Meagan looked at the assorted electronics dubiously. Students weren't allowed entertainment. Recreation cut into learning time, and doing worthless things for fun was highly disapproved of.

"Here, try it," Jacob said.

Meagan shook her head. "Maybe later. I'm busy."

"Doing what?"

"Exploring the house."

"Well, do it later. C'mon. Sit."

Meagan weighed the time she would waste arguing with Jacob against the time it would take to just do what he wanted. She dropped the jumpsuit on the couch and sat down. Jacob handed her the controller.

"Okay, this controls your movement, and this controls where you look," he explained, showing her various knobs and buttons.

Meagan looked down at just how many buttons there were. "How am I going to remember all of these?"

"You probably won't need all of them right now. Just remember those two and this button."

"What does this button do?"

"It shoots."

"Shoots?"

"Yeah." Jacob pointed to the image on the TV screen. "See those guys on the hill?"

"Yes."

"Those are the bad guys. You're trying to kill them."

"What about the people down here with me?"

"Those are your buddies. Don't shoot them. They'll help you."

Meagan took a deep breath. "Okay, here goes."

Jacob hit a button and suddenly the room was filled with the sound of shouting and gunfire. The figures on the screen started running toward the hill. Meagan tried to go forward. She found that she was staring at the ground.

"No, you want to go forward," Jacob said.

"I'm trying," Meagan muttered. She didn't see how this was fun. She jerked her controls and now she was staring at the sky. Her "buddies" were yelling at her. She lurched in their direction. She was staring at the ground again. She cursed, tried to correct, and bumped into one of her buddies.

"Hey!" he shouted at her. She shot him in the foot. Jacob was laughing. Meagan dropped the controller in frustration.

"This isn't fun," she said accusingly.

Still laughing, Jacob paused the game. "Sure it is. It just takes a little time to get used to the controls, that's all."

Meagan raised her eyebrows. "It's not that funny."

"You shot your buddy in the foot."

"That's what happens to people who annoy me."

Jacob laughed even harder.

"It really isn't that funny."

"No, it's hilarious. Just think about how you looked to the guys you were with."

"What?"

"You know, your buddies. Think about what they saw. You staring at the sky, and the ground, and lurching around in no particular direction."

Meagan started to laugh. It *was* funny to imagine what she must have looked like to those poor confused men. Suddenly, something in her mind clicked and it startled her so much that she stood up abruptly.

"What's wrong?" Jacob asked.

Meagan waved at him to be quiet. An idea was rising in her mind, and it was so bizarre, so disturbing, that she didn't want to kill it before she thought it through.

"They wouldn't," she said to herself.

Chapter 30
Games

The State trusts its citizens, knowing they will make good choices.
— Fact 994, Citizen's Handbook

"Wouldn't what?" Jacob asked.

Meagan shook her head. Could it even be true? But it made sense. Everything fit.

"I was thinking about what you said," Meagan began slowly. Jacob started to ask a question, but Meagan continued.

"What you said about how my character would look to the people in the game. People watching what I was doing trying to control it."

"Yes?"

"Well, my character would look a lot like that guy Deuce and I saw. We watched him stare into the air and wander around all jerky."

"You're saying that his behavior was similar to your character's in the game."

"More than similar, it was almost identical."

Jacob stared intently at the frozen images on the screen. "I have to get into the Space Center."

"Forget the IAS's stupid space program and listen to me."

"You're right," he said. "About the video games."

"Okay …"

"What if the IAS is developing a device that can control humans? And they implant this device in people. That would explain the scars you mentioned."

"A mind control device," Meagan said. Jacob didn't think her idea was crazy.

"Yes. Just like you pointed out with the video game. The IAS is trying to learn the controls. Only the IAS isn't playing video games."

"They're playing mind games."

Jacob nodded. "That's what they're doing at the Space Center. Remember I said it was outfitted more like a hospital? The space program is just a cover for this mind control business."

"But why would the government want mind control?" Meagan asked. "They already control everything."

"Exactly," Jacob said. "They can force people to *do* what they want, but they can influence only so much about what people are *thinking*."

"But isn't it impractical to go around physically controlling everyone on the planet?"

Jacob leaned back into the couch, his brow furrowed with thought. "With a device like that, the State wouldn't even need to control everyone all the time. They could just make everyone submit to being implanted. The ones who didn't, they would shoot as traitors. Then, even without the State controlling them, everyone would know that, at any given moment, they or their friends or their boss could stop being the person they knew and become simply an extension of the State. On top of that, maybe the State will come up with some way of controlling large groups of people all at once."

Jacob met Meagan's eyes. "It would destroy any last resistance to their regime."

"But could the State actually make something like that work?"

"Well, considering they have already started testing it on humans, I'd say there's a pretty good chance."

At that moment, Kalyn appeared at the top of the steps. "There's Public Security at the door," she said, her voice frantic. "Get up here. We have a place to hide you."

"Go," Jacob said to Meagan. "I'll be there in a minute." He switched off the TV and took a disk out of the black box.

"Come on," Kalyn urged.

Meagan turned and ran up the stairs two at a time. Kalyn already had Jacob's backpack slung over her shoulder. When Meagan reached the top, Kalyn's sweaty hand closed around her wrist, and she dragged her through the house. Behind them, Meagan heard the butler letting the search team in the door, the harsh orders as the men began to spread out. Back at the School of Information, they had had to endure searches about twice a year. Scary enough then, it was even worse now. Meagan glanced at rooms that had seemed safe and calm just moments before. Now they appeared threatening, every door a place for Public Security to come storming through.

Kalyn pulled her into a darkened room, windowless, with mirrors and wooden panels on the walls.

"Hurry," Jacob said, coming up behind them. Meagan heard a shout farther down the hall, and the sound of something breaking. Kalyn released Meagan's wrist and dropped to her knees. She wrapped her fingers around one of the panels, sliding it back to reveal a dark opening.

"In here."

Meagan and Jacob didn't wait. They crouched down and crawled forward, Meagan in the lead. The darkness closed around her and her head hit a wall. She scooted to the side to allow Jacob to enter. He took his backpack from Kalyn and pushed it through in front of him. There was barely enough room for the two of them in the tiny space.

"Be silent," Kalyn hissed as she slid the panel back into place.

They were left in total darkness. Meagan leaned her back against the wall. She felt Jacob's knees bump her as he settled down beside her.

Boots thumped on carpet. Men shouted to each other, though Meagan could not make out the words. Once she heard a woman's voice that seemed to be issuing a string of commands. There was a scraping noise as a large piece of furniture was dragged across the floor.

Meagan drew in a deep breath and forced herself to relax. Everything was under control. Random searches were a part of everyday life. Public Security showed up, searched, and then left. It was just to keep everyone obedient. She and Jacob would be okay. All they needed to do now was wait.

Meagan became aware of an oily substance on her hand. It wasn't much, just a tiny strip where Kalyn had grabbed her wrist. She raised the back of her hand to her nose and sniffed. It smelled like … foundation.

"Hey, Jacob," Meagan whispered.

"What?"

"Kalyn had makeup on her wrist. Know why?"

"No. But if I had to guess, I would say it was to hide the tattoos."

"What's that supposed to mean?"

"If you have a healthy child for the State you receive a certain tattoo on your wrist. There's a different mark for people unfit to have children. Considering Rand's line of work, I wouldn't be surprised if his servants were people he is hiding from the IAS."

Meagan mulled this idea over for a moment. She was in a house full of people hiding from the State. Just like her. She pulled her robe tighter around her.

A jolt of panic shot up her spine.

"Jacob," she whispered.

"What?"

"Did you get my jumpsuit?"

"What?"

"I left my jumpsuit on the couch downstairs. Did you get it when you were cleaning up?"

"You left your jumpsuit downstairs?"

Meagan couldn't see him in the dark, but Jacob sounded scared, angry and scared.

"I'm sorry. I didn't think. I just—"

"There's nothing we can do about it now. Just be quiet and wait."

"Maybe they won't see it."

Jacob was silent for a moment. "That will depend," he said.

"Depend on what?"

"Whether this is a random search or if they are actually looking for us. If this is just routine for them they might not search very well."

The statement sounded more like his hope than his expectation.

"And if they're looking for us?"

"Then I'd say we're in trouble."

Meagan sank back against the wall. How could she have been so stupid? Sure she needed to turn Jacob over to the authorities, but not like this. This way, Public Security would get the credit for locating Wild Card and there was a very good chance she would be shot. Jacob wouldn't just let himself be captured. In her mind, she saw a huge gun battle between Jacob and Security. And she would be in the middle of it.

Meagan's heart was pounding. She shouldn't have stopped to talk with Jacob. She should have kept looking for a computer. She should have just told him to leave her alone.

Meagan bit her lip. It was only a matter of time before she and Jacob were hunted down and caught. If she didn't turn him in before they were found, it would be too late. She would have lost value to Commander Ultan. She would not be as highly rewarded. The Commander might even think she double-crossed him. And that was only if she survived being taken by Security.

According to Jacob's wristwatch, thirty minutes had passed since the search team arrived. Time dragged itself along like a dying man in a desert until Meagan could have easily believed they'd been there for hours. The two of them sat in the dark of their hiding place with nothing to occupy them but their thoughts. Meagan was considering slipping out and trying to convince the search team of her loyalty to the State when she heard a hushed voice coming from outside the panel.

"It's all right. They're gone."

The panel slid silently open, and the darkness around them became gray. Meagan could see the dim outline of Kalyn.

"Careful," Jacob said, barely audible. "This could be a trap." He held his pistol as he crawled out of the opening into the darkened room beyond. Meagan followed.

When they were out, Kalyn slid the panel back into place. There was no one else in the room.

Meagan and Jacob wasted no time in running downstairs. Meagan's jumpsuit was where she remembered leaving it. It had become partially wedged between the arm and cushion of the couch.

"They must not have seen it," Meagan said.

Jacob breathed a sigh of relief. "We were lucky. We can't let something like that happen again." He turned and started back up the stairs.

Meagan let him go. She poked around some more in the basement, making sure Arthur's office was not there. After she headed upstairs, she made a quick stop by her room, putting on a clean tee shirt and shorts from her closet and her grey jumpsuit. She left her robe and pajamas on the bed. She didn't think Jacob wouldn't approve, considering the close call they'd just had, but in a few minutes it wouldn't matter. As soon as she found Arthur's office, the Black Fists would know they were here. Then it would be over.

Meagan found the office on the second story, the door unlocked. She pushed it open and stepped softly into the spacious room. Sunlight came in the large windows and scattered long streaks of light on the white carpet. She closed the door and crossed the room to the black desk.

A low hum told Meagan the computer was running, but the monitor wasn't on. She hesitated. Most computers were locked by a password. If she needed one, she was going to be in trouble. She leaned forward and switched on the monitor. A tight smile curled her lips. Arthur had not logged off; she would not need a password.

As Meagan clicked on Arthur's e-mail, she noticed an open file that he had left minimized at the bottom of the screen. His e-mail opened. Meagan glanced down at the file, wondering what was in it. She shook her head. Stay focused. She opened a new message and held her fingers over the keyboard. A block of ice settled in her stomach. Meagan ignored it, took a deep breath, and began to type.

Wild Card is hiding at the house of Arthur Rand. I have the information.

—Meagan

Chapter 31
Daughter of the State?

The State is your father, and the Earth is your mother. You belong to them.
— Fact 1, Citizen's Handbook

Meagan stopped. What was she thinking, writing such a direct message? She couldn't send the e-mail directly to the Black Fist Commander. She did not know how. She would have to send it to someone on Arthur's contact list and let the Black Fists figure it out. She needed to be cryptic. Meagan erased her message.

The icy feeling was spreading from her stomach into her arms and legs. Unaccountably, she shivered and glanced up. The door was still closed, so why did she feel like she was being watched?

Meagan gritted her teeth and pounded the keys furiously.

A. Rand's house. — Meagan

Meagan stopped and looked around again. The room was still empty. Nothing there except for the silence pressing down on her. How long would it take? After she sent the message, how long before the Black Fists arrived? Would she have to wait minutes? Days?

No, they could not make her wait days.

Now she felt hot all over. She was burning. She read her message again. It had to be perfect. Meagan frowned. Maybe it was too cryptic.

Meagan glanced again at the minimized file at the bottom of the page. The heat in her stomach vanished and the ice returned. The file said *Meagan.* Why would Arthur have a file with her name on it? Now she had to read it. She moved the cursor down and opened the file.

Meagan stared. Her own face stared back at her. Meagan blinked and looked closer. No, the picture wasn't of her. The woman in the picture had Meagan's red-brown hair and green eyes, but her mouth was smaller and her chin more narrow. The woman's smile dented her cheeks into cute dimples; she seemed on the verge of breaking into laughter. Meagan scrolled down to look at the words below the picture.

Valora Brent.

More pictures followed. The next was of a young man with dark hair and a serious expression. He wore the blue and white jumpsuit of a nurse. The caption read *Garvin Brent*. They both looked about twenty.

Meagan's heart started racing. Who were these people, this woman who looked so much like her and this man? She thought she knew the answer, but it made her stomach churn. Were these her parents? Were these the criminals who had condemned her to be an outcast her entire life? Why did Arthur have these pictures? Her thoughts spinning, she continued scrolling down the page.

Meagan recoiled at the sight of the next picture. Two forms lay sprawled on a concrete floor. Blood splattered the wall and pooled around the tattered clothing that covered the bodies. Meagan's throat tightened, but she forced herself to look closer. One body had fallen over the other, and, mingling with the blood on the ground, Meagan thought she saw strands of red-brown hair. Valora and Garvin Brent.

The wall behind them was gouged with bullet holes. Meagan felt her breath quicken and tears spring to her eyes. Could these bloody corpses be her father and her mother? She had been told her parents were criminals, that they had been killed for actions against the State. Is this how they died, ripped apart by bullets, left to bleed out on a cold concrete floor?

Meagan scrolled quickly past the picture. She wanted to tear her eyes away from the screen, but she couldn't. Something inside her kept her in her seat. She was compelled by a need she didn't understand. Realizing she was shaking, Meagan clenched the soft arm of the chair with her left hand and scrolled farther down the page with her right.

The pictures ended and words began.

Garvin and Valora Brent died January 14 while attempting to leave the region. We knew the danger, but they did not have much of a choice. We had managed to keep MPED off us for years, but we got wind that someone had tipped them off. Garv and Valora were going to leave. They could have made it, too. The plan was good, but the identity cards didn't hold up. Just a stupid airport security check. It wasn't MPED that got them. It was the Black

Fists. Maybe it was good that it ended the way it did. Maybe it was best that Garv and Valora resisted arrest. Everyone knows it's better to die than be captured, right? There was nothing I could do. I stood there and watched the Black Fists gun down my best friends—my only real friends. I lost their girl. Their sweet little girl, only three years old. There were so many things that I could have done. Things that I didn't do. And I lost her. They would never forgive me.

Meagan sat unmoving in her seat, staring blankly at the words in front of her. When her thoughts started moving, it felt like they were slogging through wet cement.

MPED stood for Ministry of Population, Enforcement Division. They hunted down people who had children illegally or who kept children after they were born. If her parents had been hunted by MPED that meant …

Meagan stood up so fast that the chair rolled back across the floor. If her parents had been hunted by MPED, that meant they'd had her illegally. They hadn't been arrested for smuggling weapons. They hadn't been killed for blowing up buildings. They hadn't sacrificed her future for money or rebellion. It was Meagan. She was the criminal activity they had died for.

Tears filled her eyes. She turned and ran out of the room. She didn't want to think about it—that she was the reason her family had been killed. She had always believed her parents must have hated her, bringing her into this cruel and sick world and getting themselves killed. She hated them for abandoning her. But they hadn't. They hadn't meant to abandon her at all. They had tried to take her away, to be with them.

Meagan thought of Deidre. She thought of the way the tiny baby had snuggled in her arms. She had cared for Deidre only for a few hours, yet she missed her, wanted to hold her again.

Had Meagan's mother loved Meagan that much?

Meagan slammed a door behind her, not even seeing the rooms she ran through. Tears were running down her cheeks now, and she couldn't stop them. She rounded a corner and crashed into Jacob.

He started to laugh, but when he saw her face, his eyes widened. "What's wrong?"

Meagan was in no mood to talk to anyone. She shouldered past him and kept going. Her father and her mother had planned to escape with her. Where had they wanted to take her? Had they wanted to raise her as their own? The thought was such a strange one. Why didn't they want to give her to the IAS? Who thought that way?

Deidre flashed through her mind again, and Meagan felt burning anger in her chest. She would have rather been shot than let the Ministry of Population get their hands on Deidre.

She burst into tears again. Her parents had been shot. They had been killed because of her, because they wanted to keep her. Her parents had died at the hands of the Black Fists.

Meagan sobbed harder as the gruesome picture leaped into her mind. Angrily, she smeared the tears away with the back of her hand. A soft hand touched her shoulder. Meagan jumped. She spun to see Jenni standing next to her. Her face was drawn with concern.

"Is there something I can do to help?" she asked.

Meagan shook her head. She needed to get away, to be alone. She needed to clear her head. She glanced up. She stood in the dazzling entryway, the huge oak doors in front of her. Meagan pulled away from the maid and pushed open one of the big front doors. Jenni began to protest, but Meagan ignored her, slipped out of the house, and closed the door behind her.

She wandered blindly down the streets, not caring where she went. Her parents had only wanted to protect her. They'd risked everything to try to save her.

A terrible thought exploded in her mind. Her parents had been forced to try to leave the city because they had been betrayed. Someone had reported them to MPED. Had that person been rewarded? Did that traitor feel any guilt?

Tears sprang to her eyes. She was no better than that faceless person who had destroyed her life. Here she was, preparing to sell out an entire group of people to the Black Fists—the same Black Fists who had murdered her parents. Meagan thought of the Defiance members, people who had hidden her, protected her. What would happen when she reported them to Commander Ultan? She wasn't sure what had happened to Deuce. He had already been injured for helping them. And all the patients he cared for, the people forgotten or ignored by the State, would suffer without him. And what of Jacob? She would rob him of his family like she had been robbed of hers. His mother, his grandfather, they would be killed or worse. And Jacob himself, what would the Black Fists do to him? Meagan didn't even want to think about it.

She dropped onto a bench beside the sidewalk and covered her eyes with her hands. Some people shot her furtive glances as they passed, but she didn't care. When she turned Arthur Rand over to the Black Fists, what then? His whole operation would be finished. There would be no one left to rescue children from the Ministry of Population. She would have those deaths on her hands as well. Meagan clenched the rough wood of the bench. Her eyes remained dry although her head was pounding. She had lost her footing and was tumbling down into a pit, dark and unknown, from which escape might not be possible. She had lost control, and she had lost herself.

Was that the price she had to pay for security? Must she purchase freedom from want and fear with her very soul? Did she have to become evil to escape evil?

Meagan ran her hand through her hair and took a deep breath. She couldn't betray Jacob to the Black Fists. She hadn't been able to before and now she didn't want to. She didn't want to become an aide to a powerful propagandist. She didn't want to lie and cheat and manipulate her way to the top. She had seen life at the top. It was more precarious than an ordinary life at the bottom. She would have no friends, only people who wanted to use her.

She could not win her own safety. Safety was a lie, a lie that would clamp into her with its teeth and drag her down to devour her. Meagan closed her eyes. She was tired of the game, tired of deception, and most of all, she was tired of being alone. She was done with the Black Fists. Meagan took a deep breath. A great weight had been lifted from her, but she felt exposed, vulnerable. If safety was an illusion, what was left to her?

Jacob.

She needed no more lies for him. She would willingly offer him her wholehearted cooperation.

And then, though she felt a flutter of fear at the thought, she would ask Arthur Rand to tell her about her parents. If there was no security, she might as well forget about caution.

Meagan stood up, noticing for the first time where she was. She was downtown, in the elite administrative center of the city. Office buildings rose toward the cloudless blue sky. The people passing by wore suits and ties or crisp uniforms in the color of their ministry. There were many different colors here, but the shades were all light, representing the advanced levels of the people who wore them. Someone wearing brown here would most likely be an architect or a person in charge of zoning. Even in her information gray she felt out of place.

A trill of fear shot up Meagan's spine. Most of the people around her wore dark blue suits with red trim. She searched for a name on the office building behind her. Ministry of Population.

Meagan was scared, but she didn't feel the paralyzing terror that she had felt before. Arthur Rand worked in that building when he wasn't at the CPC. She could walk in there right now and ask for him. She didn't have to wait.

Meagan discarded the idea as soon as it entered her mind. She was wanted by the Black Fists and was supposed to be hiding at Arthur's house. She looked back up the street the way she had come, realizing she needed to get out of here, and quickly.

At that moment, someone laid a hand on her shoulder.

Chapter 32
No Longer Safe

Those who defy the State will suffer the full punishment for their crimes.
— Fact 626, Citizen's Handbook

Meagan recoiled. A woman stood behind her, dressed in the yellow and blue of agriculture.

Meagan recovered and regained her breath. "What do you want?"

"Could you help me, please?" The woman looked into her eyes, imploring her.

Meagan shook her head. "No. I'm sorry. I really need to go." She turned away, but the woman held her arm in a vise-like grip.

"Please. It will only be a moment." The woman began gently pulling her across the street. Meagan wanted to yank her arm away, to run, but she was afraid to cause a scene. She allowed herself to be dragged along by the woman, her eyes darting frantically, looking for a way out.

Four concrete steps led up to the door of an office building for agricultural workers. Meagan thought they would climb the steps, but at the last moment, the woman jerked her into the corner between the steps and the concrete wall.

Meagan stumbled forward, gasping in confusion. The woman twisted her right arm hard enough to send jolts of pain up to her shoulder and Meagan let out a yelp of pain and surprise. She brought her left fist up and turned. She wasn't going to go down without a fight. The woman kicked her legs out from under her. Meagan fell to her knees, her arm still in the woman's grasp. In her peripheral vision, Meagan glimpsed another person approaching. She threw herself forward, trying to break away from the woman's unrelenting grip.

Suddenly, she was surrounded by darkness. A bag had been thrown over her head. Something—a knee?—slammed into her temple. Spots danced in front of her eyes and she stopped struggling. She became very aware of the pressure of the woman's hands on her arms, the icy firmness of handcuffs as they were clamped around her wrists. Her ragged breath seemed doubly loud as she gasped for air under the stale black cloth.

Meagan was pulled to her feet and dragged forward. She heard the sound of a vehicle pulling up beside them. Hands forced her to stop and a car door opened. The next thing she knew, she was shoved from behind. She fell forward closing her eyes and gritting her teeth, expecting to hit pavement. Instead, she tumbled into the seat of a car and someone slid in beside her. Doors slammed, the engine hummed, and she felt herself tugged backward as the car pulled away.

Meagan tried to detect what direction they were going but she had become hopelessly confused. Her hair began to stick to her forehead, and she felt sweat roll down the back of her neck and under the collar of her jumpsuit. Who were these people, and what did they want with her?

A sharp feeling of déjà vu washed over Meagan. This wasn't the first time she had been roughly handled, blindfolded, and thrown into the back of a car. Yet this time was different. This time she was alone. Jacob wasn't here beside her. Jacob, who, although captured and blindfolded, had still thought to squeeze her arm and tell her that everything would be okay. Meagan felt a sinking feeling in her stomach. This time, everything was not okay.

They did not drive far. When the car stopped, Meagan was taken into a building. She tried to keep track of the twists and turns, left, right, right, left, into an elevator. Out of the elevator and more hallways.

Finally, Meagan was stopped with a firm hand on her shoulder. She heard a door open and she was shoved forward. The door closed behind her, and she was pushed down into a chair. Not a metal chair, but one with cushions.

"Take that off," a voice said. The hood was whipped off, and Meagan blinked in the light. She was in a small office with no windows. Other than the lack of windows, the room was rather luxurious for an office. The carpet was a deep red, and the brown walls were mostly hidden behind three large cabinets filled with books and papers and small, expensive looking boxes. In front of her, behind a dark wooden desk, sat the Black Fist commander.

"Meagan. We meet again." Ultan sounded neither excited nor angry. His icy blue eyes cut into hers. Meagan forced herself to meet his gaze with a long-practiced nonchalance.

"You could have just told me you wanted to speak with me," Meagan said.

The Black Fist commander leaned slowly back in his chair. He motioned to the woman who had brought Meagan in and she removed the cuffs from Meagan's hands before leaving the room.

"I do not apologize for the method by which you were brought here," Ultan said. "Secrecy is the lifeblood of the Black Fists." He folded his hands together and rested them on the desk. "However, it was rude treatment for a woman who has served us so well."

Confused, Meagan didn't answer, only smiled a smile as wicked as his own.

"Exposing Rand was a very nice piece of work," Ultan said.

A chill raced down Meagan's spine. How did he know?

"I'm impressed that someone with no training would think to leave her jumpsuit out for the search team to find. You are lucky there was a Black Fist with the team. Success is sometimes determined by luck."

Meagan was sure there was much more involved than simply luck, but she didn't care. She had unwittingly betrayed Arthur as surely as if she had called the Black Fists herself. She felt horror rising in her, but she let no sign of it show on her face. Instead, she leaned forward, as if eager to hear what he would say next.

"I trust, of course, that you have the information I wanted on the young rebel you have been running around with?"

Meagan nodded, not trusting herself to answer.

"Good. My aide will take you to be debriefed. You will tell my men everything they want to know."

Again, Meagan nodded. Her heart pounded and beneath her jumpsuit, her tee shirt was damp with sweat.

"I need to know one thing right now. Where's the boy?"

Meagan opened her mouth but no sound came out.

"He is at Rand's house, is he not?" the commander pressed.

"No," Meagan blurted out. The confidence in her voice surprised her. "He left this afternoon, because of the search."

Commander Ultan's eyebrows drew together and his cool smile vanished.

"Where did he go?"

"Where did he go?" Meagan echoed back nervously.

"Yes."

"Well," Meagan began, her mind racing, "I was talking to him this morning and—"

At that moment, Ultan's personal buzzed on his desk. He answered it.

Meagan shut her mouth, grateful for the respite. For a moment, silence filled the room as Ultan listened. Then his face creased into a cruel smile.

"Let him in," he said. "Then cuff him and bring him to my office."

Commander Ultan returned his attention to Meagan.

"I will send you to be debriefed momentarily. There is someone I'd like you to see first."

Meagan's heart rate increased to a hammering in her chest. Had they captured Jacob already? How could they have? Meagan wanted to curl into a ball and die. She had been so stupid. Why on earth had she left the house, a house that was no longer safe because she had idiotically left out her jumpsuit?

As footsteps pounded in the hallway, Meagan wiped her sweaty palms on her legs. The door was flung open by a man whose build suggested he would be more comfortable in combat gear than in the black suit he wore. Another Black Fist entered, and then a man wearing a dark blue suit with red trim was shoved through the door by two more Black Fists behind him. Meagan jumped to her feet. Through her anguish, she felt a small prick of relief. The captive was not Jacob. It was Arthur Rand.

Ultan rounded his desk to stand beside Meagan. She felt his presence like a malevolent force at her side.

Arthur's mouth was clenched in a tight line. His steady gaze took in both the Black Fist commander and Meagan beside him. His green eyes met hers, but Meagan quickly looked away. She didn't need to see the sadness there to know what he thought. He was right. She had betrayed him. An accident had brought this about, but it was the outcome she'd planned all along. Meagan's stomach twisted.

While Meagan was staring miserably at her shoes, the Black Fist commander was having a completely different reaction. The cruel smile that seemed to come when he was genuinely pleased hadn't left his face since he had received the call.

"Mr. Arthur Rand," Commander Ultan said gleefully, "you must forgive me for detaining someone of your level."

"This time you've gone too far, Ultan," Arthur said. "For your sake, I hope you received permission from your superiors before you had your men lay hands on me."

"I have every right to detain anyone who enters this building. That's the law." The commander chuckled. "You don't want to argue law with me, Rand. We all know which one of us studied and which one spent our days in a drunken stupor back at Harvard."

"And yet, I'm still a level above you."

"We shall see," the commander snapped back. The smile had vanished from his face. "What are you doing in my building?"

"You have heard what happened at the Child Processing Center yesterday?" Arthur managed to sound both annoyed and gravely serious. "I want the Black Fists to investigate it. I'm responsible there and Public Security is not giving me answers."

"Why would I be inclined to do anything you want, Rand?"

"Well, you could certainly use something to boost your reputation."

For all of Arthur's bluster, Meagan could sense the anxiety behind his words. He was trying to keep it hidden, but she was all too familiar with using anger and insults to hide fear.

Commander Ultan took a step closer to Arthur. He made Meagan think of a snake. A snake getting ready to strike.

"And why do I need to boost my reputation?"

"You keep trying to prove that your betters are traitors to the IAS," Arthur answered. "You come after us instead of trying to catch the real criminals out there. You've failed too many times for anyone to take you seriously."

Commander Ultan rocked back on his heels. A curious expression played across his face.

"Thank you for bringing this matter to my attention. Your concern for my reputation is touching."

"It's the least I could do for my old roommate."

Commander Ultan smiled. Then, before Meagan could blink, he slammed his fist into Arthur's face, sending him sprawling on the floor.

"Liar!" he shouted. "I know you're neck deep in this." Ultan signaled to one of the Black Fists, who pulled Arthur up by his collar. The Black Fist commander grabbed Meagan's upper arm and yanked. She had to take a step forward to avoid falling.

"This girl works for me," Commander Ultan said. "She has told me everything about you."

Arthur spit blood out of his mouth, but said nothing.

"Do you doubt me?" the commander challenged.

"I had to be sure." Arthur's reply was so quiet that Meagan almost missed it.

The commander raised his eyebrows. "Is that so? See if this proves it to you." He turned on Meagan, releasing her arm. His ice-blue eyes locked onto hers.

"Where is Wild Card?" he demanded.

Chapter 33
Friends and Enemies

War, whether between two people or two nations, is caused by both parties holding onto irreconcilable points of view. In the interest of peace, let us all agree on a single viewpoint and let us and our descendants hold to it.
— Charter of the International Administrative State

This time Meagan was ready. She couldn't save Arthur, but she would protect Jacob with her life.

"After the search, he said it wasn't safe at the house anymore," she answered as smugly as she could. "He went to the First Official Hotel. I'm supposed to meet him there. I was on my way when you picked me up."

The commander turned back to Arthur.

"You are as pathetic as you are stupid. You'll give me everything I want, and then—" He hesitated. "I fear we are boring Meagan."

A jolt of adrenaline ran through Meagan when he mentioned her name. She had been studying the room, looking for some means of saving herself. She knew that if she allowed them to take her to be debriefed it would all be over. She could only construct lies for so long. Sooner or later her stories would all come crashing down around her, and she would be caught as surely as Arthur was. She had just discovered the means to achieve her salvation when the commander turned to her.

She looked up at him and smiled. "I want to get this debriefing over with. Don't forget the reward you promised me."

"Of course," he said. Meagan knew he couldn't care less. The commander looked over to one of his men. "Amden, take Ms. Meagan down to be debriefed."

Meagan nodded her farewell, then brushed past the commander on her way to the door, smoothly picking his pocket as she did so. In her peripheral vision, Meagan saw Arthur's eyes widen in surprise, but she strode quickly past and followed Amden out the door.

Amden led her down the hall. Seeing a sign on the wall,

Meagan called on one of her oldest tricks.

"Please, I need to use the restroom."

Amden didn't stop. "We're going to debriefing."

"As if I didn't know that," Meagan snapped. "Look. I'm just telling you how it is. My bladder doesn't do well when I'm nervous, and having a bag thrown over my head was a little nerve-racking. I wasn't going to mention it to your commander, but it's getting serious. If I'm going to be in debriefing for hours, you're going to have to help me out here."

"Fine."

He crossed his arms and waited while Meagan slipped into the women's bathroom. As soon as she closed the door behind her, she shoved her hand into her pocket, checking to make sure she still had the commander's pass key. Satisfied, she dashed past the rows of stalls. As she had hoped, there was another door at the far end of the bathroom and she ducked out of it.

She found herself in a long hallway. The corners of her mouth twitched in a tight smile as she caught sight of the elevator at the far end. Meagan strode purposefully down the hall, passing people wearing black suits or uniforms, carrying files or working on their personals.

Meagan reached the elevator and hit the call button. A light beside the button started flashing. On a hunch, she swiped the pass key in front of the light. With a ping, the doors slid open and Meagan stepped inside. She punched a button and rode down to the ground floor.

When the doors opened, Meagan was ready. She marched out as if she knew exactly where she was going, glancing around surreptitiously to find the way out. Down a hallway and through a lounge, Meagan came into an open area. Her excitement rose when she located the doors to the outside, but it fell right back down to her toes when she saw the security she would have to go through to reach the exit.

A glass wall divided the room, separating Meagan from escape. First she would have to surrender her personal to a Black Fist, who would check her identity and anything else he felt needed to be looked at. Then he would put her personal and any other belongings onto a conveyor belt to be scanned. She, meanwhile, would have to walk through a metal detector, and then step into a body scanner, which would deposit her on the other side of the glass wall. Meagan could see the same security measures on the other side of the wall for those entering, and beyond that, the doors out.

Meagan's mind raced. Even if she could get through security, she didn't have the time. Amden had most likely discovered her absence by now, and would be radioing down to have her arrested.

She briefly contemplated crawling on the conveyor belt, which ended on the other side of the glass, but quickly rejected the thought. She wasn't sure she would fit, and even if she did, there were too many Black Fists in the room for her to make it to the exit.

Out of the corner of her eye, Meagan noticed a man approach a lady sitting behind a desk near the metal detectors. He showed her something and she hit a button. A door in the glass wall slid open, letting him bypass security.

Meagan drew herself up and strode over to the woman.

"Open this door," she said. She kept her voice calm, but firm.

"Do you have the proper authorization?" The woman sounded bored.

Meagan leaned forward, looking her in the eye. As she did, she took the commander's pass key out of her pocket and slid it across the desk.

"The commander himself has given me authorization," Meagan said. She nodded to the pass key. "I believe this should convince you of the importance of the situation."

The lady took the pass key and ran it through the computer. Meagan's heart was pounding. Every fiber of her wanted to yell at the woman to hurry. She glanced at the door she had come through, fully expecting it to burst open and reveal a squad of Black Fists coming to arrest her. But she couldn't rush the woman. If the Black Fists felt at all threatened, Meagan's chances of escaping would drop from slim to none.

The lady handed the pass key back to Meagan. Her hand moved toward the button, but she paused.

"I should call Commander Ultan for verification."

Meagan entertained a brief fantasy of jumping over the desk and ripping the lady's hair out. Instead, she slammed her hands down on the desk and shoved her face within inches of the woman's nose.

"Did you see a man get taken down in this lobby not half an hour ago?" Meagan demanded, surprised at the words coming out of her own mouth.

The lady nodded, mouth open.

"Commander Ultan is in the middle of interrogating that prisoner," Meagan continued. "The man is spilling his guts. You call Ultan if you want, and you do all your tidy little procedures, and while you're at it, you can explain to him why his pass key wasn't good enough for you, and why you are obstructing an asset operating under his direct command."

Meagan stared into the woman's eyes until she lowered them.

"You are correct," the woman said humbly. "The commander's pass key is sufficient authorization. You can go."

"Yes, I can," Meagan snapped. "You'd be in a lot of trouble, if I wasn't in a hurry. Don't let this happen again."

"No, ma'am," the woman mumbled. She pressed a button and the glass door opened.

As Meagan strode through the door and toward the exit, she heard someone shout, "Stop that girl! Lock the doors." Black Fists came at her, but they were too late. Meagan had slipped through the doors seconds before they locked and was running for her life.

Ultan sighed and shook his head. Meagan had stolen his pass key. He'd suspected she was lying to him. She had been too nervous, too reluctant. Meagan had gone over to the insurgents. Oh, well. She had helped him enormously nevertheless.

He hit a button on his personal and spoke directly into the earpieces of his troops in the building. "This is the commander. The girl, Meagan, is going to try to escape. Let her go, but make it look good." He ended the communication and nodded to the Black Fists in the room.

"Take Rand to a cell," Ultan commanded. As much as he would have enjoyed continuing to gloat, he had other work to do.

"Ultan," Rand said. Ultan held up a hand and the Black Fists stopped.

"Don't hurt Meagan. If you leave her alone, I can make sure you come out of this with more power than you've ever had."

Ultan leaned forward. "You don't understand me, Rand, any

more than I understand you. This isn't about power."

Ultan smiled at the anger in Rand's eyes. He knew that behind the anger was fear. And Rand was right to be afraid.

"I do this because people like you have caused a lot of suffering in this country. You nearly destroyed it. I will never let that happen."

"What country?" Rand cried. "What country are you protecting? According to your IAS, national boundaries are an affront to human decency."

"The IAS is necessary. We are going to end war, Rand. End it. And end inequalities. No longer will some people starve while others throw food away."

"No, now we'll just all starve together."

"And you and those like you will stand in the way of progress, ensuring that the full success of the IAS is years in the future. You are to blame for the problems you deride."

"You are right," Rand said. "We will never understand each other."

"You know, Rand, other people, people who don't know you as well as I do, wonder why a man as important as yourself would live here instead of a more prominent city."

"And what do you tell them?"

"Nothing usually. They wouldn't believe me. But I think you stay here because the IAS largely ignores this unimportant city. You can get away with things because the State doesn't care yet."

"That must be why they sent you here."

"Childishly insulting me so that I reveal information in my defense is an old trick, Rand. You won't find out why I'm here, even though you are in no position to do anything with the information."

Ultan gestured for his men to take Rand away. He would finish with him later. He pulled out his personal and contacted his lieutenant.

"When Meagan leaves the building, have a man follow her," Ultan commanded. "She should lead you to Wild Card."

"Yes, sir."

Now Ultan typed a string of numbers into his personal, making a number more than twice as long as a regular personal's number. This communication was carefully encoded and protected and would connect him to an asset he had deep undercover. He wanted this one to be aware of the situation and ready to act.

How she managed to elude the Black Fists pursuing her, Meagan did not know. Maybe it was some skill, some talent granted to her by desperation, that enabled her to finally rest in an alley and gasp for breath. She didn't think the Black Fists were chasing her anymore. Her best guess was that they didn't want to make a scene. The IAS didn't look all-powerful if everyone saw the Black Fists chasing down one girl. Meagan didn't care how the State looked; she was simply grateful for the respite. She wasn't stupid, however. She knew she had only escaped them temporarily. They would come after her again, just more subtly, like the woman this morning. Meagan shuddered and pushed herself away from the wall. She had to keep moving. She had to warn Jacob.

Luckily, she wasn't far from Arthur's house. She had been making her way in that direction even as she fled from the Black Fists.

Turning onto Arthur's street, Meagan hurried past the elegant houses. She knew that even though she'd told the Black Fists Jacob was at the First Official Hotel, they would still want to arrest Arthur's servants. Meagan thought of the tattoo on Kalyn's arm, and her heart sank even further. She had put so many good people in danger, and she had no idea how she would ever be able to set things right.

Meagan heard the commotion before Arthur's house was in sight. Shouting. Sharp orders. When she was closer she saw the vans, two black vans parked outside Arthur's house. Meagan ducked behind a low wall that ran around a lawn several houses away. She dropped to her hands and knees and crawled along the sidewalk until she came to the fence that marked the beginning of Arthur's property. Meagan crept into the neighboring yard and crouched against the ivy-covered fence. She jerked the ivy aside and peered through the slats into Arthur's yard.

The beautiful oak front doors lay in splinters, and troops were running through the opening. Men in black suits surveyed the scene. Some spoke into radios and others shouted orders.

Meagan heard the sounds of breaking glass, of wood being smashed. Soon the Black Fist troops came out of the house and several of the men in suits walked inside. Meagan wanted to scream in frustration and despair. She was too late.

The Black Fists had found and destroyed their final haven. Tears came to her eyes. Jacob was either dead or captured, and she was powerless.

Meagan stifled a scream as a firm hand grabbed her shoulder and spun her around. She jumped to her feet and lashed out, but found her fist caught mid-swing.

"Jacob?" Meagan gasped. "I thought you were dead."

He had escaped. He was safe. He would know what to do, how to solve the problems she had created.

"You wish," Jacob answered. Meagan's eyes widened at the anger in his voice. His eyebrows were drawn together, and his mouth was set in a tight line. He still hadn't let go of her arm.

"I was afraid they had killed you," Meagan said.

"I'm sure Commander Ultan wants me alive."

"How do you know that name?" Meagan asked, her voice barely a whisper. A sinking feeling settled in her stomach.

"Arthur contacted me. Told me and the others to get out of the house. Only, I wasn't in the house. I was out looking for you. Where were you, Meagan?"

Meagan's shoulders slumped. "You know where I was. You're hurting my wrist."

Jacob didn't let go.

"I didn't betray you," Meagan pressed. "Not intentionally."

"Why were you with the Black Fists? If you weren't working for them, you wouldn't be free now."

"I escaped, okay? I came here to warn you." Meagan pulled away from his grip. "You need to get out of here. You're in danger and so am I."

Jacob shook his head. "No, Meagan. I have work to do."

"What's that supposed to mean?" Meagan snapped.

Then she saw the man.

Chapter 34
Betrayal

Entrust your well-being to the State, for you can trust no one else.
— Fact 85, Citizen's Handbook

The man stood across the yard behind Jacob, holding a pistol. Jacob's eyes followed Meagan's stare, and he spun, drawing his weapon.

"Freeze!" the man shouted. He was not wearing a uniform, but Meagan knew he was a Black Fist. He had followed her.

However, the Black Fists still wanted Wild Card alive. Jacob had no such restraints. He emptied his clip into the man before he or Meagan had a chance to move.

The sharp pops from Jacob's gun drew the attention of the Black Fists in Arthur's yard.

Jacob turned to Meagan. His face was pale, but full of fury.

"Tell your friends they'll have to do better than that to catch me." He sprinted around the back of the house. Meagan didn't know what to do, but she couldn't stay here. The Black Fists would be all over this yard in seconds, and they knew she was a traitor. Her feet were moving even before she'd made a conscious decision. She dashed across the street, in the opposite direction from Jacob.

She wasn't fast enough.

"Over there!"

Meagan heard the shout behind her. She didn't look back. Her feet thudded into soft grass as she raced across a well-kept lawn. She plowed through some ornamental bushes and came to another street. She hesitated. Cars whizzed by in this high-level section of the city. Meagan charged ahead anyway. A horn blared. She hopped onto the sidewalk on the other side and ran. Glancing back across the street, she saw several Black Fists but didn't think they had spotted her yet.

Meagan winced at the sound of screeching brakes. A small red car pulled up next to her. She was about to dart away, when through the open window, the driver hissed, "Get in."

It was Tina. Meagan flung herself into the backseat and Tina pulled away, hitting a button that rolled up the window.

"Thank you," Meagan gasped, trying to catch her breath.

"The Defiance heard there was trouble," Tina said. "I was sent to get you and Wild Card out."

Meagan leaned back in the seat and closed her eyes. There was no way Jacob would believe her now. She couldn't blame him. It looked like she had brought the Black Fists right to him. Which she had.

Meagan rubbed her eyes. Could nothing work out right? Jacob had vanished thinking she was a Black Fist spy. Commander Ultan had her followed, so he must know she had betrayed him. And Arthur was a prisoner. She had severed all ties to the State only to have her allies yanked away from her. She thought she'd been alone before, but to have the hope of friendship, only to see it vanish, created a loneliness in her that was almost a physical ache. Now she truly was alone.

Meagan opened her eyes and looked at the back of Tina's head. Her brown hair seemed almost blond in the light of the afternoon sun.

"Well?" Tina said.

"Well what?"

"Where is Wild Card? We can't leave without him."

"I … I don't—" Meagan stopped. Tina would want to know why Meagan didn't know where Jacob was, and Meagan would have to explain. She would have to explain how she had betrayed him and Arthur, and how Jacob never wanted to see her again. Tina would dump her on the street and leave her for the Black Fists, or she would take her back to the Defiance and execute her. Tina was Jacob's friend. She wouldn't understand.

"I can't tell you," she said, which was true enough.

"How am I supposed to help him if you won't tell me where he is?"

"Wild Card is fine," she answered, which may have been true. At least she hoped it was.

"Meagan, I can't do this with you," Tina said with an exasperated sigh. "Wherever he is he's in great danger."

"The Black Fists won't find him," Meagan said, but her voice quivered uncertainly. She was trying to convince herself.

"How did you know we were in trouble?" Meagan asked.

Maybe the Defiance already had a plan to fix this disaster.

"We don't have time for this," Tina growled. "You have to tell me where Wild Card is. Or do you want him to end up like Rand?"

Neither of them spoke for a moment. Silence expanded and filled the car.

"How did you know about—"

"The Information Ministry announced it on the radio," Tina interrupted.

The hair on the back of Meagan's neck prickled.

"Where are you taking me?" she whispered.

"To find Wild Card," Tina said. "As soon as you decide to tell me where he is."

Meagan was shaking her head. "The Black Fists don't give news to Information that isn't at least a day old. And even if they did, they would first give it to the television stations. They have an arrangement. How did you know about Arthur, Tina?"

"Where is Wild Card?"

Meagan didn't answer. She was looking out the window. They were coming to a turn in the road.

"Meagan," Tina snapped, but Meagan had already yanked open the door and thrown herself out.

The car had appeared to be going slower when she was in it. Meagan tumbled onto the sidewalk. The concrete tore at her hands and knees, but she regained her feet. Ahead of her, brakes squealed as Tina slammed the car to a halt. Meagan crawled under some tangled bushes and came out into a narrow, weed-choked space between two houses.

Behind her, Tina cursed as she struggled through the bushes. Meagan hurried over the muddy ground, but as she reached the other side of the alley, fingers closed around her collar. Tina yanked her backward and spun her around.

"You're with them," Meagan yelled.

Dirt streaked the knees of Tina's red jumpsuit, and in places the fabric was torn. Her face was furious.

"Tina, how could you be with them?"

Tina slapped her hard enough to make her eyes water. "*You're* asking me that?"

"The Defiance trusts you. They accept you."

"Like they accepted you?" Tina shot back. "You are no more

clean than I am. Or were you with the Defiance all along?"

"No, I—"

Tina gripped Meagan's shoulder, and a layer of ice formed at the edges of her words. "Do you really think you're special? Do you think you're the first girl Ultan rescued from a desperate situation in return for her loyalty?"

Tina released her and stepped back.

"You are nothing special, Meagan."

"Are you jealous of me?" Meagan asked.

"Of you? Please. Why—"

"No, you are. I can hear it in your voice. You—"

Tina hit her in the mouth.

"There is nothing about you that I envy," she said. "You have betrayed the Black Fists. Your allies have deserted you. How about Wild Card, Meagan? Still think he will save you?"

Tina's eyes searched Meagan's face. Meagan wondered what she expected to find there. Fear? Hope? Resignation? Meagan straightened. All she felt was anger.

She kicked Tina in the shin. Tina cursed and backhanded her. Meagan stumbled back, but didn't fall. Tina grabbed her jumpsuit and yanked her forward.

"Where is he?" Tina hissed.

"You'll never find him."

Meagan aimed a blow at Tina's stomach, but Tina shoved her backward. Tina sighed, a short exasperated sigh, and drew a small silver pistol from a holster strapped above her ankle.

"Last chance, Meagan."

"Are you going to kill me?" Meagan tore her eyes away from the barrel and met Tina's gaze.

Tina smiled, but her eyes were like daggers. "No, but you'll wish I had."

Meagan felt the blood drain from her face.

"Put your hands up," Tina commanded, "and turn around."

Meagan obeyed. What else could she do? She felt cold metal against her wrists, scraped from her dive out of the car. Tina deftly cuffed her hands behind her and pulled her back to the street.

"Get in," Tina ordered, opening the door behind the driver's seat. She shoved Meagan down into the seat and fastened the seat belt over her, pulling it so that it would stay tight. Meagan tried to move, but between the belt and the handcuffs there was not much she could do.

To Meagan's surprise, Tina did not take her to Black Fist Headquarters. She drove into one of Government's sectors, heading toward the river. Meagan sat up a little straighter. She had been here before.

"Are we going to the Space Center?" she asked.

"Shut up," Tina answered. "You'll find out soon enough."

A short while later, their footsteps echoed loudly in the almost deserted halls of the New Worlds Space Center. Tina had taken Meagan in through a back door and now they were in the employees-only part of the first floor. Meagan half ran and was half dragged along by Tina, who strode purposefully down the white corridors.

They passed several Space Center employees who kept their heads down and their eyes on the floor.

"Attention all workers," a voice announced over a loud speaker. "The Space Center is being evacuated. Please gather your belongings and go to your designated stations."

"Where are you taking me?" Meagan asked as they rounded a corner.

"I'm making you someone else's problem." Tina didn't turn her head. "I have a meeting with the Defiance."

"How come?" Meagan asked. "Did they figure out you're a traitor? I bet the Defiance shoots traitors."

Tina laughed. "You really are a nasty little girl, aren't you? For your information, the Defiance is planning something."

Tina paused by a wall.

"Once I find out what they and Wild Card are up to, how they plan to get in here, I'll take care of them."

She waved her pass key in front of the wall. Meagan's eyes widened as a door opened to reveal an elevator. Tina pushed Meagan inside.

"How does that sound, Meagan? How about I finish the job you didn't have the guts for, and kill Wild Card?"

Meagan stared at the floor. "You'll never find him," she said.

"We will. We always do."

Tina punched a button and they began to descend.

"Not that you'll ever know or care," Tina continued. "You'll be too busy wishing you were dead."

Meagan felt as if she had turned to jelly. She leaned her head against the cool wall of the elevator and tried to regain her breath. Tina just kept smiling at her.

The ping of the elevator made Meagan jump. Tina grabbed her by the collar and dragged her forward into an empty hallway. Florescent lights spaced far apart in the ceiling made the halls darker than the ones upstairs. One light flickered ominously. Meagan didn't think it was a good sign that the floor had changed from vinyl to concrete.

Tina stopped outside a drab blue door. She swung the door open and shoved Meagan inside.

A florescent bulb in the low ceiling dimly illuminated four concrete walls. There was no furniture. Tina stepped into the room and closed the door behind her. Meagan tried to suppress the bitter churning inside her as Deuce's words came back to her. She wanted to be strong. She had always been strong. But now, one thought crowded out every other in her brain. Better dead than captured.

Chapter 35
Interrogation

Those who rebel have signed their own death warrants.
— Fact 627, Citizen's Handbook

Meagan watched Tina type on her personal. A minute later the personal beeped and she answered.

"This is Anderson, sir. I brought Meagan. We're in room 17 B1."

They waited in silence. Meagan tried unsuccessfully to calm her racing heart. She was in over her head, and she couldn't see a way out. It was strange, she thought, Jacob wanted so badly to get back inside the Space Center, and here she was. Not that she could do anything about it.

Meagan started as the door opened. Commander Ultan stepped into the room and she felt her heart sink down to her feet. Tina gave him a sharp salute, but Ultan turned to Meagan.

Meagan wanted to shrink back against the wall, but she didn't. She tried to keep herself from shaking. She wanted him to see that she wasn't afraid, but she *was* afraid, and she knew he could tell. Meagan kept her eyes locked on his face.

His gaze traveled over her. Meagan saw his eyebrows draw together slightly and the corner of his mouth twitch. He turned to Tina.

"She fought you?"

Tina blushed. "Not really, sir."

"I see." He sounded almost amused. Then he grabbed a fistful of Meagan's collar, lifting her off her feet and shoving her back against the wall.

"What is the plan?" he demanded.

"I don't know," Meagan gasped, finally crying from fear and pain. "I don't know, okay? Jacob wouldn't tell me. He thinks I betrayed him. He wants nothing to do with me. I don't know where he is. I don't know what he's doing."

Ultan's icy blue eyes stared into hers. He let go of her jumpsuit and Meagan dropped to the floor. She tried to stop crying, but she couldn't.

"So, his name is Jacob," Ultan said. "An interesting name."

He paused, perhaps waiting to see if she would reply, but she said nothing. She had done too much damage as it was.

"I believe you truly don't know what he is doing," Ultan said.

Meagan sniffed. Ultan didn't look very bothered by the fact that she couldn't give him the information.

"You have a meeting, Anderson," he said to Tina.

"Yes, sir."

"Find out what the Defiance is planning."

"Yes, sir. I'll be out of touch for a while."

"If they are planning to help *Jacob* investigate the space program in some way, go along with them until you are able to sabotage them or get a message back to me. I have reinforcements standing by."

Tina saluted and turned to leave.

"Oh, Anderson," Ultan added with a smile on his face.

"Yes, sir?"

"You might want to get cleaned up a bit first."

"Yes, sir." Tina shot Meagan a dirty look and left the room.

Ultan turned back to Meagan. "You gave me a name," he said. "I'll give you one as well."

Meagan met his eyes.

"Brent," Ultan said.

"What?"

"That is your surname."

Confusion rose in Meagan's mind and swirled in dizzying circles. "You know about my parents?"

"Oh, I know all about your parents."

How did he know? There was probably some file somewhere. But there was something in his voice. He made this sound personal.

"You knew them," Meagan said.

"No. I didn't know them at all." Ultan tilted his head to one side. "Learned more about them later, though."

"What do you mean?"

Ultan smiled down at her. Meagan's eyes grew wide.

"You killed them."

"I was the officer present. I ordered it done. But no, I did not kill them."

Meagan stood.

"You can't say that!" she shouted. "Just because you didn't pull the trigger doesn't mean you weren't responsible."

"Oh, I agree."

Ultan slammed the side of his fist against the wall only inches from her head. His face was level with hers.

"They killed themselves the moment they decided to disobey the State."

Meagan had forgotten how to breathe. Ultan gripped her shoulder. She did not move.

"That's something you should have considered, Meagan, daughter of the State." He watched her carefully. "Anything else you want to tell me?"

Meagan shook her head.

Ultan straightened and took a step back.

"You won't be completely useless to me," he said.

He spun on his heels and left the room, slamming the door behind him. When Meagan's breath returned, she counted to two hundred, then tiptoed to the door. Her hands were still cuffed behind her back, but after some effort, she got the commander's pass key out of her pocket and waved it in front the door, hoping to trigger the sensor and unlock it. But the door remained immobile. She sank down against the wall and sobbed.

Meagan sat against the wall for some time, thoughts spiraling in despair. She realized her throat was dry, and she was very thirsty. Would she spend the rest of her life in this cell?

No, Ultan would come back.

Meagan trembled and fought back tears. Jacob wouldn't save her; she had no one, nothing to hope for.

After perhaps several hours, the door opened and four Black Fists stepped into the room. Two of them grabbed her arms and ushered her into the hallway. They escorted her down the corridor at a brisk trot before turning down another, longer hall. Near the end, they wheeled to the right and hurried down yet another corridor. Meagan began wondering how big this building was.

The men finally halted outside a thick metal door. Meagan clenched and unclenched her fists, trying to keep circulation in her hands. The cuffs pinched painfully. One of the Black Fists swiped a pass key over the lock. It beeped and the lead Black Fist swung the door open. Meagan felt a shove from behind and she stumbled through the doorway.

Meagan quickly scanned the concrete room. Directly ahead Commander Ultan stood with his back to her. At least ten Black Fists were gathered in front of him. To her left, strange equipment sporting an overabundance of needles and sharp-looking objects surrounded what appeared to be an operating table. Two men in blue and white doctor's scrubs stood by. On her right was a metal door, and on the far wall she thought she saw another metal door, but the crowd of black uniforms obstructed her view.

As her escorts marched her forward into the room, the commander turned.

"Meagan Brent," he said, but he wasn't speaking to her. He stepped to the side and Meagan's heart sank. Arthur stood there surrounded by Black Fists, and beside him stood Jacob. How had they found him?

Like hers, Jacob's and Arthur's hands were cuffed behind their backs. Arthur's eyes met hers and she saw such sadness and pain in them that her heart almost broke. Meagan could tell he was blaming himself for what had happened. Arthur looked even worse than she did. His face was bruised and cut, and his hair was matted with blood. He still wore his blue and red suit pants, but the jacket and tie were gone, his white shirt torn and flecked with red.

In comparison, Jacob appeared almost completely unscathed. Megan could see a bruise on his left cheek, and a packing peanut stuck to the shoulder of the black shirt he wore. She saw another in his hair, which looked like someone had rubbed it with a static-filled sweater. A large box sat open on the floor. Had he mailed himself to the Space Center?

Only his backpack was missing. Two Black Fists were examining its contents and another Black Fist scrolled through Jacob's personal.

Jacob's reaction to her sudden appearance was less readable than Arthur's. His eyebrows drew together and his mouth compressed into a tight line, but he made no other movement.

"Farley." Ultan turned to a tall, thin Black Fist.

"Yes, sir?"

"Bring me the data I was downloading."

"Yes, sir." Farley left the room.

Ultan folded his hands behind his back. "So," he said to Jacob. "You figured out what we are building."

He was completely ignoring Meagan, which was fine with her.

Ultan took a step closer to Jacob. "It's interesting," he continued. "Mind control is so impractical. It takes eighteen scientists to physically control a single person. You'd be surprised at the complexity of the human body."

"Sounds like the perfect project for the IAS," Jacob said. "It's expensive, impractical, and will probably cause wide-scale disaster."

Ultan gave him an amused smile. "Of course, there's a much more applicable model in the works."

"And when it's finally ready, what then?" Jacob said. "World domination? Oh, wait."

Ultan chuckled. "You'd like to know, wouldn't you? However, despite what you may believe, this little science lesson is not for your sole benefit."

"Why are you telling me this? Just to hear yourself talk?"

The commander held up a hand to silence him. Farley had slipped back into the room, and he now handed Ultan what Meagan thought was a flash drive. Ultan put the device in his pocket.

"I was told," he continued, turning back to Jacob, "that the surgery required to implant the necessary devices is incredibly risky. It's only recently that people have started surviving the procedure. Even now there is only a fifty percent chance of living through it."

He nodded and Meagan felt her arms grabbed by one of the Black Fists behind her. He started dragging her backward, toward the table.

"No!" Meagan screamed. She lashed out with her legs. The man holding her cursed and tightened his grip.

"What are you doing?" Arthur gasped.

Ultan laughed. "Meagan decided she didn't like being a Black Fist spy." He breathed a sigh. "She never could just follow orders."

The Black Fist brought her to the edge of the table. Meagan saw the instruments gleaming above her. She threw herself from side to side and kicked as hard as she could, but she couldn't break away from his grip.

"Of course, soon that won't be a problem. Right, Meagan?"

"I'll never obey you," Meagan shouted.

The Black Fist holding her spun her around and slammed her onto the table. Meagan gasped in pain as her hands were crushed under her and the metal cuffs dug into her wrists.

"Ultan!" Meagan heard Arthur shout. "Do the procedure on me. We always have hated each other."

Ultan laughed. "I wouldn't hurt you, Rand. Not yet, anyway. You're too valuable. As is Jacob."

"So's Meagan," Jacob challenged.

"Meagan's only value is that you two seem to have some incomprehensible affection for her. So, you can start giving me names, or you can watch Meagan become a docile little puppet." He paused. "Memory loss is an unfortunate side effect, so don't be surprised if she doesn't remember you."

The commander motioned to the Black Fist who was holding Meagan down. The man rolled her onto her side and another Black Fist, a woman with red hair in the same buzz cut as the others, removed her handcuffs. Meagan was pushed onto her back again.

"You will both end up telling me everything anyway," Ultan said. "You may as well make it worth your while."

Meagan looked past the Black Fists leaning over her to Arthur and Jacob. Tears were running down Arthur's face, though his mouth was firmly closed. Jacob's eyes were wide.

When neither answered, Ultan continued. "Of course you might agree with me that Meagan isn't worth it." He shook his head. "She could have been very good."

Meagan's respite from the handcuffs was brief. The woman clamped her fingers around Meagan's wrist and forced her hand down onto the table. She grabbed a leather restraint, preparing to strap Meagan down.

Ultan looked over his shoulder at her. "You could have been better than Tina, Meagan. You have a fire she didn't."

"Go stick your face in a blender," Meagan said.

Ultan shrugged. "Have it your own way, then."

"Stop."

The command was low and even. To Meagan's surprise, it was not Arthur who had spoken.

"Let her go, Ultan," Jacob said.

Ultan held up his hand. The Black Fist woman dropped the strap, but she and the other Black Fist still held Meagan firmly against the table.

"All right, Wild Card," Ultan said, "what are you planning?"

Jacob looked at him. "This."

Chapter 36
Jacob's Plan

Progress can come from the peaceful agreement of parties or it can be forged in blood. The IAS supports peace and unity in a drive toward world progress.
— Fact 401, Citizen's Handbook

Confusion flickered across Ultan's face. Jacob glanced at his personal, still held by a Black Fist.

"Forty-seven sierra tango," Jacob shouted. "One niner seven two."

That was all he was able to say before a Black Fist hit him in the mouth. Jacob reeled back but recovered quickly. He threw himself forward, past Ultan. Meagan's eyes widened when she saw that his hands were free. Jacob shoved aside the Black Fists near Meagan, pulled her down to the ground, and covered her body with his, all before she had time to react.

Jacob's personal beeped once. The Black Fist holding it threw it into an unoccupied corner of the room. Meagan noticed that Arthur had also dropped to the ground, although his hands were still behind him.

The personal hit the floor. Meagan braced herself for an explosion. There was a small pop and the personal melted. The room filled with a nasty burnt smell, but that was the extent of the damage. Meagan bit her lip in disappointment. She tried to raise herself, but Jacob was still on top of her and hadn't budged.

Ultan looked at both of them and laughed out loud.

"Get up." Worlds of contempt filled his voice. "You should have stayed with the Black Fists, Meagan, then you would have seen real explosions."

"I hate you!" Meagan shouted at Ultan. As she spoke, the left wall exploded, shooting flame and debris into the room, covering her words with the roar of crumbling concrete. Jacob's arm over her head pressed her face into the floor. She squeezed her eyes shut. Above the din from the collapsing wall, another sound rose. Gunshots.

All the battlefields of the world couldn't have sounded louder.

The tempo of the shooting did not let up. It increased.

Over the thunderous noise, Jacob shouted in her ear, "I'm sorry I didn't believe you. Rand told me you didn't betray me."

"No, I'm sorry. I—"

Meagan felt Jacob's muscles tighten.

"Stay down," he shouted before rolling off her.

"I'm not planning on going anywhere," Meagan muttered to no one in particular.

A body hit the ground beside her, its arm flopping over her back. Meagan lifted her head enough to see that it was the Black Fist who had dragged her to the table. He had been shot repeatedly in the chest. Dust filled the room and packing peanuts dotted the air. Blood was everywhere. Meagan shoved the Black Fist away from her.

Almost as suddenly as it had begun, the roar faded, and the gunshots slowed and died. Through the ringing in her ears, Meagan heard shouting. After a moment, she began to distinguish the words.

"Wall is stable, y'all!"

"Cover that door!"

"Arrow?"

"I'm on it."

"They know we're here now."

"Check the stairwell."

Bam! Meagan jumped at the sound of another gunshot.

"I found Princess."

Meagan felt a hand on her shoulder. She looked up to see Par. Gray dust coated his hair, forehead, and eyes. A dust-choked bandanna had been pulled down to reveal the clean lower half of his face.

"You okay?" he asked.

"Yeah."

Par helped her to her feet.

Bam!

"Got Rand!" Jack shouted.

"It's Rich Dude," Par muttered. "I gave him Rich Dude as a call sign."

"Call signs is pointless if they all know who you're talkin' about," Jack answered.

The dust was starting to clear. Meagan looked at the gaping hole in the wall. Beyond it was blackness. They must be belowground. The floor was slick with blood and littered with the bodies of Black Fists. Diamond was covering the door through which Meagan had entered.

Bam! Bam!

Meagan whirled toward the sound. Sword was walking through the bodies, methodically shooting each one in the head. Meagan shuddered. A loud click to her right made Meagan turn again. Jacob's mother was pushing open one of the big metal doors.

Ace stood in the third doorway, peering into a stairwell.

"Y'all are not going to be able to keep the stairs clear," he said. His steady drawl cut through the frantic shouting. "There's an awful lot of entry points."

"Jack, take the prisoners." It was the Manager, Jacob's grandfather, who spoke. "The rest of you get to the data storage room."

The team began running toward the stairwell.

"Par—" Meagan began. She had to warn them about Tina.

"Wait, Meagan." Par grabbed the Manager's arm as he passed. "I've got Meagan and Rand, but Wild Card is gone."

"Where is he?" The Manager turned to Meagan.

"I don't know. He was here, but I haven't seen him since the shooting started. But sir, Tina—"

"What're we gonna do?" Par interrupted.

The Manager shook his head. "Stick to the plan. It's his after all."

"But—" Par protested.

The Manager held up his hand. "We don't have time to discuss it. I trust Wild Card. He knows what he's doing."

The Manager turned and ran into the stairwell before Meagan could say anything. Par followed him. Meagan glanced around the room. She saw Jack and Arthur. What was going on? Where was Jacob?

"Let's get to work," a gravelly voice said from behind her. Meagan whirled around. For the first time, she noticed a small woman, her mess of graying hair contrasting with her dark skin and eyes. Her lined face was still half-covered by a bandanna, and she carried a deadly looking rifle slung over her shoulder. She was old but she looked dangerous. Meagan didn't remember her from the Defiance meeting.

Arthur came up to the remaining group. His handcuffs were off and he had armed himself with a Black Fist rifle.

"Rand, we don't got Wild Card," Jack said. "So you gotta cover those doors." He pointed to the stairwell and the door Diamond had left open.

"There are other prisoners," Arthur said. "People waiting to be the next test subjects."

"I know," Jack answered. He jerked a thumb toward the old woman. "It's why she's here."

Arthur nodded. Jack and the woman ran for the door Jacob's mother had opened. Meagan ran after them. Through the open door she could hear shouts, crying.

"How did you get here?" she asked Jack, coming through the door on his heels. She found herself in a long hallway lined with cells.

"Get those doors," the woman said, shoving a pass key into Meagan's hands. Jack had already gone to the first cell and swiped a card. The door clanged open.

"Empty," he said, and jogged to the next. Meagan and the woman started down the row opposite him. The first cell she came to was also unoccupied.

"How are you here?" she asked again.

"Wild Card's plan. His mind control theories convinced the Manager to get involved." Jack answered, helping a man out into the hallway.

"Stay in the hall," he instructed the growing number of ex-prisoners. To Meagan he
explained, "Wild Card figured out where our tunnels ran next to the Space Center. Then the kid sneaked in here in a delivery truck. Friends in the business or something. When he signaled us—boom."

"What is everyone else doing?" Meagan asked. "Yes, get out of there," she snapped at a young boy huddling in the back of a cell. "This is a rescue. Do I look like a Black Fist?"

"Blowing this place," Jack answered. "No mind control on our watch. Defiance is covering Ace so he can get into the server room and destroy all their stored information. I gotta keep our retreat open, and set it to blow after we're out."

Jack gestured to his belt. Thin plastic cylinders were strapped around it.

Meagan glanced at the old woman, but she carried no explosives.

"Who's she?" Meagan asked.

Jack shook his head. "Don't know her. Wild Card has contacts in the Rails. She'll handle the prisoners."

Meagan had not followed that, but it probably didn't matter.

"Tina is a Black Fist agent," she blurted out.

Jack stopped and turned to her. "What?"

"She's planning on sabotaging the mission."

Jack crossed his arms. "I barely know you. Just because you're with Wild Card won't convince me she's a traitor."

"It's true. She's the reason I'm here."

"You can't—"

"Please," Meagan begged. "You have to warn your team."

Jack took a radio off his belt. "We'll see what the Manager thinks."

Meagan swiped her card in front of another door impatiently, but turned to Jack when he cussed and started punching buttons on his radio.

"What's wrong?" Meagan asked. She didn't like the scowl that had come over his face.

"Jammed. No communication."

Meagan felt rage bubbling up inside her. Her hands clenched into fists, and her face grew hot.

"I bet you a week's rations Tina's responsible," she growled. Before Jack could stop her, she was running back down the hall and ducking out the door.

Arthur had turned the operating table on its side and moved it farther into the room to provide cover. He had piled some of the bodies in front of that. The dead Black Fists had been stripped of their guns. Meagan noticed a nice stack of weapons behind the table on Arthur's right side, and a pile of grenades on his left.

"Tina's a Black Fist, and I'm taking her down," Meagan shouted to Arthur as she dashed across the room.

"Meagan, wait—"

But there was no waiting. Meagan would not be stopped from getting her hands around Tina's neck.

"Ultan wasn't with the bodies," Arthur yelled after her. "He's still alive."

Meagan didn't care. She burst into the stairwell and paused, glancing down. She had thought they were on the lowest level, but the steps spiraled down three more stories. They went up much farther. Meagan remembered counting eight stories on the night of the gala, and that was just aboveground.

Gunfire broke out. She could hear the sharp cracks mixed with shouting below her and farther away in the building. Meagan hurried cautiously down the stairs. Two levels down, she met Par. He was crouched beside a half-open door, holding a heavy black rifle. Somewhere beyond that door, closer to the building's interior, someone let off a short burst of automatic fire. More gunshots answered.

"What are you doing here?" he yelled at Meagan.

"Where's Tina?" Meagan demanded.

"She went to try to get our communications working," Par answered. "Why? Is something wrong?"

"She's a Black Fist spy. She probably jammed you herself."

Par's eyes widened and his face went pale. "I can't believe that."

"Par, she slapped me around, handcuffed me, and dragged me here to be interrogated by Ultan."

Par was shaking his head. Confusion, hurt, and disbelief mingled in his eyes.

"I don't—" he began.

"Just tell me what level she's on," Meagan interrupted.

"The next level up. But, Meagan," he shouted after her as she darted up the steps, "let it go."

Meagan hesitated, turning back to Par, who had risen from his crouch and was facing her. "Any minute, these stairs could be swarming with Black Fists," he warned. "I don't know why they're not here already."

Meagan shook her head. "She won't be satisfied with destroying your communications. She has something else planned."

She didn't wait to hear his response, taking the stairs two at a time. When she reached the next level, she took a deep breath and opened the door as quickly and as quietly as she could, hoping that any noise she made would be covered by the intermittent gunfire.

Two Black Fists standing in the hallway a few yards ahead of her turned when she came through the door. Meagan dove forward, yanking open the nearest door and darting through it, barely registering that its sign read *Communications*. She slammed the door behind her and locked it just as the Black Fists rattled the handle. Meagan plunged forward into the dark room.

Chapter 37
Tables Turned

The IAS ensures that all citizens are able to live a healthy, active lifestyle.
— Fact 101, Citizen's Handbook

A sliver of light from beneath another door guided Meagan across the room. She heard Tina's voice.

"I'm almost ready … Keep your men off the stairs until I get back into the data room. And warn them about the gas … I should be able to take out anyone the gas doesn't. I'll let you know when to send in your men, just don't, don't start firing. I'm risking my neck to render them unconscious; I don't want them killed unless there's a legitimate threat. Understood. Anderson out."

Behind her, Meagan heard a gunshot as the Black Fists shot at the door's lock. She was trapped between Tina and the Black Fists. A plan rushed into her mind. It was hazy, and she didn't have time to think it through, but she really didn't have a choice.

Meagan slipped into the lighted room just in time to see Tina put on a brown jacket to cover the gas canisters attached to her belt. She had a pistol strapped to her thigh.

"Tina," Meagan whispered sharply.

Tina whirled, drawing her pistol. "You!"

Meagan allowed a smile to creep across her face. "I told everyone about you."

"I'm glad we don't want you alive," Tina said, leveling the pistol at Meagan's face.

Meagan's heart beat wildly. Behind her, she heard the Black Fists moving into the room. She forced her voice to be mocking.

"Go ahead, kill me. Par and Sword will take care of you before I hit the floor."

She noticed Tina falter ever so slightly.

Meagan's eyes stayed riveted on the pistol in Tina's hand. Adrenaline coursed through her body. She saw Tina's finger tighten on the trigger and didn't wait. She threw herself out the door. Tina cursed and dove after her.

One of the Black Fists gave a shout when he caught sight of

Meagan. Meagan turned sharply and scrambled backward in the darkness. Tina froze when she saw the two dark shapes. Meagan backed into a table and threw herself under it as Tina opened fire.

Not looking back, Meagan crawled the length of the table. She reached the end and sprang to her feet.

"Meagan!" Tina shouted from behind her. There was no mistaking the pure rage in her voice.

Meagan glanced over her shoulder. Tina was crouched over the bodies of the Black Fists. She rose to her feet and began to walk toward Meagan. Her steps were slow, deliberate. She did not bother to raise the pistol; her hands were clenched at her side.

Backing away, Megan kept her eyes locked on Tina. She felt the door behind her. It swung open when she pushed. She turned, stumbling into the hallway and lunging through the door to the stairwell, Tina right behind. On the landing, Meagan spun to face her.

"I'm not going to shoot you, Meagan," Tina said. Her voice was ice. "I'm going to throw you over the railing. The fall probably won't kill you. Not immediately anyway."

Meagan felt the cold metal railing behind her. She knew she needed to run, but her mind still raced frantically, not willing to accept defeat. She needed stop Tina.

Tina holstered her pistol. "You shouldn't have come after me, Meagan."

Tina's arm shot out, grabbing Meagan's neck. Her other arm was across Meagan's chest. One good shove would send Meagan tumbling headfirst to her death. Meagan tried to struggle, but Tina held her pinned against the railing. Knowing she shouldn't, Meagan twisted her head, looking over her shoulder to see the stairs twisting downward to the concrete floor below. Tina shoved, and Meagan knew that the next push would send her over the edge.

"Did you really think you could go against the Black Fists and live?"

Crack! A shot split the air. Blood splattered Meagan's jumpsuit. Tina released her grip and took a step back, her eyes wide with surprise and confusion. The sleeve of her jumpsuit was turning red. At first, Meagan thought Tina was only wounded. But then Tina lifted her arm and Meagan saw blood beginning to stain under her armpit. The bullet had gone through her limb and into her chest.

Meagan ducked away from the edge. She glanced down and saw Par a level below. His rifle was lifted to his shoulder, and he gave Meagan a brief nod. Tina crumpled to the ground at Meagan's feet. She lay still, a growing puddle of red beneath her. Meagan shuddered. The rage had gone, and she was left with only cold horror.

As she started down the steps, two of the doors above her burst open and Black Fists poured out. Par immediately began shooting, and the first few Black Fists went down. Others opened fire. The echoes of automatic gunfire filled the stairwell.

"Meagan," Par yelled. She threw herself down the remaining steps. Par was already backing into the door behind him. As Meagan dove into the shelter of the room, Par cried out and fell backward through the door.

Meagan whirled toward him. A crimson stain was spreading out from a bullet hole in his thigh.

"Par!"

"I'm okay." Par kicked the door closed. "We need to get back."

Meagan looked down the long white hallway to the open door at the far end. Par pulled himself to his feet, and they both ran.

"Black Fists in the stairwell," Par shouted.

Jacob's mother leaned out the door. "Get in here," she said.

Black Fists smashed through the door behind them. Meagan and Par launched themselves past Jacob's mother as she opened fire.

Par leaned against the wall.

"You sure you're okay?" Meagan asked. The bloodstain on Par's pants was still spreading.

Par waved her away. "Just gotta wrap it up," he said through gritted teeth.

Meagan turned. The air was thick with a sharp smell that tickled her nose. Rows of servers filled the room. Ace crouched next to one of the servers. Like Jack, he had plastic cylinders hanging from his belt. Meagan watched as he opened one of the cylinders and poured two silver disks into his waiting hand. Meagan's eyes widened as she realized that about half of the servers already had small silver disks attached to them.

Bright flashes and an explosion of gunfire drew Meagan's attention. Across the room, Diamond and the Manager crouched behind a big metal cabinet that they'd used to block a doorway. They fired down a long hallway. Their weapons were smoking and a pile of spent cartridges covered the floor around them.

"I need some help here," Jacob's mother shouted, slamming another magazine into her rifle. Sword rose from where he too had been setting explosives, and joined her at the door.

"Ace, how much longer on those charges?" Jacob's mother asked.

"I'm gonna need eight more minutes, ma'am," he answered.

"Where's Arrow?" Sword hollered over the noise.

Par shot Meagan a quick look.

"She's not coming," Meagan answered.

"What do you mean she's not coming?"

"She's dead, Sword," Par said.

Sword stopped firing and turned to Par. "No," he said. "No, she can't—" He fell silent.

"I'm sorry," Par said. There were tears in his eyes.

Sword shook his head. With his fingertips, he touched his forehead, chest, left shoulder, then right.

"*Perdonanos nuestras deudas*," he said, but his voice broke. He clenched his jaw and began firing again.

Par slammed a fresh magazine into his rifle and replaced Diamond at the other door. Diamond began helping Ace set the charges.

"Where's Wild Card?" Meagan shouted. Jacob wasn't here, and he wasn't downstairs with Jack. Where else could he be?

"He's with Jack," Diamond answered. Meagan didn't reply, knowing he wasn't. He had better get back quick. The Defiance was going to blow up part of the Space Center. But what if he couldn't? What if he was trapped somewhere? She had to find him. Make sure he was okay. Make sure he got out. But how?

She took her personal out of her pocket. If she could remember the password, if Jacob had his backpack, if they weren't all killed first, she might be able to find him using the locator she had planted on his backpack.

Meagan racked her brain trying to remember the password. What was it? Something about angry seas? Into the angry sea?

That didn't sound right.

Meagan had a good memory, but, when she finally decided on the phrase and punched in the words, she had no idea if they were right. She bit her lip and waited. The reverberating clamor of the firefight subsided. The Defiance reloaded; the sharp clanks of their weapons replaced the noise of the firefight.

Meagan's personal beeped and a red dot appeared on the screen.

"Now I've found you," she said. Then the excitement she felt seeing the red dot plummeted. She muttered a curse. She didn't have a map of the Space Center. She had Jacob's location, and a white dot that marked her location, but not in relation to anything else. But the red dot seemed to be nearby. Staring at her personal, Meagan walked toward one end of the data room, watching the gap between the dots on the screen start to close. Then she came to a wall. She looked up at the smooth barrier that halted her progress. She was next to the red dot, so where was Jacob? Suddenly, her mind flashed back to something Tina had done only hours ago.

Meagan pulled Ultan's pass key out of her pocket and waved it in front of the wall. A little to her right a door slid open, revealing a hidden elevator. Meagan's heart leaped at the sight of Jacob's backpack inside. But where was Jacob? She stepped into the elevator and scanned the buttons until she found the one she wanted. She punched the button to return the elevator to the floor it had come from. Then she slipped Jacob's backpack over her shoulder. He would be wanting it back.

When the doors slid open, Meagan stepped cautiously into the white hallway. It was surprisingly quiet here after the din in the data room, and there was no sign of any Black Fists. Then she heard a gunshot. A grim smile twisted her mouth. It had to be Jacob.

Meagan ran down the hall in the direction of the sound. She came to an open door and hesitated, afraid of what she might find. She heard a shout and stiffened. The voice sounded like Ultan's. She knew Ultan had escaped the Defiance's entrance. Had Jacob gone after him? Why would he do that?

Meagan let the backpack fall to the ground. If there was shooting going on, she wanted to move without hindrance. She took a deep breath and stepped through the doorway. The room was brightly lit and filled with small labs divided by glass. At least, some of them were divided by glass. Others had ragged edges where glass used to be. Jagged shards littered the floor.

The sound of another gunshot split the air. Meagan dropped to the floor. She lifted her head in time to see a figure dive behind a desk to her right. Was that Jacob? Meagan started crawling in his direction, trying to stay low. Out of the corner of her eye, she caught a brief flicker of movement to her left, farther back in the room. Her heart started racing. She was crawling into the middle of a two-man gun battle.

She craned her neck to see who it was she was crawling toward. She hoped it was Jacob, but it could be Ultan. All she could see was a bit of black clothing. That was no help. Both Jacob and Ultan were wearing black. The person nearest her fired two shots in quick succession. Meagan crawled into the relative shelter of a table. She had to hurry. The Defiance would blow the data room any minute. When they pulled out, the Center would be swarming with Black Fists. She had to get Jacob out.

The person crouching beside the desk was just out of sight. Meagan crawled out from under the table on her stomach. If she could just get a little closer …

The person dove forward to take shelter behind a thick concrete support beam. Now, although his back was to her, she could see who it was. She wasn't on Jacob's side. She had crawled over to Ultan.

Meagan was thoroughly disgusted. She was disgusted with herself, with Ultan, and most of all, with the whole situation. A familiar rage, fueled by both fear and anger, began to burn in her. She raised herself to her knees and looked back at the objects on the table nearest her. Measuring tools and glass vials wouldn't serve her purpose. Her eyes fell on a thick metal rod. She had no idea what use it served science, but she snatched it up. Meagan crawled quickly and quietly behind the desk that Ultan had formerly used for shelter.

Out of the corner of her eye, she saw Jacob move. He was closer than she expected. He threw himself to the right, behind a long wooden desk. Meagan realized that Jacob was trying to get around to flank Ultan.

Ultan saw it too. Meagan heard him curse, saw his muscles

tense as he prepared to move to a better position. She knew she had to act now. She rose to her feet, stepped forward, and raised the metal rod.

Ultan must have heard the broken glass crunch under her feet. He spun, bringing his pistol around to face her. The move threw him off balance and he fell backward.

It didn't stop him from firing.

Chapter 38
Into the Night

Some agency must bring peace. Without a mediator, what will keep the whole world from dissolving in blood and fire?
— Charter of the International Administrative State

Meagan heard a hiss as a bullet whizzed by her ear. The same instant her right arm, raised to strike, was wrenched back and a burning pain shot through it. Meagan screamed and fell to her knees, the metal rod falling uselessly at her side.

The instant Ultan's attention was distracted, Jacob moved. He jumped on top of the table and fired down at Ultan. Meagan saw two bullets hit Ultan in the chest. Then the pistol's slide locked back. Jacob dropped his gun and jumped down. Ultan weakly raised his pistol, but Jacob dashed forward, grabbed his arm and wrenched the weapon away from him. He turned and fired into Ultan until he was out of bullets.

Even after he had stopped firing, Jacob stood over the bloody body, the gun shaking in his hands. His face was white and his whole body trembled. Meagan knew she needed to tell him something, but she was having a hard time recalling it. Her entire upper body was on fire, and there was a roar in her ears. She scrunched up her face trying to remember. Then it came to her.

"We have to get out," Meagan said. "The Defiance—"

A sharp rumbling shook the room. Glass that had remained intact now crashed to the floor, adding to the swelling sound. Meagan saw a thin crack race up the far wall and spread onto the ceiling.

Jacob dropped Ultan's empty gun and turned to her. Was the panicked look on his face caused by the explosion? He said nothing, but ran back, snatched up his gun and shoved it into his belt. He crouched beside Ultan's body. Did he take something? Meagan wasn't sure.

Jacob slid his arm under her good one, pulling her to her feet. He half helped, half dragged her back through the broken glass to the door. Black spots began to dance in front of her eyes. Her arm was burning and slick with blood. Meagan fell to her knees before

Jacob could stop her.

"Jacob, I can't," she gasped through the pain. "Give me a minute."

Jacob shook his head. "Jack's been planting explosives on the support beams of the prison level. When the Defiance pulls out of here, they are going to set off the charges to stop anyone from following them. The whole building might collapse."

"How long?" Meagan spit out.

Jacob glanced at his wristwatch. "Five minutes."

He yanked on his backpack and slid one arm around her shoulders and the other under her legs. When he lifted her off the ground, Meagan bit back a scream and threw her good arm around his neck. Jacob stumbled forward. Meagan closed her eyes and gritted her teeth against the throbbing pain.

She opened them again when Jacob kicked open a door. Thick black smoke poured out of the stairwell. She didn't hear any shooting, but everything was lit by an eerie red light.

"Hang on!" Jacob shouted. He started down the stairs, half running, half sliding along the wall to keep his balance. Meagan started coughing. The smoke stung her eyes and made them fill with tears. She became aware of a sharp, crackling noise. Fire was racing up the walls.

Meagan's head spun. With every cough, new jolts of pain shot out from her arm. The spots in her eyes thickened, then everything went dark.

She wasn't unconscious long. She opened her eyes as Jacob stumbled into the room with the operating table. Only three people were still in the room. The Manager was standing at the gaping hole in the wall, the tunnel opening behind him, a detonator in his hand. His eyes were riveted to the stairwell door. Jacob's mother had her hand on the Manager's arm.

"I'll go back and look for them." Arthur said, but then he caught sight of Jacob and Meagan and shouted, "Hey!"

Meagan was aware of every Defiance member and Arthur running toward them from the tunnel. The Manager started shouting orders. Jack scooped Meagan into his arms.

She heard Sword say, "You okay?" to Jacob.

"Meagan—" Jacob started.

"I got her," Jack said. They retreated back toward the tunnel.

She heard shouting coming from nearby, and knew the Black Fists were preparing to attack again. Let them come. They were already too late.

The Defiance members plunged into the tunnel, their feet echoing loudly on the concrete. A few seconds later, Meagan was deafened by the roar of the explosions detonating.

"Keep moving!" the Manager shouted. The flashes of light illuminated the tunnel ahead of them. For a brief instant, Meagan saw the ceiling stretching above them. Looking back over Jack's arm, Meagan caught sight of the freed prisoners, huddled in a mass, far down the tunnel. They were going the opposite direction.

"Don't stop," she heard the old woman shout.

The roar did not subside; it was merely joined by deep thundering as parts of the New Worlds Space Center began to collapse. The fugitives continued running, away from the destruction, their destination a mystery to Meagan. She closed her eyes, and let herself be carried.

They traveled quickly through the subway tunnels, the sounds of the collapsing building echoing around them.

"The Black Fists had evacuated the workers from the building," Par told Meagan.

"Yeah, no loyal followers turning on them when the fighting started," Jack added.

"So we hope there aren't too many people in the building when it collapses," Par finished.

"Just a lot of Black Fists," Jacob said grimly from her other side.

More explosions shook the tunnels. The Defiance was detonating explosives that had been laid years before. By tomorrow, the Black Fists, or what was left of them, would find only rubble in place of the tunnels.

Blackness hung over the street that ran along the river. A drizzling rain blurred the outlines of the dilapidated buildings and of the warehouses that concealed the movements of the small group of fugitives. In the shelter of a low brick building, the group stopped.

"Took you long enough to get here," said a voice from near

their feet. Through the pain, Meagan smiled. The voice belonged to Deuce. He sat against the door, shielded from the rain. Meagan clenched her teeth as Jack set her on the ground.

"Hang on, Deuce," Diamond said. "Princess is wounded."

Ace crouched next to Meagan. "Shine a light over here."

"It's my arm," Meagan said. She was feeling lightheaded.

"I see that."

"How is she?" Jacob asked.

"Bullet went through her arm. It looks like it missed any bone or arteries. Once I get the bleeding stopped, she should be fine."

Ace took a bandage out of one of his many pockets and pressed it tightly to her arm. Meagan gasped and bit her lip to keep from crying out. Sword, Par, and Jack positioned themselves to guard the group.

"It's just her arm?" Jacob pressed. "She's covered in blood."

"That all don't belong to her," Ace said. "Remember all those Black Fists getting shot above you?"

"You're a mess yourself if you didn't notice," Diamond added.

Jacob turned to Meagan and she could see the relief on his face.

"Will you come with me?" he asked. "I'm leaving the city. It'll be a long trip."

Ace had finished with the bandage and Meagan gulped down some water and pills Deuce held out for her. She thought about teasing Jacob, saying maybe she wouldn't leave with him. But she was too tired, and her arm hurt, and honestly, she'd go just about anywhere with anyone to get away from this city.

"Deuce is coming," Jacob added.

"Yes," Meagan said.

"Rand?" Jacob turned to the man who was keeping quiet in the back of the group.

Arthur shrugged. "Where else would I go?"

Jacob turned to the rest of the Defiance. "Thank you. I don't think I can ever repay you for what you did for me."

"You don't have to," Jacob's mom said. She pulled Jacob toward her and leaned up to kiss his cheek. "I love you, baby."

She said it so softly that Meagan doubted anyone else heard.

Jacob shook his grandfather's hand. "Good-bye, sir."

"Good-bye, Wild Card. You did a good job."

"Thank you, sir."

Jacob helped Meagan to her feet. Diamond and Ace assisted Deuce, who grimaced as he stood.

"Pleasure to meet you, Princess," Ace said, with a nod in her direction.

Meagan looked at all the faces gathered around. "Good-bye," she said. The Defiance moved back down the street and vanished in the darkness.

"Now," Arthur said, "where are we going?"

Jacob held a finger to his lips and motioned for them to follow him.

The four fugitives arrived at the wharf that ran along the river. The city behind them glowed red and a chorus of sirens wailed. Jacob gave a low whistle, and then led them down a short flight of stone steps. A small black boat bobbed in the water.

Two men dressed in dark clothing sat on the concrete next to the boat, smoking cigarettes. They both stood when Jacob appeared. One stepped forward.

"You only arranged for one," he said. He flicked his cigarette into the river.

"So I did," Jacob agreed. He slid his backpack around and opened a small pouch on the side. He took out a chip and handed it to the man. The man took a personal from his pocket and slid the chip into it. After he'd viewed the screen, he said, "Well, I guess that will cover it."

He motioned for the group to get into the boat. As she passed, Meagan heard him say, "I still don't like surprises like that."

Jacob raised his eyebrows. "For that much, I could bring a troop of performing elephants and you couldn't complain."

The man gave a short laugh. "So you could."

He followed Jacob into the boat. There was no joking or cigarettes now.

"Stay low," the man told his passengers, "and get comfortable now, because you don't get to move around. No noise, no lights, and you do exactly as my partner and I instruct. Understood?"

Four heads nodded.

The second man started a small motor on the back of the boat, and it made hardly more than a whisper. Meagan took one last look at the city looming over her as if forbidding her to go. She smiled at it. She would not miss this place where she had spent her entire life. Turning away, she settled back as the boat sped into the night.

Epilogue
Belonging

Embrace diversity, but unite in purpose. Firmly believe in Equality.
We are the hope of peace for Planet Earth.
— Motto of the International Administrative State
— Fact 1,000, Citizen's Handbook

One week later, Meagan sat on the deck of a cargo ship, towering stacks of crates surrounding her. The rumble of the engine as it powered the ship relentlessly south through the Atlantic was inescapable.

Meagan closed her eyes and let the hot sun warm her face. She rubbed her arm gingerly. It was still sore, but Deuce—no, Jasper—despite his own injuries had bandaged it well and said she was healing quickly. Meagan took a deep breath of the fresh air. She was finally out of the cabin she shared with Jacob, Jasper, and Arthur.

Now she sat alone in the open air, enjoying the glorious freedom of the sea, as she tried to blow bubbles with the gum Jacob had given her. Gum was new to her, but she was determined to be able to blow bubbles like Jacob could. Besides, she had to admit, it sure beat the flavored cardboard that passed for food that Jacob had been buying from the cook to feed the four passengers. With three extra people to provide for, Jacob was being extremely conservative about their expenses, and the rationing now was even stricter than Meagan was used to. Still, she'd spent little energy cooped up in a cabin all week, and she wasn't about to complain. Meagan had lived her whole life with rationed food. Jacob had told her chewing gum would help her feel less hungry and he was right.

Jacob had insisted that the group needed some fresh air. While the ship was near land, the fugitives had to be content in their crowded cabin, but now that they were in the open sea, they were ready to be free. The captain at first refused, but after some arguing, and bribing on Jacob's part, he allowed them to move about the deck. It was an expense Jacob considered a necessity. At least Meagan had not been seasick like Jasper.

This ship would carry the fugitives along its given route, and when it reached port, they would be expected to fend for themselves. It was understood that Jacob and his friends would not do anything unreasonable that would incriminate the crew. Transporting illegal, but well-paying passengers, was, Jacob had explained, a convenient opportunity for the captain and crew to earn money and rations they were not normally allowed. They would keep their mouths shut, and gather what profit they could. It was purely a business arrangement. As far as Jacob knew, they were not a part of any rebel group. Meagan could believe that. Jacob certainly had to negotiate with the captain before they were let onboard. Moving from the river and a small boat to the open sea on a ship, without being detected, had been an adventure all its own.

Jacob had paid a lot of attention to her during the time they were cooped up in their cabin, trying to make sure she was comfortable and had what she needed. He had done that for the whole group, but, whether it was her imagination or not, Meagan chose to believe he'd singled her out for the most care.

Jacob had some minor burns and a few cuts himself, but other than that, he was fine. Waiting in the room, Jacob had been restless and fidgety. He would sit down, only to get back up again; he unpacked and repacked his backpack, checking all his supplies. He cleaned his weapon multiple times. The others, though, had been more than happy just to have some time to rest. Conversations were short, fading away a few minutes after beginning.

Still, one afternoon when Meagan had been in a more talkative mood, she asked Jacob, "Why did you go after Ultan? You could have just let him be blown up like the rest of the Black Fists."

"A hunch," Jacob answered.

"Not back to that, Jacob," Meagan said. "I'm going to be mad if you don't have a better reason, considering what I went through to get you out of there."

"Okay. Call it an educated guess. Back when you, Arthur, and I were all in that room with Ultan, he sent one of his men to get some data he had been downloading. I figured he must have been getting the most essential information on the mind control program, and keeping it with him in case something went wrong."

"Which it did," Arthur added.

"Exactly. I went after him to keep him from getting away with the information."

Jacob held up a flash drive. "The added bonus is that I can take this information back to some friends of mine, and they can come up with a way to counter it. Then we can sell that technology to the Defiance, and they'll be ready if the IAS ever tries again."

"I guess you're not as crazy as you look," Meagan said.

"Hey!"

Now Meagan glanced up as she heard Jacob's voice, raised in conversation. He and Arthur walked along the deck toward her, Arthur limping. Meagan's heart started pounding. She had been avoiding discussing recent events, especially with Arthur. She still felt miserable about the way things had turned out and the role she'd had. She knew most of Arthur's problems were her fault.

Even in the cramped quarters they were confined to, avoiding the topic had not been hard. Meagan had lost enough blood to leave her feeling weak, and of course, her arm hurt terribly.

Arthur hadn't been in much better shape. He had been beaten by the Black Fists, and the harsh trip down the river was harder on the older man. Meagan stared miserably out at the rolling waves. All she could think of was the look on his face when he'd been brought into the office by Ultan. He had been so disappointed.

The conversation between Arthur and Jacob stopped. Jacob said something about going to see the captain and hurried off.

"Mind if I join you?" Arthur asked. Meagan shook her head, and Arthur sat down beside her.

"You have a lot of courage, young lady," he said. "Defying the Black Fists is something few people dare to do."

Meagan stared at the deck.

"You went against them," she mumbled. And was almost killed or worse because of her.

"Meagan, I know you're feeling bad."

"I'm seasick," Meagan snapped.

"Don't lie to me. You haven't been seasick since we cast off. Let me rephrase that. I know you're feeling guilty about what happened."

"Yes I am," Meagan said. "I caused the problems. I was working with the Black Fists. It's my fault that you got captured. Ultan destroyed your life because of me. Jacob could have died. Everything is my fault."

Arthur glanced at the bright sun and the clear sky. "As far as faults go, if any of my mistakes turned out half as well as yours did, the world would be a very different place."

He put his hand on her shoulder. "Okay, Jacob almost died, but he didn't. Don't think about what could have happened, look at what did happen. Jacob is fine, he's here, you're here. Jasper's here."

Arthur moved his hand from her shoulder and raised her chin so she met his eyes. "Those people might not be alive now if not for your actions. And I would not be with you here on this boat, so, thank you."

Meagan stood abruptly. "Look, thanks for trying to help, but I don't think you understand how I'm feeling. You may have ended up here through my actions, but let's not forget that those same actions were what got you captured and tortured by Black Fists; the Black Fists I was helping."

"Sit down, Meagan."

There was no mistaking the command in his voice. Meagan sat.

"First of all," Arthur began, "you don't get to blame yourself for my actions. I chose to walk into Black Fist headquarters knowing full well what the most likely outcome would be. I happened to see you be picked up by them from my office window."

"But you had no way of knowing I was working for them."

"Don't flatter yourself." Arthur said sharply. "I suspected you were with the Black Fists ever since you asked for my identity back in that house, after you rescued the baby girl."

"Then why in the world did you tell me?" Meagan demanded.

"Well," Arthur began slowly, "that is something you should know about me. I do understand the guilt you're feeling. I've had to live with that guilt for most of my life."

Meagan's eyebrows drew together.

"Did you read the information about your parents that I left for you on my computer?" he asked.

"Yes," Meagan answered. He had left it for her?

"Then you know what happened. But I didn't tell you it was my fault. I'm the one who got them killed."

"What?"

"It was my job to get the identity cards. That was all I had to do. I was the rich one with the famous parents."

Arthur's hands clenched and now it was he who stared at the deck. "The identities I bought weren't good. They didn't hold up to airport security. I had arranged to have a flight that day. I was in the airport. I was watching to see if they made it." Arthur shook his head. "They didn't."

He looked up at Meagan. She was surprised to see tears in his eyes.

"They were my best friends, my only real friends in the world. You were their love, their most precious possession. I couldn't even save you. The Black Fists turned you over to the Ministry of Population. They didn't even give you to the Ministry of Education, which is where you should have been at your age. So even then, I knew that they were going to reform you, that they would treat you terribly. For that, I am truly sorry. I tried to find you. I got a job processing children from the Ministry of Population into the Education Ministry. But it was too late. I had lost you."

"So you devoted your life to helping save other children," Meagan whispered.

"I couldn't change what I had done, but I thought maybe I could do some right to make up for my wrong. But I never could forgive myself."

He looked out over the water.

"So when I saw you standing there, at that party, looking exactly like your mother, but a little like your father too, I knew who you were after all those years. I had to do everything I could to find you. And when I started to suspect you were working for the Black Fists, I did what I could to rescue you. I was sure you would reject me outright if I approached you too soon. That's why I wrote you the notes and instructed Kalyn to leave them for you. I don't know how much good it did."

"You pushed me over the edge," Meagan said softly. "You made me reject the Black Fists."

Arthur smiled at her. "You are a wonderful young lady, Meagan. Whatever else you may have done, you have taken a great burden off of my chest. Your parents would be proud of the woman you have become."

Now Arthur wasn't the only one with tears in his eyes. No one had ever said anything half so nice to her before. Hardly knowing what she was doing, much less why, Meagan threw her arms around Arthur and sobbed.

She didn't know whether she was happy or sad. Maybe she was a little of both.

Arthur patted her on the back. Meagan sniffed and let go.

"So is Meagan my real name?" she asked. "Do you know how old I am? I have plenty of questions, you know. You better be ready to give me some answers."

Arthur smiled back at her. "Your parents named you Meagan after your mother's sister. You are seventeen years old, and your birthday is March third."

Meagan laughed. "I always did like spring."

"It isn't springtime," Jacob said coming up behind them. He gave them both a huge smile. "How does it feel, Meagan, to be well and truly rid of the International Administrative State?"

"Wonderful."

"Where are we going?" Arthur asked. "You've pulled off some impressive stunts, but I've spent this past week wondering how you plan to escape a world government."

Jacob glanced quickly around, making sure they were alone. He sat down next to Meagan.

"Well, safety protocol is that I don't tell anyone until we reach our destination. That way, if any of us is captured, no one but me could tell where we are going."

Meagan gave him a disapproving look.

"But, considering I was the one who came up with that rule," Jacob continued hastily, "and considering I came up with it this week, and since I really do owe both of you—"

"You do," Meagan and Arthur said at the same time.

"I'll tell you, but you have to keep it to yourselves."

"We will."

"We are going to my adopted home," Jacob said. "Antarctica."

"Where?" Meagan asked.

"Why?" said Arthur.

"The research bases were shut down the spring before the War," Jacob started.

"Where is Antarctica?" Meagan demanded.

"It's the continent at the bottom of the world," Arthur said absently. "It's cold."

"There's another continent that I wasn't told about?"

Jacob nodded. "During the War, it was mostly forgotten about. There just wasn't really anything that valuable down there."

"We had been researching there for years before the IAS really gained any support," Arthur added. "Back when they were just another faction."

"Anyway," Jacob continued, "after the Great Crash, the UN sold the land. They needed a lot of cash very quickly to offer to 'help' governments financially. Some very wise men, who could see the way things were swinging, bought the land. They prepared it as their final retreat, the last free land they could flee to."

Jacob gazed out over the ocean. "They were very secretive about what they had done, and we believe that the records of the sale were destroyed when the UN building was burned to the ground at the beginning of the War. They believe that event, in a way, was God's provision for them. Whatever else may have come from the fire, it enabled this group of people to drop almost completely off the radar of the IAS, which, at that time, was taking control. The State may know that these men exist, but if they do, right now the IAS has bigger problems to worry about. We have been able to live in relative peace. It's a hard life, but at least we're free."

"And you're a part of this group?" Arthur asked.

"Sort of," Jacob answered. "I'm a bit of a novelty even among such a diversely talented group as they are. I was very honored to be able to join them almost four years ago, when I had just turned fifteen. I stayed there for a while, but I was accustomed to a much more active life, working with Rails and all. I headed back to the mainland, but this time my work was a little more … unique."

"What do you mean?" Meagan asked. She may have changed a lot in the past few days, but she hadn't lost any of her curiosity.

"I guess you could call me a spy. I'm a liaison between the Exiles, that's what the Antarctic group calls themselves, and certain Defiance cells here on the mainland. The Exiles sometimes sell the Defiance tech, mostly in exchange for information. I also do information gathering of my own. The Exiles may not be a part of the world government, but our leader likes to keep an eye on what's going on."

"So you were gathering information when we met?" Meagan asked.

Jacob nodded. "Yeah."

"Why exactly did you want information on the State's space program?"

Jacob hesitated. "I don't really know. What I do know, I can't tell you."

When Meagan gave him a look, he raised his hands in surrender. "I'm not just saying this to annoy you, honestly. This is serious. This is like, kill yourself before you talk, serious. I really can't tell you anything."

"Fine." Meagan turned away. Let Jacob dodge her questions, she would find out sooner or later. That's what she was good at, after all.

Meagan leaned back against a crate, getting comfortable. Arthur sat on one side of her and Jacob settled down on the other. Meagan closed her eyes, knowing she didn't have to be afraid anymore. Jacob and Arthur were here beside her and they would keep her safe. She felt Jacob's hand take hers, and she smiled. The sun was hot on her face and the wind tugged at her hair, and here, of all places, she had found where she belonged.

ABOUT THE AUTHOR

Esther K. Bowen is one of those people who will lose sleep to a good book. She likes penguins and movies, and being completely involved in a good story. She enjoys reading science fiction for its ability to explore religion, politics, science, philosophy, freedom, tyranny, and the human mind and spirit. She lives with her family in Indiana. She would love to hear from you. Contact her at estherkbowen@gmail.com.

Made in the USA
San Bernardino, CA
13 February 2016